DISCOVERY

SOUL SEER CHRONICLES, BOOK 1

S.J. CAIRNS

Cover design by Getcovers
Logo created by S.J. Cairns
Logo image by CNuisin depositphotos.com ID 265803116
Tree vector by chachar depositphotos.com ID 489800234

ISBN 978-1-7782426-0-1 (ebook)
ISBN 978-1-7782426-1-8 (Paperback)
ISBN 978-1-7782426-2-5 (Hardcover)

Previous editions printed 2018, 2016

Black Thumb Publishing
Ontario, Canada
www.sjcairns.com

✱ Created with Vellum

ACKNOWLEDGMENTS

Dreams begin somewhere. For myself it was when someone contacted me out of the blue and wanted to see my series grace the pages. Without their random act of kindness, Sophie's story would never have made it within readers' hands. You know who you are. Thank you for changing my life.

On a more personal note, I wouldn't have made through the mushy middle, overworked energy slumps, or all-night writing marathons without the Quillies, the online writing group that elevated a whimsical hobby into a personal mission. Each of you deserve a warm cuddle, a heap of cookies, and ample alcohol.

To my mother, the enabler and progenitor of my reading addiction, thanks for being the first to read my crappy writing and providing direction with unwavering support. To my husband, thank you for enduring cold nights in bed alone as I sat at my desk and wore down the letters on my keyboard and for never once thinking I was a weirdo without saying it with a smile. I promise, one day, I'll get back to gaming again.

To my Aunt Marj:
An avid reader who will never get to read this, but rests in peace and
survives within my words and always in my heart.

1

———————

LACKING

Change is terrifying. Terrifying and destabilizing, but I crave it. I need distance from where I was. Space to re-evaluate the unsatisfying hollowness that yearns for fulfillment, an escape from neediness and indecision.

My soul craves sustenance, more than something to chew over and spit out. Something of substance, of worth. Right now I am starving. And all I have to feed on is a job serving drunks and college kids angling to get laid.

My checklist of "Ways to Get Your Shit Together" grew every time I ticked something off, and the never-ending hamster wheel was too exhausting to reflect on, at the moment, feeling physically drained was my biggest issue.

I rejected introspection and focused on my footsteps clapping cement, each one bringing me closer to The Lush, the bar where I work, only a fifteen-minute walk from my downtown apartment.

Passing a couple of customers smoking outside, their shoulders up around their ears to protect against the light rain and cool breeze, I exchanged quick greetings to plant the seeds of good tips. I scanned familiar faces, looking for anyone known to cause issues before I got my night started.

"Where the hell have you been?" Drew, my boss, scowled at me when I was two feet in the door.

Behind the bar, Eddie, a co-worker, mouthed something to me, but I couldn't decipher what.

"Sophie!"

My attention snapped back to my seething boss. When I didn't say anything, he filled in the blanks.

"You were supposed to work the day shift. Eddie is pulling a double because I couldn't find another bartender on short notice."

"What?" I looked to Eddie again. He was cutting limes. "No, I work tonight. Clearly, or I wouldn't be here."

"My schedule says day shift. Which means you missed your shift. Again."

"I'm—"

"Full of weak excuses. And damn lucky I like watching your tight ass behind the bar and hate doing interviews." If I hadn't switched off my 'give a shit' supply as soon as my boss laid into me, I would have introduced Drew's balls to my Chucks. "There's a line of people outside the welfare office begging for jobs. Miss a shift again, and it won't matter how tight your ass is, you can shake it on the street and pray for a handout."

Drew stormed into the back office. Eddie dropped the knife and looked at me with a rigid expression, waiting for me to blow a gasket. The fact I hadn't was evidence of my growing numbness. Drew could have been right. Maybe I was supposed to work a day shift.

Being right didn't make him any less of a grimy asshole.

"If it helps, I don't think your ass is that tight."

I glared at Eddie.

"Well, all right then," he mumbled, and went back to cutting limes.

"Why the fuck didn't someone call me?"

"He's called all mornin', chick. You never answered. I assumed you were up late working on your psych paper and slept through the day."

A gasp punched out of my lips.

Eddie's pierced eyebrow peaked at my reaction. "Didn't finish it?"

Dread broke through my emotional fog. I slipped my purse under the bar with shaking hands, the ghost of future failure already haunting me. My vision clouded with anger and disappointment so thick I was blind to whoever Eddie served next.

After hours of research and revisions, I had forgotten to email the paper to my professor. So much for losing sleep over writing the damn thing. I'd have to pull off near-perfect marks the rest of the semester or I may as well drop out.

If I had the energy to laugh...

Helping with payroll after closing would earn me a few extra bucks, but also meant I'd have to wait until much later to send in the paper attached to a desperate email pleading for partial marks. If it meant a passing grade, the hit to my pride was worth it.

Helplessness gripped me, and I felt my control over my thin emotional stability threatened as tears gathered and blurred my vision. With Eddie staring at me, I beat down the compulsion to lose my shit and held my breath until numbness began to take over again.

I needed this degree. I needed my plan to work.

And I needed to not humiliate myself by passing out.

Letting go of the air I held left me too unsteady to speak. I held up one finger and zipped off to the staff bathroom to collect myself before Eddie could see how badly I was shaking.

This was nothing like what my psychology texts outlined. I'd played the depression and anxiety game before, was well acquainted with the symptoms, as well as the medications I refused to take because they removed me from the world around me. Normally, my waning focus on the here and now was easy to shoulder aside. I was too exhausted to concentrate on anything more than the day-to-day: work and school. Missing assignments and shifts indicated how months' worth of nights with minimal sleep was breaking me, and my well-laid plans, down.

But more sleep meant more nightmares. I bit down on my lip to prevent my whimper from being heard outside the bathroom. More dreams? I couldn't take it.

I pushed away the spiral of negative thoughts, reminding myself that bedtime was far off and I could lose myself in the monotony of the job. The smell of cheap, industrial hand soap grounded me. This wasn't my paradise, but I've been in worse places, and I refused to slip back into that black hole. Cold water over my hands dissipated the last of my anxiety as numbed-out resilience settled into place, protecting my sanity.

I washed my now-steady hands and left the small room to focus on my first drink order. Pouring a rum and coke in a tall glass with an extra lime for the floral skirt in front of me was manageable. The rest could wait.

———

By the time I got through payroll, the sun was lightening a new day's sky. With a few extra hundred lining my pocket, I considered my night a success, even if I was sleeping upright on my walk back home.

Ugh, living the dream.

When I twisted the key in my apartment's lock, Bosco wailed on the other side of the door. Getting inside and calming my lonely little pug had nothing to do with the neighbours and everything to do with the headache knotting between my eyes. Having been subjected to the neighbours' screaming orgasms, I didn't care if they complained about Bosco. And their children had to be sound sleepers because the sex-capades sounded like someone was beating a Chihuahua.

I plopped down on my old, faded green couch while Bosco wagged his fawn-coloured tail and danced his little feet on my lap. My welcome home was interrupted by a knock on the door. Bosco flew off my lap and sprang over the faux cherry wood coffee table, sending an old cup of grape juice flying. Purple liquid sloshed across everything on the table and dripped down onto my neutral carpet.

"Shit balls!" The glass bounced to the tune of my mother's voice in my head chastising my "unladylike" outburst, using each of my given names like a mischievous child, "Sophie Olivia Saterlee, that mouth of yours..." Bosco was barking at the door. As he never barked unless excited, he knew who our visitor was before I did.

I swung the door open for the only neighbour I enjoyed seeing. After grunting a, "Hey Kim," to the red-haired beauty who had to catch the door before it shut in her face, I went to the kitchen to the right of the entrance for a rag and stain remover.

"Wow. What's with the bags under your eyes? If you expect tips tonight, you'll need more cleavage and cover-up. I've got the perfect shirt."

"I don't work tonight. And you always have the perfect shirt." I blotted the slash of colour on the cheap carpet and sprayed it with cleaner. I doubted it would make a difference to the funky new design.

"For tits like yours? Damn right I do."

A product of working at a high-end retail store with a great employee discount.

"You smell like bleach." Kim's face screwed up in distaste as I returned the cleaner to the cupboard beneath the kitchen sink.

"So do my jeans." I angled my leg to display the discoloured splotch near the cuff from cleaning at work.

"Ain't that a bitch. Perfect timing, actually. I have a friend with access to designer jeans. Fifty bucks a pop, if you're interested."

"A friend?"

She shrugged. "Friend of a friend."

"Cuz that doesn't sound shady at all. They your weed dealer too?"

She laughed and left the question unanswered, though, which made me wonder if that's why she was so bubbly all the time.

"Besides, my pay grade doesn't allow for snazzy clothes. Even at trunk-selling prices."

"Let me know if you change your mind."

When Kim hovered at my door with a tight, edgy smile, it was obvious she had something more on her mind.

"Kim, it's too early to swallow the anticipation of whatever you're about to say, but I warn you, if it involves the words 'blind date' you're going to lose a good six inches of hair." There's a reason I'm single. Kim was ignorant to that reason, but it existed.

She gasped and clutched strands that reached the middle of her back. "The hair? You'd go straight for the hair?"

"Always know your opponent's weaknesses. And when they're deflecting. Spit it out already."

"Fine." She leaned against the waist-high partial wall separating the kitchen from the living room. "There's this group thing I go to on Sunday nights. I thought maybe you'd be interested in coming?"

My forehead wrinkled. "Is it a nudist thing? 'Cuz I have issues getting into bikinis."

Kim snort-laughed. "No, no nudity." She gave it a moment's thought. "No, just a bunch of people who get together and"—her pause had me holding my breath—"we read, um, tea leaves, stuff like that. You don't have to come every week. You mentioned, ah, a family friend that does tea leaf readings, but you never got around to doing it. So, I figured you might want to join in on a little fun." She gave a nervous laugh, while I locked down my poker face.

This awkwardness was incongruous with the self-assured Kim I was used to. Seeing the shift in personality was unsettling.

The moment stretched as I tried my best not to look judgmental. Things like tea reading were all fun and games, but Kim said she went every week. Offending Kim was off-limits, and since I had no plans, I chalked it up as a girls' night out and agreed to go. We didn't socialize outside the building, but her quirky enthusiasm was infectious. I was young, unattached, and childless, yet I had little time for socializing because I was focused on rebuilding myself from the core outward. With all the stress I wasn't handling well, and getting little to no sleep, I needed to get out of the apartment for something other than work.

Kim squealed like a sorority girl. "You won't regret it. I promise!" Then the excitement vanished from her blue-green eyes. "Forewarning, *different* types of people attend. They can be a bit intense, so don't laugh if they say something that, you know, is kind of odd."

Immediately I reconsidered. "Maybe you should ask them first."

"I already did, a while ago. Like I said, you mentioned that tea leaf reader you know, and as long as you don't spread what happens in the group around town, and don't insult anyone, they're cool. I've never brought anyone before, but I thought you'd like it."

I nodded and swallowed as my throat tightened with nervousness.

"Sweet-beans." Kim re-adopted a tight smile. "Be ready for eight-ish?"

"Coolio. Are you up early to work out?" I scurried from the awkward topic.

She slapped her hips. "Gotta keep this booty in check for beach weather. Plus, I have to open the store this morning, and my legs will be too tired to do squats after work."

"Ugh, you exhaust me just talking about it." I really hated mornings. Add exercise this early, and I'd look like a greasy, panting giraffe for the rest of the day.

Deep-voiced screaming that made me flinch reverberated down the hall, and Kim missed my reaction as she looked toward where the voices came from. We listened a moment, recognizing the owner. I hid my clenched fists by crossing my arms.

"Ugh." Kim flicked her hair over her shoulder. "Jack is such a dick. You're lucky you don't live across the hall from them."

Across the hall or not, it didn't stop the whole floor from being witnesses to the cycle-of-abuse playing out every few nights. I grit my teeth. "Theresa needs to leave him."

"Don't bother getting involved. You don't have good enough cover-up for those bags, let alone a black eye."

"True that," I said with my jaw still clenched.

Kim shook her head and headed back to her apartment.

Closing my door to what Theresa was dealing with broke my heart, but I had to do it. Taking online and day classes to earn a psychology degree was how I coped after a tumultuous relationship had obliterated my life plan. Now I wanted to help people, to understand the mindset of those like Jack and Theresa, abuser and victim. I wanted to understand human nature. What I did know was that Theresa wouldn't leave until she was good and ready, but she still needed support during and I couldn't give her what she needed.

Refocusing on my future was easy after hearing Jack and Theresa. I went straight for my computer and emailed my professor the late paper, made my plea, and left it in her hands. Then I carried Bosco with me to the window in the living room, overlooking the park, and wished I had a balcony. Cloud cover shadowed the green-space that hosted my dreams. After six months of a bitter cold Canadian winter, drain-clogging slush had melted, and the rains came in as the seasons shifted. So far, it was late June and all we'd seen was rain and more rain as summer struggled to take root.

The feeling of crisp energy through the screen, the bold scent of wet earth and asphalt, the sound of rain drumming against the windows, and the air thick with the woody taste of park brought me back to my childhood. Cheapest entertainment available.

Heavy with the tension of adult stress, I sank onto my couch and turned the flat screen on. I tried to bury the shame of not breaking Jack and Theresa's door down to beat the shit out of the guy. Leaving the woman to deal with his abuse another moment was cowardice I couldn't face.

Deluding myself into believing Kim was right not to get involved with our neighbours, my lids grew heavy, and I lay down with Bosco tucked into my side.

——————

Torrential rain soaked my grey shirt. The fabric clung to me, and water dripped down my arms and legs onto muddy gravel beneath my dirty feet.

Where the fuck am I?

Raindrops hit my lashes, making me squint to scan my surroundings. The gravel pathway may have been cold and the colour of filth, stretching out in front and behind for an immeasurable distance, but my narrowed eyes captured a sea of unnaturally green grass thrown around by a fierce wind. Flanking me on both sides of the path were rows of thrashing willows, sugar maples, and hickory trees. Wind and rainwater battered their branches, ripping away leaves that disappeared into sheets of rain.

Lucidity hit, and I recognized the park a stone's throw from my building. Access to the park was across the street from my apartment's entrance, down a staircase constructed from disintegrating railway ties. The park itself circled around a twelve-mile creek like St. Catharines' own Central Park.

While the memory of the park grounded me, it also reminded me of the dark, unforgiving reality of the park's seedy side.

Unlit at night, the greenspace became a place most people shied away from. In fine weather, it housed the homeless and was where sex trade workers brought their customers. At the moment, the park was clad in that seediness. Fear sparked in my gut, yet I continued to stand in the muddy gravel, sopping wet and terrified.

Why am I here?

I turned around, searching through the rain for the exit to the street above. The soles of my feet were numb, submerged below rapidly rising water. I lifted a foot, but had to sink it back into the dark water, the crunch of gravel now only a slight pressure against my skin. The creek was flooding into the park, water rushing toward me. Debris from the trees wrapped around my ankles as the stink of the creek wafted into the stirring air. The rain and wind battered the blanket of liquid taking over the park, while an uncomfortable tingle grew up my calves. Cold took root within my body.

A shudder skittered along my spine and crawled under my skin as my panic intensified. This wasn't just the wind or the rain, or even the cold. The sensation of being watched sparked my hyper-vigilance and kept my eyes open wide despite the rain.

I spun around, looking for what had me in its sights. Although I saw nothing through the pouring rain but trees in the darkness, the feeling grew into an urgency to escape.

This urgency should have got me moving. Instead, I froze, unable to will my body to listen to my brain.

Whatever was in that darkness was close.

Too close.

At my back.

Could I run fast enough to get away? Not with the water now up to my knees. Should I run for the safety of the stairs or confront the thing? Every muscle quivered in fear of either choice. Like a frightened child, I snapped my eyes closed, wishing for a blanket to hide under.

I held my breath and slowly turned around. Tense moments passed as my lungs burned. Still with my eyes closed, I felt the presence move closer. I had no doubt something was there.

Come on, Sophie. I goaded myself into rummaging up a hint of courage.

As soon as I peered through my lashes, the black mass in front of me made my heart stutter. No distinguishable features were illuminated. There was no way of knowing what it was, but its oppressive size made me want to sink into the water now grazing my thighs. I shivered.

Terrified curiosity made me fully open my eyes. The darkness rushed forward, and the shock of seeing, yet not seeing, what was coming for me, woke me up with a gut-wrenching scream.

I flailed to catch the coffee table before landing tits-down on the floor. Bells rang and an echoing scream ripped through my vocal cords. If I lived anywhere besides downtown, the cops would be booting my door down, expecting to interrupt a murder scene. As it was, the neighbours were probably used to my horror-movie wakeup calls after so many months of hearing them. The fact Kim never mentioned it meant she heard me and was being respectful by leaving it unquestioned.

That, or she wasn't prepared for my answer.

The ringing bells were on the TV, part of an infomercial for jewelry so gaudy only an eighties beauty pageant contestant would appreciate it. The host claimed to only have ten units left on a sale *"you just can't miss!"* The bell was a selling prop that could rouse the dead and, in my case, save me from recurring nightmares.

The phone shrilled and threatened my full bladder. I answered the cordless with as much finesse as I had displayed waking up.

"Hello?" A voice asked.

"Yes, yeah, I'm here," I told Kim, realizing who the caller was.

"You okay?"

Maybe she did hear me. "Why?"

"You sound distracted."

"Oh. No, I'm good. What's up?"

"I was just wondering if you had any rosemary."

I didn't answer.

"The herb," Kim prompted.

Again, I remained silent.

"Unless you used it all, there's some in the spice carousel I bought you for Christmas."

"Used it? I don't even know what to put rosemary in."

"Oh...plenty of things." Again, her awkwardness was off-putting, but she recovered. "I thought a spice carousel might inspire you. I smell take-out coming from your place far too often."

"And I appreciate the effort, you're not the first, I'm just lazy when it comes to the kitchen."

"Fine." Kim sounded relieved it was my failure and not her gift-giving. "Are you still coming tonight?"

My eyes burned, temples pounded, and my hands were shaking from anxiety caused by my dream. I was a mess.

Being a hermit had done nothing to chase the dreams away. Dream was more accurate, since it was always the same one. A night out might be exactly what I needed. So, I reassured Kim I would be ready in time and would get the rosemary to her then.

I hung up on Kim and then I scooped up Bosco's pudgy body onto my lap, steadying my shaking hands by smoothing his fur. "At least I slept, Bosco."

After months of the recurring dream that had me standing nose-to-nose with an oppressive mass in the darkness, without a glimpse of the mass's identity or motive, my nerves were shredded. Why couldn't I dream about something else? And now the resulting exhaustion threatened my degree and the job I needed to pay for it. Something had to give. I prayed it wasn't me.

———

Bosco ran around like a maniac, using the hallway from the bedrooms to the living room as a racetrack, sprinting back and forth to air-dry his short coat. He'd insisted on jumping in the shower as I readied for Kim's "group thing." His huffing smile lifted my mood until Kim knocked on my door. The reality of what I'd agreed to kicked in my anxiety. I didn't know the people in the group, and Kim seemed nervous about asking me to come along. That didn't exactly help my trust issues.

"Ready to go?" Kim sounded afraid I might renege after thorough consideration.

"Almost." I went to the cupboard for the rosemary.

She looked at the small container. "It's still in the original plastic."

"I told you I don't cook."

"Are they all unopened?"

"Do you really want to know?"

Kim shook her head and ripped the plastic off before putting the container into a bag slung over her shoulder.

As we headed out, I refused to focus on Bosco's honey-brown, googly eyes. They were glossing over, trying to fill me with guilt for leaving my fur-baby alone.

The ride in Kim's burgundy car, a new-to-her vehicle with a small crack in the passenger window, was tense and awkward. She looked more nervous than me and began talking about safe topics while she white-knuckled the steering wheel.

"You okay, Kim?"

"Totally." She paused, forcing a smile as she looked straight out the windshield. "I just hope you don't think I'm mega freak-tacular after tonight."

"Don't worry. Like you said, if I don't like it, I won't go again. I can put up a mask and hide my true opinion. The bar's certainly honed that talent." And real life, for that matter.

If it wasn't the things my customers did, it was the stories they told. Every bartender is a therapist, a stranger people unload on when loaded. I'd learned to suppress my reactions lightning quick. Good practice for a future in psychiatry. Tonight, I was glad to have the skill at the ready just in case I was blindsided.

To make conversation, I asked where the party was.

"At Aunt Lacey's, in Niagara-on-the-Lake." Kim was, apparently, confident I knew who her aunt was. I didn't remember her bringing up the name before now.

My whole life I had called St. Catharines home. The Garden City was on the cusp of busy-city-meets-family-town. Not as touristy as neighbouring Niagara Falls, it was still big enough for mall crawling without running into every person you've ever met.

Niagara-on-the-Lake had that small town feel. Tours of the area included battle re-enactments at the old Fort George and beautiful historical buildings, all supposedly haunted. Most importantly, NOTL was known for money. I had a feeling Kim's Aunt's house was going to be huge.

My prediction was correct.

We parked at a grey stone mansion reminiscent of a small castle. After seeing the outside, I would bet a ham sandwich there were a handful of rooms inside meant only for looking at. In my previous experience working with a cleaning service, the rich loved to showcase their things rather than use them.

Kim led me through the front door without knocking. Breathing deep, I had no clue what I was walking into, but I hoped no one was slaughtering a goat in there, or our friendship was going to become a tad strained.

2

ONCE VEILED EYES

O h! Cold floor. Removing my sandals, I chided myself for not wearing shoes and socks.

Kim spun around and raised her hands. "Can you wait here a sec?"

I didn't want to be left alone, but wasn't given a chance to refuse before Kim raced off.

Distracting myself from my nervousness, I took the opportunity to investigate the room off of the foyer. The mansion's decor was straight out of a catalogue, not to mention maintained by a professional. The floor was lickably clean. Personal touches peppered the room. Photos covered surfaces with smiling faces of all ages and ethnicities. Maybe Lacey was a teacher? Maybe they were the photos the frames came with? Or trophies stolen from Lacey's victims' homes? I was braced for any possibility.

Wooden masks hung on one wall, remarkable pieces painted with small dots in an array of colours. Bizarre next to the modern theme. I got up close and personal to the blank eyes of one large mask with a mane of wild, wiry hair I thought might be real. Compelled to touch it, the sound of footsteps had me jumping back like a kid caught wandering, my bare feet squealing on the floor.

"Follow me, Soph." Kim's blue-green eyes danced with excitement.

Down a long hallway, we passed many open doors, each room highlighting a particular historical era. Victorian brilliance dripped from wallpapered walls and a high-backed red velvet couch as I paused to peek inside. A portrait of a woman straight-faced in a frilled collar, regal yet utterly bored, hung over a fireplace. Farther down the hallway was the patriotism of the Civil War era, then the rustic charm of a western brothel.

Oh, to have money.

"We're good to go," Kim told me as we walked. "Just had to remind the group I was bringing someone new."

"All righty." Why they needed a warning, I had no clue. I worked to keep my expression neutral. My heart beat in my throat.

Kim opened a white door, and I gulped at the thought of descending into a stranger's basement. Pausing in sudden panic with a paralyzing feeling of entrapment, I was hyper-aware of placing myself at the mercy of whoever was down there. Underground. Whether Kim vouched for them or not, they *were* strangers, and survival included knowledge of your surroundings. This was the antithesis of safe. My ability to trust people I knew, let alone strangers, was a slowly draining sieve. Right now, I was all out of sand.

Could I fake a stroke?

I swallowed my paranoia and tailed Kim, strangling the railing as I forced myself to take each step toward whoever waited for us.

Low light flickered at the bottom as muted voices grew louder with my descent. My sweaty feet slipped off the last stair, my iron grip on the railing keeping me from landing on my ass. Candlelight danced along surfaces. The only other light sources were dimmed sconces along the walls. Cozy yet awkward. Expectant smiles and eager-eyed bodies rounded the floor in a ceremonious circle.

As Kim waved me forward, I felt no better. Every muscle too tight with anticipation. Approximately fifteen people smiled at me as I forced a grin. I was surprised those smiles weren't all from women. As un-feminist as it sounded, I assumed this would be a ladies' only night. No guy I knew would show interest in this kind of thing, regardless of the tail they followed through the door.

When we joined the circle, the relief that I was closest to the stairwell—my escape—was so palpable, the tips of my ears tingled.

"Everybody," Kim's voice rang, alive and eager, "this is my friend Sophie Saterlee."

"Hey." My wave was weak.

This cued the blonde on Kim's left to introduce herself, then her neighbour, and so on, the group sounding off, used to the routine. Forgetting their names as soon as they were spoken, I only catalogued which woman introduced herself as "Aunt Lacey."

In her mid to late fifties, Lacey had inviting eyes and smooth, lightly tanned skin. What aged her was her long, grey-streaked brown hair worn gathered at the back of her head in a bun. A long, flowing dress with a large colourful pattern draped over her knees. She was clearly reluctant to let go of the 1970s.

As I scrutinized the details of this woman, Lacey's face triggered a memory of the painting of the bored woman in the Victorian room. Other than a clear difference in those dresses, they were identical. Maybe a recreation to add to the room's ambience? Sitting amongst the others, her hazel eyes glinted with pride for her eclectic group.

"Thanks for having me," I said once I realized I was scrutinizing her longer than socially acceptable.

Aunt Lacey countered with a congenial smile. "Pleasure to finally meet you."

The stares of the others made my skin itch. The raw sensation of new-kid-on-the-playground was impossible to shake with all this concentrated attention.

Lacey instructed the group to hold hands. Kim grabbed mine. A woman to my right with frizzy, orange-red hair gave a lopsided smile that said "I know we don't know each other, but I promise I'm not contagious" so I held on, hoping this wouldn't last long.

Lacey spoke, "Blessed is this gathered Coven, be it whole and unbroken. Our divine Goddess Hecate, shelter your children, encasing all within the arms of your protection. Light the way with your torch as we explore your teachings this night. Welcome those within our circle of trust, and guide our essences to a higher understanding of each of our rightful paths. Blessed be."

Coven? As in voodoo dolls, blood sacrifices, and black cats? What the shit? Talk about right-hooked. A coven gathering was far from a ladies' night.

Fuck me, was she serious?

Another glimpse, and yes, Lacey was definitely serious. No pointy hats or broomsticks, yet the meeting just got started. I eyed a closed door half-way along the long, rectangular room, envisioning what could be stored inside. Maybe that's why Kim had to warn them I was coming.

Poker face, poker face, poker face, I repeated to myself as my anxiousness shifted my imagination into overdrive. I looked at Kim, who returned an apprehensive smile. She must have known that I caught what Lacey revealed about the group. Before my expression faltered, I looked away.

Now Kim's nervousness made total sense. Why would she invite me to a coven meeting?

I silently wished this were a blind date.

Concentrating beyond the coven reveal before I freaked my shit, what Lacey expressed in the blessing sounded simple enough. My discomfort bloomed when the others around the circle gave each other side-eyed and uneasy glances. Was it new to them?

Maybe things had been altered because I was a newcomer? And protected by a Goddess. Who the fuck did I need to be protected from that would require intervention from a Goddess?

The only thing to make this worse would be if it turned into an orgy, and the Trojan Man galloped into the room with a condom cannon. Now there's protection. I was in too much shock from the ass-deep mess I was in to ask questions.

The blessing was nothing familiar from childhood summers spent in Bible camp at my Grandma Lizzie's request. I rebelled by wearing my mother's Rolling Stone t-shirts. Religion was never my thing, so I hypocritically prayed this wasn't a conversion attempt.

Introductions and Goddess blessing over, everyone broke into groups amongst the thick carpet and grey suede couches. Kim motioned me to follow her and Lacey toward the back of the long sage green painted room to a hand-carved wooden table with four chairs. My fight or flight mechanism roared and had me envisioning drop-kicking the old lady and using the chair now under my ass lion tamer style on anyone between me and the exit.

"Tea?" Lacey offered in a sweet, powerful voice, drawing me back to reality.

Having never become accustomed to the flavours of tea or coffee, and only fifty percent certain it wouldn't be laced, I reluctantly took her up on her offer.

Watching to ensure nothing was slipped into the small cup but loose tea leaves, I planned to gulp it down so as to not prolong the charade. I thought of my mother's tea mugs—big enough to chug beer. Thankfully, this cup was small and delicate, painted white with a green farmhouse and trees.

Lacey served my cup and sat across from me, immediately asking questions. I explained my work at the bar and my schooling. My suspicions about what Lacey really wanted to know, or what the point of separating us from the herd was, distracted me. I had no intention of bleeding my business to a perfect stranger without paying them per hour and enjoying the rich smell of a leather couch. But I droned on about my divorced parents and two younger brothers anyway, unable to satisfy Lacey's intense curiosity. I felt like a rambling fool.

With each sip of my drink, I did my best to prevent the tea grits from pouring into my mouth. Sitting around strangers who didn't care if I had grits in my teeth was too much tonight. I hoped, if Kim weren't too busy with the cult recruiting process, she would let me know.

I eyed the others over the rim of my cup, searching for signs of brainwashed automatons or figures in a play putting on a show for my benefit. Instead, I found only engrossed individuals content with whatever was happening in front of them. Proficient actors, pleasantly delusional, or genuine fun times? Too early to tell.

When I finished choking down the tea, I placed the cup on its saucer. Lacey smiled, took hold of the cup, and peered inside. Twisting the cup around so the handle faced me, she leaned forward so I could peer into the cup with her.

Then it hit me: I'd been subjected to the tea leaf reading I signed up for. Kim was on the ball and pulled out a legal pad from her bag, her pen scratching the surface as Lacey began.

Starting at the handle and working clockwise, Lacey pointed out what looked like a bunch of nothing, until she started talking.

"The spade," she said, and I saw a spade shape in the tea leaves, "a person who created disappointment and unrest in your life, perpetuating a self-imposed loneliness. While you're content alone, the sense of shame resulting from this spade's actions brought you to the harp." She pointed out a harp shape. "Once overwhelmed, you broke, and then lost a sense of self and control."

My blood thrummed through my veins as heat built inside and burned in my cheeks. A moment stretched as I restrained outward signs of distress to ensure Lacey wasn't reading my facial responses like a stage medium. *"Hmm. A male with the initial "J" in your life has passed on. He wants to tell you about the red wagon. Does this make sense?"*

"Since then, you've swam upstream through these stones, which represent instances of worry and vexations collapsing well-intended plans. Now, you're trapped with balloons,"—I saw the cluster of balloons—"much attempted, so little achieved, reinforcing your sense of failure and unworthiness."

My teeth clenched at the word "failure."

She moved along, "The open book, a thirst for knowledge to provide a window into yourself and that which broke you, as well as the world around you. Seeking answers, direction, and the wisdom to discern what is meant for you.

"And while all that scars a young life, the bones seen here represent misfortune surpassed with courage, already evident in your metamorphosis from the recent past. While I would love to confirm you're in a stage of completion, you, my dear, have yet to toe the threshold of change."

I struggled not to squirm as Lacey dipped the cup and peered inside, murmuring, "So much beneath the surface," and neglecting to explain.

"Clouds," she pointed at the mass of leaves, "overcast plans since the moment you made them, but it's the dragon you should fear." In the bottom were the knobbed nostrils, razor-backed skull, and long jagged tail climbing up to the lip. "More changes, sudden, dangerous, unknown origin or result." She shook her head, her expression knotted in grief.

Lacey placed the cup down and folded her hands. "Laced through all this darkness," she fluttered her fingers toward the cup, "is hemlock. Aspects of your past pop up and add layers of confusion, but they're not all together tragic. Great love paints your future, as does greatness through powerful friends, all evident in the lion." She pointed at the lion's mane completing a full circle of the cup.

"You contain inner strength and immense power, innate and unrealized. Not cast aside, rather tucked away. You would be wise to trust yourself instead of forcing decisions when left without alternative choices. You will prosper here, Sophie. If you allow yourself."

Prosper in what way wasn't outlined. Nor was how I was "tucked away" from some power, but I kept quiet.

Lacey's expression twisted from examination to restrained excitement. Her hazel eyes were bright as she sat forward and said, "Tell me of the dream."

My eyes widened. So much for facial control. I couldn't have been more surprised if Lacey had told me she was half-unicorn.

"What dream?" Kim asked with focused curiosity.

"My dream?" I stalled, making sure Lacey wasn't implying my career aspirations.

"Yes, the one that presents itself every time you sleep. Tell me about the storm, the water, the shadow figure. Do you know where you are? Some type of forest maybe?"

No one knew about the dream. It scared me too much to repeat them to anyone, and since I lived alone, it was easier to hide the screaming or blame it on the TV if anyone asked, but they never had, not even Kim. I stopped labelling this old lady as a loon and explained the dream in as much detail as I remembered. I had to put my hands between my crossed legs under the table, to hide the fact they shook.

"This shadow, you call it a monster?" Either she cared, or was excellent at pretending to care.

"Feels like a monster to me."

Lacey nodded. "A dream of this nature is usually something or someone vying for our attention. Showing us something repressed or undiscovered. This figure could be the manifestation of something else altogether, too difficult to discern at this time. The next time you dream, do not close your eyes. Turn and confront this figure, demand its purpose. Once it sees your strength, this figure may reveal itself, and the dream should proceed to its natural end."

She made it sound effortless. "How am I supposed to control that? Every time, I'm automatically terrified. There's *no* thought process, it just happens. I don't even realize I'm fucking dreaming!"

Lucid dreaming was far from an exact science and not something I have ever done. By now, my curiosity about the park dream was overripe, but would identifying the dark figure be enough to make the dream stop? Not only did she make it sound too easy, it had to be. After all the dream had put me through, I couldn't believe in an easy fix.

Lacey was as helpful as a Magic 8-Ball.

Lacey looked pointedly at Kim, clearly a frequent non-verbal order as Kim left the table and returned with a handwoven basket. A magnificent earthy and sweet scent emanated from the basket before Kim removed the burlap cloth over the top, revealing a plethora of fixings that looked like dried weeds.

With keen curiosity, I watched Lacey lay the cloth down and pick through the greenery, placing sprigs on the fabric.

"Rosemary?" she looked at Kim who reached into her bag, handing Lacey the container from my kitchen.

Kim smiled at me. "See? Used for many things."

How did she know she would need it? I didn't ask, though my thoughts were tangled over the possibility. Lacey must have needed it for something else as well. I couldn't wrap my thoughts around the alternative.

"In this case," Lacey took over, "to alter the aspects of your dream which prevent you from understanding. Rosemary,"—she shook a sparing amount from the container into her palm and then sprinkled it onto the cloth—"along with anise, cedar, and mullein will repel nightmares. If this dream is of that sort, a good night's rest will follow. If one of deeper meaning, clary sage will clarify the fog, artemisia will assist your recall where before you were blind, and agrimony will remove fear and release inner blockages preventing you from deciphering this being's intent."

Lacey's hair fell in tendrils as she plucked a leather thong from the bun. She then tied the fabric around the herbs creating a pouch.

"Place this dream pillow inside your pillowcase. It will strengthen that which is already within you, clarifying your visions to your sleeping self."

"Vision?"

Her smile tightened. "Dream."

I nodded, then thanked Lacey in a meek voice. Because I was desperate to try anything to shed the dream and get my life back on track, I took the dream pillow. I didn't know the herbs Lacey mentioned by name and would have no clue where to find them. I had a handful of weeds that, for all I knew, would work better if I smoked them. If anything, the delightful aroma might help me sleep.

"Sophie, may I please speak with Wiccum alone for a moment?"

The moment lingered until Kim's smile revealed Lacey meant her. I leapt to excuse myself, hoping the dismissal was innocuous, suspecting otherwise.

Lost little lamb now more than ever, I was without my ally in a room brimming with small group activities that I wasn't comfortable enough to approach. Needing to appear preoccupied, I found a comfortable seat on a couch and hoped no one noticed when I smelled the little bundle again. Whatever it was, I wanted to store it in my sinuses.

Around the room others were tarot card flipping and dice tossing, plus more doing I had no clue what. I was too overwhelmed to process anything, but I was impressed with their apparent confidence in their skills.

The cushion next to me depressed. Wearing a spritely smile was a young woman with long blonde hair and the bubbly personality to match. "Hi, I'm Denise Cartier." She offered her hand, with professionally manicured nails, to shake.

"Sophie Saterlee." I managed a light smile. Denise either forgave or ignored my hesitance.

"I've been a member for some time," Denise explained, though no one had asked. "Aunt Lacey seems to have taken a shine to you. What do you do?"

Not about to argue Lacey's interest, I noted Denise called her "Aunt Lacey" like Kim, which I now assumed everyone called her, relation not required.

"Um, I'm a bartender at The Lush in downtown St. Catharines while I get my psychology degree." Considering the due date I'd missed and Lacey's reading, was it something I should even bother with anymore?

"So, you're hired help?" Denise hid the majority of her disgust under her bright smile, but I detected more than she wanted me to. There's no way she missed the expression of insult I flashed. When I didn't answer, she said, "I mean, unless you want to head shrink us or pour a drink, I figured there was more to you." She looked at a group sitting on the carpet in front of us. Their focus was on bones that a reedy blonde rolled in between them like dice. I really hoped she was playing with chicken bones.

"Right, well, I guess I don't *do* anything." My irritation was thick. I was still stuck on the "hired help" comment. Who was this chick? "Um, I have a set of tarot cards I've had since I was a teen that took me forever to talk my mother into buying, but I can shuffle better than tell you your future." My mental snapshot of inept attempts years ago was laughable. Sifting through the handbook trying to decipher the cards as something good or bad was impossible.

"Bring them next time. They work better when they're consecrated."

"Yeah...I'll do that."

Denise's stiff posture told me she doubted my sincerity. Obviously, she was someone Kim would classify as "taking things seriously."

My hands were clammy, heart rate too high, thoughts a blur, and my agitation at Denise's questions was beginning to boil over.

"Are you returning next week? I get a good aura from you. That's what I do, I read auras, and I know Aunt Lacey sees something there. She said so, didn't she?" she asked with a hint too much transparency. Denise's eager smile and invasive stare revealed her true intentions.

Denise's forward introduction was a veiled information hunt, a ruse she was confident in pulling off. Two-faced people were among the worst, and my patience for Denise and her questions had run dry.

"Well...she..." Before I could give an evasive and rude response, someone touched my shoulder. I turned and mouthed a thank you at Kim for saving me, though I felt cheated of the chance to crush Denise's hopes.

"Let's find Donovan. He does palm reading." Kim didn't address

Denise as we walked away, leaving the blonde to sulk over her failed mission.

Some people never leave their adolescence behind.

I followed Kim to a spot on the rug where a group of women had assembled. Kim ordered them away with a snarl I was shocked anyone acknowledged. Once my line of sight cleared, the reason the crowd rallied was obvious. He must have snuck in late, because no matter my shock, this guy would have stood out during introductions.

Holy-shit-Fig-Newton, Donovan is gorgeous. Palm reader? No fucking way.

Adjusting his seated position, running his hands over his jeans, was a guy who could fit snugly in one of The Lush's barstools, after he posed for his own calendar. I would never have picked him out as someone who would entertain the concept, let alone read palms himself.

As we sat in front of him, Donovan looked irritated, scratching his head, and running his fingers through shaggy, dark hair. Almond-shaped, deep brown eyes rimmed with thick lashes surveyed us with something close to apathy. He had a strong chin sporting panty-wetting, kissable lips.

Donovan stated Kim's name. She responded with his, in the way of pleasantries, but sounding everything but pleasant.

Distracting myself from checking out the set of hard pecs beneath his plain, grey t-shirt, I had to say something. "Why don't they set up small tables?" I shifted my feet beneath me. "Sitting on the floor isn't made for tall people."

Even sitting, Donovan looked tall. "What? You don't like feeling like a kindergartener at story time?"

I was elated to hear sarcasm, his husky tone enough to make me want to keep him talking. I forgot all about Denise. "Do we get nap time?"

"Nope. No chocolate milk either."

"Just whiskey?" Though he appeared sober, the scent of spiced alcohol wafted my way, my nose for it honed.

He made a throaty sound coupled with a sly grin that dimpled one cheek. "Only for the teacher's pet."

"Well," Kim interjected with impatience, "can the teacher's pet manage another reading?"

"Now, now. Don't be jealous, Second Fiddle." Donovan's jaw clenched. He kept his gaze on me and held out his hand in a prompt for mine.

"I'm not..." Kim started, but Donovan ignored her rebuff, starting in on the reading.

Holding my hands firmly, he traced the lines on my palm and spoke with confidence. Mesmerized, I forced my attention on his words, but not without difficulty.

Donovan was accurate about past and present events, so I paid close attention when he spoke of days to come. Still holding onto my hand, he peered up to catch my eye. "A shit-ton of chaos crashes your future. You got plans?"

"Doesn't everybody?"

Both cheeks dimpled this time. "Apparently. Be prepared to drop them." I kept my expression neutral despite the raging emotion his statement evoked. He looked at me with such purpose, I straightened my posture. "You've got more important things to worry about. Though you think you can handle that, and more, you need to prepare for the shitstorm or it'll take you out. Play the observer all you want, learn from your textbooks, and unravel the brains of everyone while trying to please every jerk-off but yourself, but indecisiveness isn't an option." He let go of my hand and sat back against the wall, crossing his arms over his chest. "Those choices would be easier if your talents were better taken care of."

The accusation I was being intentionally neglectful, or rebelling against whatever talents he assumed I possessed, was clear. In reality, I had absolutely no fucking clue what the hell he was talking about.

Stunning good looks only afforded so much leeway. Donovan's was exhausted by the scowl he sported.

"So, that's the answer, huh?" I snapped at him. "Shape up and the shitstorm coming my way will fuck off?"

Donovan's dark eyes narrowed. "You came to me for a reading—"

"No kidding. A reading doesn't involve you judging me for doing what you're assuming I'm doing. What the hell are you doing with your life, huh? You got plans? Do they involve something more than scowling and sitting in this basement telling other people how to live their lives?"

"Sophie!" Kim interjected, but Donovan answered anyway.

"I don't have a single plan past the hour I'm living. Right now, I'm here. In two hours? Who the fuck knows? But it won't be here, taking your shit."

Suddenly, I was happy to leave the palm reader alone. When I looked back as our empty spots filled, that scowl morphed into something else, like he was trying to figure something out—figure me out? —and coming up short.

Kim didn't comment on what was said between me and Donovan, but I took a few minutes in the bathroom at the back of the long room to collect myself. Cold water on the back of my neck only did so much. It took me longer than I wanted to get a handle on my emotions.

Kim waited outside the door and asked me if I was okay when I finished up.

"Yup, what's next?" I wasn't letting this run me out of the meeting, even if I didn't want to be here. Instead, I fell back into that numb place where I found comfort and went through the motions.

Exact opposite in temperament to the scowling palm reader was Gwen, the orange-haired woman I held hands with during the blessing circle. She read my tarot cards in a ten-card spread I recognized. Overall, Gwen created a better experience than Donovan. We bypassed an aura reading with Denise as Kim claimed Denise was book-learned and could barely detect a hint of true auras. I assumed Denise made it up when she briefly mentioned reading auras anyway. Plus, I wouldn't be able to contain myself if she made another off-hand comment. It was safer for everyone.

Apparently, I'd missed the memo, as each member who read me with cards, auras, bones, or chakras had something to say about my lacking drive and expectant talents, lessons I should have already learned, and warnings they shouldn't have had to warn me of, though they couldn't pinpoint what to watch for. Thankfully, Kim had the forethought to write it all down. My brain was stuffed with "What the fuck?" too many times to organize it all and I couldn't drum up the energy to ask questions about what half of what they said meant.

Two hours after I white-flagged it, the night ended. Nothing remained. No veiled snarky remarks, no energy to pretend I understood a lick of what they claimed, not even the capacity to screen my boredom when someone went on about the healing properties of boswellia.

Before our escape, Aunt Lacey stopped us and dropped a silver chain in my palm, which I then shoved into my pocket without a second glance. Aunt Lacey made no comment on my rudeness. "The charm will balance your mind and make your past, present, and future clearer to your opaque eyes. We are all connected, Sophie."

Her intense stare conveyed an indiscernible message. She meant well in passing along the advice, cryptic as it was. To my surprise, she followed up with a tight embrace before wishing us safe travels back to St. Catharines.

Ten minutes had passed before I thought about the reading with Donovan and snapping at him. What was I doing with my life? According to Aunt Lacey's reading, I was wasting my time with my current plan. Some unknown "dragon" was waiting to decimate everything I had worked for anyway, so what was the point?

Giving up never looked so attractive.

3

THE CONTINUUM EXISTS

Kim passed over folded sheets of paper when we got off on our floor. "Here are the entries from your readings. Read them again and see what makes sense."

I took the papers for my mushy brain to mull over later. "Thanks. No way would I've remembered all that stuff." Referring to the readings as stuff caused Kim to flinch.

"Do you think you'll go again next weekend?" Despite her smile, Kim's frail voice made it seem that a negative response could shatter her.

"Next weekend? Hmm, not sure. I might have a conflict with my *other* coven." I added a small laugh to cut the tension.

Kim grabbed my arm and talked too fast. "Shit, I'm so sorry. I should've told you what it was, but I figured if you liked it, the fact it was a coven might not matter. You did have fun, didn't you? You got the pouch for your nightmares, so it wasn't a total waste."

"It's fine, Kim, really. You're right. I would have faked a ruptured tonsil if you were upfront."

"Eww, can that happen?"

"Who cares when you're avoiding a potential blue Kool-Aid situation?"

She swatted at me.

"So, yes, oh lovely red-haired enchantress, the night wasn't a total wash. I just need to unscramble the Rubik's cube in my head."

Kim nodded, her smile small and twisted.

I wanted to say yes to the weekly invitation. Believing in the obscure wasn't a huge stretch, most lore is derived from somewhere, but the fiction I read is labelled as such for a reason. Reading palms, auras, tarots, bones, and whatever else was entertainment in my world. Organizing a coven meant they believed in their abilities. Even if I tabled the debate over extraordinary talents, how could I expect to find a niche within the group with nothing of equal value to offer? Showing up for free readings, and to gawk at Donovan, would be frowned upon.

Though the man candy may be worth a trip or two to the mansion, as long as the asshat kept his fucking mouth shut.

"Will this actually work?" I held up the pouch.

"Absolutely." Kim's confidence returned. "Aunt Lacey knows her shit. If she says it'll help, it will."

"She's not really your aunt, right? Other people called her Aunt Lacey too, and I assume you don't have a dozen siblings. Please tell me you're not related to that bitch, Denise."

"God, no. I'd change my name and move to Alaska. No, it's just what Aunt Lacey likes being called." She shrugged, so I dropped it.

"Wish me luck." I moved toward my door.

"Good luck. Let me know how tonight goes."

"I will," I promised over Bosco barking at the sound of my voice.

Back in the normalcy of my small space, the smell of my mixed-berry air freshener increased my calm factor as I sank onto my comfy couch with my pug sidekick. No neat collection of words could sum up how I felt. Kim had reached beyond her comfort zone by intro-ducing me to how she spends her Sunday evenings. I had no intention of causing her mental anguish over the decision, but I was sapped of energy and mentally battered.

Did I really just attend a coven meeting?

I listened to my messages. My mother's voice chimed, "Checking in," adding Dr. Konnor's office called her place by accident to remind me of a yearly physical coming up. After sending her love, the line went dead.

"You bring such wonderful news, mother."

Dr. Konner had known me since I was in utero. If he heard about my dream and how I spent my night, even he would scratch out a script so fast his gold-rimmed glasses would slide off his nose.

Nervous anticipation kept sleep at bay. I dreaded the freezing, flooded park. If the pouch failed, besides heading to Dr. Konner's office, what solutions did I have? I realized how desperate I was and felt utterly stupid.

Stubbornness won out.

Postponing sleep, I retrieved the silver necklace from my jeans pocket, taking my first look at the charm. At the end of a simple silver chain dangled a Celtic knot. Aunt Lacey told me what it meant, but I needed to do my own research.

I jumped on my computer. Hundreds of images depicted variations of an interlocking, three-point knot, yet many also had a circle running through the knot. Mine did not. Finding a near identical rendition, the site claimed it was one of the most well-known knot symbols, called a *triquetra,* with a long history including 500 BC Macedonian King Coins and the Norse God Odin.

My favourite explanation was of the Maid, Mother, and Crone. What it boiled down to was exactly what Aunt Lacey had claimed.

Of course.

I thought back to what she said. "We are all connected, Sophie." The symbol represented those connections as we evolve from one stage of life to another. This continuum exists regardless of our struggle to hit pause on the good years. It remains steady during the ruts that breed wisdom through heartache and despair, even if we wished to fast forward through them. Life was, itself, a revolving cycle we can't escape.

The concept of "everything happens for a reason" was bunk, as far as I was concerned. Denying that evolving equalled happiness was the worst case of selective blindness. Personal evolution I could swallow. Fate? Hooey slathered in codswallop or plain and utter bullshit.

"Fine, you were right, smarty pants," I mumbled and powered down my PC.

I poured chocolate milk into my favourite childhood blue Kool-Aid man plastic cup, craving simple comforts. I chuckled to myself, remembering the reference with Kim in the hall and joked about the drink with Donovan before he became a dickhole.

With Bosco at my side and my book begging to be read, I tucked the pouch thingy into my pillowcase. Hoping it didn't fall out during a restless sleep, I shoved it into the further corner. Given Bosco's history, it would be his new chew toy, and I had no idea what it would do to him, plus no clue what to tell a vet he'd gotten into. "Oh, you know. Just a bunch of poisonous weeds I keep handy for bad dreams. No biggy, Doc." That would be worse than the time he got into an entire tub of butter while I was at work. I laughed until my stomach hurt trying to catch the slick, butter-basted bugger as he tore through the apartment. Luckily, he turned out fine.

Thirty minutes of reading and a belly full of chocolate milk later, the book's words slipped together, begging me to give up on this tug-of-war. After re-reading the same line four times, I tapped out.

———

I winced as a bolt of lightning cracked and illuminated the sky for a pulse that whipped my trembling hands to cover my ears. A biting wind chilled my rain-soaked body. My jaw ached from chattering teeth as my polka-dotted pj shorts left me unprotected from the elements. Water covered my ankles, rising fast as I remained rooted in place like the thrashing willows dancing in the storm. Fear caught in my chest while my breath shortened, making me dizzy.

A sense of danger at my back poured steel into my spine.

The rain fell harder as if taking stock of my emotions. How? I didn't understand, but the storm raged in stride with my fear. Strands of wet hair whipped across my face as the wind picked up.

A tingle crawled beneath my skin, goosebumps littering every inch. Even with the frigid winds, this stirring inside warmed me a few degrees.

Willing my arms to straighten to my sides, I clenched my fists against the impulse to run as I closed my eyes.

Don't! Don't be a coward. Open your eyes! Open your eyes! Open your eyes!

I forced them wide, needing to see a face, needing more than shadows and oppression.

Gathering my fear, I let it coil into an anger within to keep me rooted. With a strengthening inhale and exhale, I sprayed water off my lips, making the feared decision to turn around.

If only slow motion took over as in the movies. Instead, the scene was chaos, water rising up my bare legs, the park refusing to allow a moment's rest from its perpetual storm as I twisted to face the shadow.

I did it!

In other dreams, if I managed to turn, it was without conscious decision, just a scripted scene progressing on cue. Choice empowered me.

Let's do this, fucker.

Clear-headed, feet rooted and braced for confrontation, I faced the obscured figure. My blood raced, and every muscle was alive with adrenaline-filled fear. I refused to back down. Lightning struck in spiderwebs, chasing away the shadows hiding the ambiguous figure.

A man's stark face filled my vision as he stood in front of me looking down from his oppressive stature, his eyes capturing my attention. Grey as a winter's sky behind narrowed lids and thick, furrowed brows with wolf-like intensity, those eyes stole my confidence.

Shocked by the reveal, and the jarring thunder that followed, I snapped out of the dream and back into my bedroom.

———

Amongst tangled sheets, a second skin of cold sweat caused me to shiver. Bosco jumped up and whimpered while making feverish attempts to lick my face. Minutes passed before I could take in satisfying amounts of oxygen.

"I'm fine, buddy." Stroking his back reassured him as much as myself.

After months of agonizing confusion, I finally knew who the figure was. No, not who, but what he looked like. I woke up too quickly to ask questions, but one mystery was solved. No monsters, no demon to possess or kill me, or anything else fitting my worst-case scenario imagination. Actually, remembering the strong set of features, I was captivated.

He was beautiful.

Lying back on my pillows, I tried to remember the striking man who appeared in front of me. Why does he do that? I had to strain my neck skyward, he at least five inches taller than me, his skin pale, short hair shining black and dripping with rainwater.

Hot damn.

Next, I tried to decipher his expression. Anger? Why was *he* angry? He was stalking me. He scared the shit out of me night after night. What gave him the right to act like I was the asshole? My own anger swelled at the audacity.

Propelled by this fury, I shot out of bed and started pacing until I found myself in the living room with more space to tread. Bosco's feet pattered on the carpet at my heels. If only I was the work-out-in-anger type, or the punch-things-or-smash-dishes type. At least then I could expel the feeling in a burst of energy. Instead, it simmered. I paced and gnawed on already pathetic fingernails, a bad habit that felt like progress while I was too amped to drop back into the dream for another round of "Who the fuck are you?"

After fifteen minutes of snacking on my nails, I plunked onto the couch, ready to burrow my hands inside my skull to pull out answers. Did the pouch work? Was that why I finally saw his face? Maybe Kim was right, and Aunt Lacey wasn't an old coot hawking even older wives tales.

"Now what?"

I contemplated my options. Though my gut told me only one thing made sense, calling an old lady in the middle of the night was not a viable option. Besides, I didn't know Aunt Lacey. Was this the pouch thing? If it was, the old lady deserved to be woken up in the middle of night.

Frustration brought me back to my computer, this time as a distraction. I couldn't focus enough to do schoolwork. Email was mostly junk since I had no interest in finding "LOCAL SLUTS NOW" so I popped onto social media hoping for more than annoying game requests and cat videos.

"Kim!" Her chat was enabled.

My fingers swept across the keyboard typing *IY QIRKWD!!* into the chat box and hit enter without catching the blunder.

???? Kim typed back.

Ugh...It worked.

Tell me!

In the middle of typing, another message blipped through:

I'm coming over!

Less than two minutes later, Kim and I were on my couch. Her excitement matched mine, which was good. If she wasn't as excited as me, I would have screamed because I was so worked up.

"It was a man! A gorgeous man, but he looked at me funny."

"What do you mean 'funny'? Like you had a booger or something?"

"No, though considering the cold and rain, it's probably happened at some point." Kim giggled as I moved on. "He seemed confused about why was I there, like I strolled into his man-cave without the password. And was as surprised to see me as I was to see him."

"Did he say anything?"

"Lightning hit, and I woke up before he could. I learned nothing besides the fact he's not a snarling beast who wants to eat my face."

"You can't rule out cannibalism just because he's hot. Not all monsters are ugly."

"Don't I know it." My history with good-looking monsters was what dismantled my life in the first place. Not that Kim knew anything about it. "I'll remind myself of that while he's snacking on my liver."

"Let's be real, he'd probably cook you first."

"Then he better pair me with good wine."

Both laughed and then a moment of contemplation drew out.

"I always felt like he was coming after me. I don't know. Now it seems like something else."

"Okay. Give me a play-by-play."

I recited every detail, including his weird eyes and that I'd realized, in the dreams, I was often wearing only little pyjamas, underwear, or even nothing at all. I wondered how much of me he saw. Kim and I analyzed the sequence of events to death for over an hour. I appreciated her effort, knowing definitive answers were impossible.

Kim sighed. "I can speak to Aunt Lacey in the morning, and will, but I know what she'll say. You need to dream again. Sorry I can't be there to coach you through it. The herbs Aunt Lacey gave you are working. Let them do their thing."

"What if he attacks me? I usually wake up too quickly but, just 'cuz he's hot, it doesn't mean he's not dangerous."

"Mmm. The best ones are little bit of both."

"*Pfft.* You know what I mean."

Kim giggled. "Sure do." Her tone was lascivious. "You said the dream begins with him farther away, and then he gets up nice and close."

"This isn't porn, Kim. Remember...dark and looming."

"Sounds like porn to me."

I laughed and laid back into the couch. "Sounds like someone's overtired."

"And apparently lonely."

"Don't even get me started on comparing cobwebs. I gotta deal with this guy before I can concentrate on anything else."

"Cobwebs? Eww." Kim fake gagged, relieving the last bit of tension in the conversation. "'Kay, back to Danger Dude. My point, before I was distracted by lack of penis, is that he could've taken you to your knees, but he just left you standing there."

"Now you're using euphemisms?"

"Too easy, right? But I'm not wrong. He's had ample opportunity and did nothing but stand and stare. He could be into that whole watching thing, especially if you were showing up naked, but you won't know anything until you see him again."

"Okay, fine. Thanks for talking me through this, Kim. It's nice telling someone without being chemically restrained."

"No prob, Soph. Get some sleep."

After goodbyes, the search for answers continued. I was so energized that sleep would only happen with an over-medicated stupor unavailable from my medicine cabinet. Instead, cleaning was the best energy dump available.

After wiping down my faux cherry wood coffee table, side tables, and new-to-me desk, I graduated to the bathroom, my most dreaded chore, but it consumed time and worked up a sweat. Once those tasks were done, I dropped my wet gloves into the sink and checked the time. Still too early to vacuum. Noise complaints were no help to my situation.

Rummaging through the heap of dirty clothes, it became apparent I'd waited too long to do laundry. Even while separating whites, colours, and reds I fixated on the image of *him* in the lightning-bright park, his expression, the way his eyebrows contrasted those pale grey eyes, and trying to guess why he was there, who he was.

Reading while the wash cycle did its job was useless, focusing on the story was impossible while daydreaming more than usual. How did he get into my dreams? Were the weird eyes a clue? Was he trying to tell me something? Maybe he was some type of spirit guide, though it sounded too hokey, and I wasn't sold on the existence of spirits.

My thoughts reverted to their pessimistic comfort. What if these dreams were just dreams? Nothing sinister, nothing to interpret, and didn't mean a damn thing. All this time just a by-product of imagination and stress.

The fact he wasn't real was depressing. Geez, was I scared of him or not? Technically, I didn't know this person enough to decide. Despite the possibility he was a predator, albeit a beautiful predator, I tried to force my thoughts to flow in a positive direction. Nonetheless, I was at odds with myself, volleying between what I preferred and what I could handle.

Achy from cleaning with unnecessary vigour, I plunked the full laundry basket on the coffee table once I'd fetched it from the laundry room. I decided to lay out on the couch and rest for a moment as my limbs felt too heavy. Bosco shimmied himself against me and got comfortable after he exhaled a snot-filled sneeze.

———

A crick in my neck evoked a groan, the sun in my face blinded me. Trying to escape it by rolling away to hide from it only made my neck feel worse.

Wait. Why is the sun up? Did I fall asleep?

Mentally foggy, I looked through my sheer drapes as if the light had to be something other than the sun of a new day. Then I checked the TV guide station to corroborate the sun's high position, astonished it read 2:53 pm.

Not only did I sleep. I slept without dreaming.

"What the fizz?"

4

———

SPEAKING UP

Mystified, I peered around the room expecting to see a layer of dust from countless years of sleep. Why didn't I dream? Without Aunt Lacey's pouch under the couch pillow, I should have had the original blind-and-shitting-my-pants nightmare. I suppose it was possible I didn't remember if I dreamt or not, but I doubted it. The dream was too terrifying to forget.

I tried to recall the last time I'd slept without being drawn into the nightmare. The sense of being stood-up soured my mood. I expected to see *him*. While trying to figure out why I felt such disappointment, I dug my fingers into the knot in my neck.

My phone blinked, indicating I had messages. That meant even though I didn't dream, I did sleep. My off switch must have been stuck if I slept through my phone blaring next to me.

The first message was from my mom. She wanted me to see my brother Adam's alternative rock band play that night with her and my cousin Serena.

The next message was from Adam himself. "Pick up the phone, d-bag!" Dead air hung until he continued, "'Kay, you better be coming tonight. Mom and Serena are, so stop being a coward and getchyer ass over here."

No hello, no goodbye. Gotta love brothers.

With hours left until rock-god heaven, I checked my email and was happy to read a response from my professor agreeing to take my late paper, docking twenty-five percent of the mark. Better than a zero. Regardless of Aunt Lacey or Donovan's assessment of my future, I wasn't ready to give up on my studies, and signed into the school's site to find a new assignment to dive into while Bosco perched on my desk.

Ready to prove Aunt Lacey and Donovan wrong, I powered through a paper for my Ethics class, a worksheet for Statistics, and outlined another paper on Sensation and Perception. I felt accomplished and restored from my earlier apprehension about giving up on school. Learning is never a negative path, and I refused to believe it a waste of my time.

To better focus on a working plan, so I didn't miss more assignments or shifts at work, I printed out a simple schedule and taped it to my wall.

Pfft. Give up. Not until I'm forced to.

A group chat popped up when I checked social media. My childhood friends were trying to pin down a date when everyone was available for dinner, a near impossible task. Most had babies or full-fledged little people having playdates and school trips, a level of responsibility foreign to me. I wrote back, including dates of availability, confident they were correct since my handy schedule was in front me, conveying my excitement with as many emoticons as were endurable.

After powering down my PC, I crushed a layer of crackers onto the surface of some tomato soup. The meal was necessary so I could drink at the concert without puking like a college freshman. Plus, I had to show up to work sober. I refused to give Drew another excuse to fire me. While eating, I argued with myself as to whether or not to tell my mom and Serena about the grey-eyed man, Aunt Lacey, and the Coven. Sharing with the two people I confided in the most was natural.

Not in all things.

I'd hoarded the details of my asshole ex and what he put me through. They asked questions, countless questions, but I sidestepped them like a pro, assuring them I was fine. The biggest lies I've ever repeated involved him, and were ones I hoped to rectify when I felt stronger and less shameful for falling into my ex's trap.

Serena would think the Coven was the coolest thing since she grew boobs and want to tag along to the next meeting. My mom, well, I wanted to spare my mother the worry.

What if these people were nutbars or Aunt Lacey was playing me? Getting my cousin involved without knowing for sure was too risky. Could I have been so desperate for the pouch thing to work that a placebo effect took over, unveiling the mysterious grey-eyed man? Could a placebo connect me to my body or grant me control to change the outcome of the dream? I had no clue. Suspicions aside, Aunt Lacey knew things she shouldn't, and until I figured out how, I was keeping Serena far away from the group.

The only thing I was sure of was that soup made a piss-poor dinner.

———

Serena was the closest thing I had to a sister and couldn't look more different than me with her light eyes and fair hair. Her mother—my mom's sister, Karen—was my second mom. My memory was filled with times when the sisters, who married a set of brothers, listened to oldies while playing Scrabble or cards. Serena was the outgoing one of us too and wouldn't let me skip the concert. Secretly, I looked forward to the distraction. With music that loud, cohesive thought was impossible.

Parking downtown was a pain in the ass, so Mom, Serena, and I walked from my apartment to the bar in which Adam had made part of his rise to fame. After paying our ten-dollar entry fee, we stepped into loud voices and the smell of packed bodies.

"Ugh," Serena tried to push through the crowd. "We trekked our asses to Florida for that battle of the bands thingy on a stanky, pukey bus that broke down in some hick town with only a Pizza Hut, and he can't pitch us free tickets? Custy bird, that kid."

Countless concerts, diligently paying the ten- or twelve-dollar ticket price, added up, but we kept paying.

"We'll get ink poisoning from all the hand stamps before that happens." I couldn't wait to wash it off already.

My mom fidgeted with the edge of her v-neck as we found an open spot and scanned for Adam. "Am I dressed okay? I'd rather chew pinecones than compete with chickies twenty years younger than me."

Serena appraised her with her ice-blue eyes. "Who cares what these bitches think, Aunt Lu? Plus, half can't see you through their emo bangs, and the rest are too busy making sure the right man-meat notices they're not wearing underwear." Serena pointed to our right at an example in a short skirt perched on a high stool and laughed. I looked away in time, but it was a close one. My mom wasn't so lucky.

"Don't worry, Mom. You're wearing all my clothes, and I don't go commando for anyone." I recognized the outfit she'd borrowed for a date and neglected to return.

"While I'm overjoyed my parenting never needed to include instructions on keeping your legs closed, you really should wear more skirts." I rolled my eyes, but that didn't stop her. "And it's precisely my point. I'm wearing *your* clothes. I want to blend, not look like I'm running a free show." She poked my ribs, chiding me for the risqué, low-cut top I'd decided on last minute.

I may not be looking for a date, but it didn't mean I had to walk around in a muumuu.

We caught up with Adam, who introduced us to his girlfriend-of-the-month or week or night. We never could tell. Knowing Adam, this Hailey with the trendy, cropped hairstyle was probably perfect right down to her pedicured toes.

"Okay!" Serena slapped her hand down on my shoulder after awkward small talk. "Who wants a fucking drink? I'm buying." Adam and his girl already held beers. Serena was orchestrating an escape for a true account of our opinions on Adam's new squeeze.

As the show began, we avoided the rowdier bunch by sticking to the edge of the crowd, our shoes Velcroed to alcohol-soaked floors.

Adam owned the performance with captivating stage presence. He played the guitar and screamed through songs, but he loved writing music. The lead singer strained for high notes, yet had improved since the Florida battle of the bands.

Serena hit the bar while my mom hit the bathroom, leaving me to save our spot. Denise and another girl from the Coven, whose name I couldn't remember, caught my eye and headed through the crowd. I saw them first but couldn't look away fast enough.

"Well, hello there," Denise's voice trilled. Her eyes were glassy from the drink in her hand. "Big fans?"

"Guitarist is my brother. What are you doing here?" As light as I attempted to keep my tone, the snark was unavoidable.

"Bartender gives free drinks." She held up her glass, which I assumed she earned with shameless flirting. "No other reason to come to this shithole." I nodded, her friend huffing with impatience. "Maybe you know him?"

"Why would I? Is he...?" I didn't want to say "a part of the Coven" out loud, but she seemed to catch my drift.

"No,"—she flicked her blonde hair, more straw than Serena's gold—"blissfully ignorant. But you're in the same business, figured you'd cross paths in your...circles."

Her transparent dig was laughable.

"I need a refill," Denise's friend whined.

Denise nodded and then asked me, "Do you know how to make a sloe gin fizz?" Her tight smile mocked me. I returned it in kind.

Serena returned with her hands full of drinks a moment later.

The crowd surged when the next song switched to a harder beat. Since she's a pro, Serena saved our drinks. Denise wasn't so lucky.

Sometimes karma's a quick bitch.

Denise swiped at the front of her wet dress. Refraining from laughing was impossible. "Cheers for free drinks!" I yelled over the music. Denise fumed as I took a sip of my own and moved with the crowd.

Denise pushed back at the guy who dumped her drink, her friend stumbling behind her. Both managed to escape by ineptly dodging a few drunken moshers.

"Free drinks?" Serena's voice sounded strained.

I waved her off and focused on the band, satisfied that my assessment of Denise was spot on. I'd misjudged others and been spanked with unjust consequences; it made me second-guess my perceptions about most everything and everybody. Being right about Denise had me on a high. With renewed energy, I downed my drink, and jumped with the crowd.

After a complete set, Adam swiped at his dark, matted hair as we laughed about the drummer trying to use his hand when he broke a drumstick before Adam switched topics. "What'd you think of Hailey?" With Hailey preoccupied at the merchandise table with a couple friends, he had an opportunity to get feedback.

His smile widened as we spouted off words of praise. "She seems really nice,"... "She's pretty,"... "She has perfect teeth."

"Will this one make it to the next show?" I asked in a sisterly manner.

"*Pfft*, don't get ahead of yourself, sis." He chugged his beer, plonked it down on the bar top, and gave us all a sweaty hug before setting his charm on selling tank tops and keychains to Hailey's friends.

We left before the next band started screaming.

I invited them back to the bar with promises of a free drink and nachos. My mom tried to bail, but Serena wouldn't let her.

We bypassed Jack, the yelling-and-abusive-to-his-wife neighbour who lived across from Kim, standing in a cloud of smoke in front of The Lush. A sneer creased his pock-marked face when he caught me glancing at him before we headed inside.

Mom and Serena sat at the bar so I could multi-task with work and socializing, still floating on a high from the concert and Denise's soggy dress. I put in an order of nachos and got drinks for my mom and Serena.

I waved at Jack's wife, Theresa, who sat with a plate of fries in front of her at a small table against the wall. She smiled and waved back as Jack came inside and ordered another beer from Eddie. He didn't know Jack was an angry drunk, but when he passed Jack his beer, I wanted to punch Eddie anyway. Heavy on the sauce meant heavy with the fist. I cringed at what that meant for Theresa, who stopped smiling when her husband sat in his chair.

After a few customers, I plunked the plate of hot-and-ready nachos in front of my mom and Serena and got them another round of drinks.

"How's life, my Dolly?" Mom asked me over the loud crack of the pool table being used.

I shrugged, not wanting to lie by pretending to be "fine", handed a customer a beer, and then deflected by asking about hers.

"Brian took me out again last night."

"What's that now?" Serena popped a salsa-and-cheese-slathered chip into her mouth, speaking around it, "Six or seven dates?" She looked at me with a knowing leer. "You know what that means."

"Shut it. I don't wanna know what that means."

"Definitely gettin' some," Serena muttered as I paled.

"Just because I'm a mother, doesn't mean I'm not still a woman who—"

"Who looks beautiful in my clothes," I interrupted. "Will I ever get them back?"

"They're probably what got her laid," Serena mumbled.

"Certainly helped." My mom laughed. They clinked glasses while I wilted.

Mom mentioned planning this year's family reunion with Grandma Lizzie. Never a thrilling experience. At least the event would include an unending supply of Uncle Roger's lewd jokes, as well as delicious home-cooked food.

I sloshed vodka over the lip of the glass when Jack raised his voice above the music. Theresa looked around and coloured in embarrassment as people stared. She tried to calm Jack. Instead, he surged to his feet, knocking his beer to the floor. Glass smashed in a spray of alcohol.

"See what you did!" Jack yelled at Theresa.

"Hey!" I shouted.

Theresa apologized and bent to pick up the broken pieces.

"Theresa, don't." I rounded the bar, grabbing the broom on my way.

"Take your drama outside," Eddie tried. Jack was too focused on supervising his wife, on her knees, cleaning up his mess.

I knelt next to her. "I got it."

"What are you doing?" Jack grabbed the handle of the broom and pushed it away. That threw me off balance, knocking me to my ass.

"Sophie!" my mother called.

I stood up and gave her and Serena a look that kept them only a step from their stools, before I turned back to Jack. He stared me down, his nostrils flaring like a drunken, infuriated bull. Being the subject of an oppressive stare from a power-tripping bastard sparked flashes of my ex and created a horror film that clouded my vision. The difference was Theresa loved the man in front of me, and I wanted nothing but to kick his balls up inside his pelvis.

A light touch on my hand re-focused me. Theresa stood close, her eyes pleading for me to back down. For her sake, I did.

"Sorry." My forced apology caused another flashback to grittier times when an apology was expected no matter who was at fault. "It's staff duty to clean up anything that might hurt a customer. Liability issues and all that."

"She would've fucked it up anyway." Jack sniffed so hard I heard the mucus dance in the back of his throat. "Go!" he told Theresa, who dipped her hazel eyes to the ground and marched off as instructed.

As I watched them leave, I gritted my teeth so hard my jaw hurt.

Vibrating while I cleaned up the mess, I finished and retreated behind the bar, fielding my mom and Serena's questions about Jack and Theresa. I told them the couple were neighbours, but refrained from more detail. No need to tell them he was an abusive prick, the whole bar had caught his aggressive vibe.

From the look exchanged between my mom and Serena, they knew there was more. Not only more to the situation, but more to my reaction to it. They knew and, for whatever reason, weren't asking questions. They never did and I wondered how much they knew.

With the "Jack and Theresa Show" over, the bar patrons went back to their drinks. I struggled not to imagine the horror Theresa was going through right now and to shake off memories of my own struggles.

Putting aside my thoughts before they drove me out of The Lush to outside Theresa and Jack's door, I focused on my dreams. I could only do a fraction more to figure out the dreams than I could the hot mess that had walked out of here, but it was something.

Since it weighed so heavily, my mom picked up on this and pressed for explanation. I conceded in hopes the small admission might prove cathartic. Once I began, the dream was highlighted in detail. The coven stuff stayed secret, but the storm-ravaged park, the dark mass, the flooding, and the grey-eyed man was all out there.

As predicted, Serena thought the dreams were "Badass!" Mom, equally as predictable, assumed I was reading too much before bed and worried about my lack of sleep, then went into a story a recurring of her and I on a sinking ship.

Lemon and lime juice coated my fingers as I prepped them. My focus was far from my mother's story, too distracted by thoughts of the grey-eyed man. I had to admit, speaking of the dream, even if not in its entirety and quietly so others wouldn't think I was insane, to people who truly knew me, downgraded my restlessness, but I still needed answers.

Plans of the next get-together were made before my company left and Mom promised to have me and Serena over for some macaroni and tomatoes, a household favourite.

As satisfying as good tips and time spent with my mom and cousin were, it was equally satisfying to be home alone once my shift ended. An introvert at heart, socialising was exhausting. My head pounded with the echoes of Adam's band, the bar patrons, my mom and Serena's chatter, plus Jack and Theresa's fight.

Kim had left a cryptic message to call her with an update no matter the time. Unnecessary discretion, yet appreciated.

"Hey Kim, were you sleeping? If you were, it's your fault for telling me to call you at any time."

"Nope, I'm up. Worked the late shift, though not as late as you. What happened after I talked to you last?"

"Diddly-squat. I worked off the energy by cleaning until I dropped. I guess I was too exhausted to dream again."

"Yeah. About that." She paused. "Aunt Lacey thought you needed a break."

"Excuse me?"

Kim's exhale vibrated the receiver. "After we talked, I called her."

"You called her?"

"I swear, the woman never sleeps. I knew she'd be up and would want to know the herb mix worked. I also thought she could give some advice to pass on."

"And her advice was that I needed a break?"

"No, that was my advice, actually. You deal with this every night. I thought maybe a little sleep would help you function like a human being. She took it to heart and gave you a break."

"She stopped my dream!"

"Temporarily made you unreceptive to the dream. Temporary. Just enough for a few hours of uninterrupted sleep."

"How the hell can she pull that off? Is that even possible?"

"She can do a hell of a lot of things. And after dreaming every night for forever, you didn't dream, right? So, yeah, it's possible."

I pulled the phone away from my ear, contemplating hanging up. What right did they have to fuck with my head? And how the hell could they get into my head to mess around in the first place? How could Kim believe this? I warred with the possibility and tried to follow Kim's logic.

No matter what, I needed to move on with my life. These nightmares were fucking up my plans. Now that I'd seen that face in my dream, I felt compelled to find out who it was, to understand why this was happening night after night. Even if Aunt Lacey *could* stop them from happening, did that solve the issue?

No. It was avoiding it. Something I did all too much, and was what got me into this trouble in the first place.

"Sorry, Soph." I heard and put the phone against my ear again. "I was just trying to help. So was she. She won't do it again if you don't want her to, I'll make sure of it." My thoughts were a tangled mess. "So, what do you want to do next?"

"I...I don't know. Dream again, I guess."

"Okay. Call me tomorrow if you find out anything more. Okay?"

"Sure."

"You okay?" Kim asked when I didn't hang up.

"Um...weird night." I told her about Denise at Adam's concert and the run-in with Jack and Theresa, leaving out its full effect on me.

"Man, I hate that loser. Both of them. Jack and Denise should shack up and leave everyone else alone."

"Jack is a classic douchebag bastard who I'd love to leave bleeding for a starving hyena. Though I'm sure he has a fucked-up story of his own to make him the dick he is. Denise is just one of those chicks. I take it as a compliment she doesn't like me. I might go to the meeting next week just to fuck with her."

"I wouldn't even hate you for it."

Sometimes we bond with others over mutual hatred.

Walking Bosco one last time, I felt the temptation to visit the park, but I knew *he* wouldn't be down there while I was awake, and it was dangerous this time of night.

Upstairs, I slid on pyjamas, making sure they were long pants and sleeves, and crawled into bed with Bosco snuggled at my feet.

Twenty pages into a book and I put it aside, checking that the pouch was still in place.

Closing my eyes, my last thought was a hope to see *his* face again.

5

INTERFERENCE

Fear cocooned my body.

Panic staved off a chill from the cold rain blanketing me. I attempted to convince myself I was safe from the grey-eyed man. It was an optimistic rationalization for such a pessimist, but I craved to believe this guy wasn't infiltrating my dream for some nefarious purpose, fearing the result if not.

Equipped with new, flimsy optimism, my nerves shook as the water around my ankles rose and my anticipation built. I squinted through the darkness and rain, seeing nothing.

The presence was at my back. I knew this without him touching me or turning to prove it with my eyes. My skin crawled and itched as I gathered courage. A long moment passed before I managed to face him.

His silhouette was visible, looming over me as always. My patience thrummed at having to wait for lightning to strike.

I need to see. I need to see.

My mind raced as fast as my heart in my chest and the breath in my lungs.

Lightning struck, thunder on its heels, so abrupt I cringed. My shoulders bunched beneath my ears. Multiple strikes followed, the park assaulted by a lashing of light and vibration.

Forcing my eyes open against the barrage gifted me the chance to see him again. His beauty made me gasp. He looked at me with that same inscrutable expression.

"Why did you bring me here?" he shouted, his voice laced with confusion and pain. Lightning struck closer, three bright flashes in quick succession.

He spoke! Answering him was impossible. His words had stolen every syllable from my lips.

"Why are we here?" His brows furrowed, creasing his forehead while my chin trembled. His frustration matched my own, and I fought for composure.

Lightning struck a tree fifteen yards away, dousing us in sparks like reckless fireworks, pulling me violently out of the dream.

I fell into darkness. Impact with the floor knocked the wind out of me. I rocked in a shocked panic as my body cramped. Once the pain subsided, whimpering overshadowed my wheezing. Bosco's cold nose nudged my face, scaring the shit out of me before I realized what it was.

Able to focus now, I laid on my bedroom floor, tangled in my sheets.

After biting back tears of frustration, I untangled myself to sit on the edge of the bed. All I could think was, why is this happening?

The moment of self-pity passed quickly once I berated myself into getting a grip.

Why did he think I'd brought *him* there?

Dreaming was supposed to provide answers, not frustrate the fuck out of me instead.

Sunlight poured into the room when I moved the curtains, stinging my eyes. At least I had slept. The clock showed 10:30 am, early by my standards, but better than nothing. It amazed me how short the dream was, yet it consumed the whole night. Why I didn't dream of other things as well was another conundrum.

Holy-shit-god-damn-it, those eyes!

I felt like a stupid little girl.

I sought distraction from obsessing by taking a trip down the street to the convenience store for work snacks that didn't come from a vat of grease. I brought Bosco along. We both needed the fresh air, and the owner always spoiled him with mystery treats.

Around 5:30pm, I finally remembered to contact Kim as promised. She worked until 4:30pm anyway, so it was good timing. I detailed the dream, sparing nothing, every syllable he spoke, every feeling I felt, even falling out of the bed.

"Let me call you back," Kim said once I stopped rambling. "I'm calling Aunt Lacey."

"Okay."

I wasn't sure if her jumping to call Aunt Lacey meant she was worried, but it wasn't reassuring. By the time Kim called a half hour later, I was back to pacing a track in the living room carpet.

"Hey Soph. You work tonight, right?"

The question prickled my suspicion. "Yeah."

"After your shift, me and Aunt Lacey are gunna swing by and pick you up."

"I won't be done until at least three o'clock. You might not mind, but Aunt Lacey isn't exactly...young."

"It was her idea. I told you, she barely sleeps."

"Oh, okay. Then, I guess I'll see you then?"

I wish I'd asked why they needed to physically come to me, because she said good-bye and hung up, leaving me confused. Maybe Aunt Lacey had a stronger pouch? Wishful thinking, but the possibility of any forward motion in figuring this out cured my restlessness.

Bypassing dilapidated houses and an abundance of emaciated street cats, I walked to work enjoying blaring music from an old MP3 player through my ear buds and the cool, fresh weather.

Outside The Lush, Jack was having a smoke. Both of us were content to ignore each other.

Eddie was cleaning broken glass from the floor behind the bar, Drew giving him a speech Eddie ignored. Drew then retreated into the back office, probably adding a note to dock Eddie's pay. Guy was a real peach.

Jack came inside as I was getting set-up. Ordering a drink from Eddie, Jack sucked down half the bottle before heading to a small table against the wall, this time without Theresa. I forced myself to look away from his glare and to help Eddie with the dustpan.

Throughout the night I felt Jack's stare on me and ignored him the best I could.

Around midnight, my asshole neighbour approached the bar for another drink while Eddie was in the bathroom.

"No."

"S'excuse me?"

"I have a right to refuse serving you. You've had enough." And he had. I'd kept count in case Eddie didn't, which he hadn't, considering he should have refused Jack two drinks ago.

"You're cutting me off?"

"Yes, I am. Unless you want to order some food to soak up what you've already drank, you won't be having any more."

Eddie returned.

"I'll take a beer," Jack said to him.

I stopped Eddie from opening the fridge behind us. "No, I refused you. You don't get to play bartenders like we're your parents. Order food or hit up another bar."

Eddie didn't argue.

Jack looked between the two of us and said, "Fuck you both," before spitting at the counter.

Eddie laughed. "Oh yeah, old man?" He wasn't intimidated. Neither was I. "Leave now or you get bounced. Your choice."

Outnumbered, Jack left in a huff.

"Thanks for backing me up, man." If he had served Jack anyway, I couldn't have stopped him. Drew only cared about paying customers, so complaining would have done nothing but leave me pissed off.

"You trying to be a real angel?" He was referring to the shirt I was wearing with angel wings on the back. "Last night and now tonight? You can't save that woman if she won't leave a douchebag alcoholic. He'll go somewhere else and drink and still go home and use her as a punching bag. It won't be good, we both know it, but you can't stop it."

"I know, but I also don't need to stand for it when I see it."

He raised his hands, conceding the argument, and we dropped the topic.

At 2:00am, the last patrons decided on an after-party elsewhere. It was my turn to close. Drew had left hours ago and Eddie was free, leaving me to clean up and count the till for the nightly report, which took about an hour, enough time for Kim and Aunt Lacey to come and do whatever they planned to do.

When I had finished with the report, I left it on Drew's desk and locked up the cash in the safe. Cleaning was a time-suck, perfect for distracting my anticipation in waiting for Kim and her Coven Leader to arrive. Coven. The concept was still a shocking one. I never would've guessed they truly existed before Kim took me to one.

I was bending to grab a garbage bag to bring the bins outside when I was shoved to the floor. Pain shot through my back.

Landing awkwardly with only one hand to brace my fall, I smacked my chin off of the hardwood, my other hand still gripping the garbage bag. Black spots filled my vision. Sparks of pain shot through my jaw. Spinning onto my back, my vision cleared, revealing Jack's dark expression. I scrambled to my feet, leaning on the back of a chair as a dizzy spell had me swaying.

"Should've locked the door, bitch," he told me. "Don't worry, I locked it for you."

He locked us in? I couldn't concentrate.

"You interfere too much. Put thoughts in Theresa's head."

He kept talking, but I couldn't focus on his words. Nausea stole my focus. My hand pulled away from my chin with bright red blood pooled in my palm. I felt more dripping down my throat, dotting the front of my white shirt.

When I looked up at him, Jack's face contorted with hatred. He closed the gap.

I inhaled to scream. Jack hauled off and clocked me full force across the left side of my face. The metallic taste of blood spilled through my teeth and down my throat.

I never expected shock to cripple my reaction.

Stunned by Jack's audacity, I didn't lunge at him, raise my hands in defense, or try screaming again. I did nothing, absolutely nothing to defend myself.

Pain incapacitated my thought process, rendered me powerless.

The second blow to the skull jellied my knees. My ears rang, and the world spun. My breath escaped in a bloody huff, the second strike to the temple only a half-second after the first. My knees gave out, my limp body crumpling to the hardwood.

With a grunt, Jack dragged me up onto both feet. His hands gripped me with bruising pressure as his face came within inches of my own. The smell of stale beer, cigarettes, and decay billowed out from behind broken teeth. His eyes were blood-shot, hard as marbles, and held no remorse.

I was stunned, eyesight blurred with tears. I swayed as my equilibrium had been beaten senseless. My feet were on the ground without holding my weight. If it wasn't for Jack's arm bracing me, I would have collapsed again.

I tried to raise my arms. Jack batted one away easily.

Numbness flowed through me.

Jack's hand came up around my throat, squeezing so hard I felt things in my throat break. My temples pounded. I tried to claw at his arm but couldn't do more than hold on with weak fingers.

Stealing what power I had left, Jack squeezed tighter, and spoke over the sounds of my strangled wheezing, "You think you can tell me what to do, huh? Now what? Go ahead and try it. Can't, can you?

Just some stupid bitch who doesn't know when to shut her mouth. I promise you won't say another word."

White-hot pain lanced my left side, under my ribcage. I didn't understand what it was and couldn't get away from him. My hand went to my side and felt something hard. A knife handle.

In a last-ditch effort—instinctual self-preservation?—I clasped the handle. If he removed it, I would bleed out on the floor, losing consciousness in less than five minutes, and dying in about fifteen. Thank you, TLC special.

Jack threw me down like a discarded beer bottle.

Finally I could breathe, but when I did, a jolt of pain thrashed my throat. My hand was still on the knife handle, unable to break my fall. I cracked the back of my skull off the floor. My vision blackened.

When I came to a moment later, I vomited rice and veggies. A favorite meal I would never eat again without the reminder.

Nothing felt real after that. With the sensation of floating outside my body, I called myself a piece of shit and told myself to get on my feet. I fought to do it, but my energy was gone.

Fighting to sit up, my head reeled. I was unable to see straight as bile washed over my tongue again. When my stomach clenched so I could stand, the knife wound screamed. The worst pain I'd ever endured sent me flat on my back.

Terrifying clarity hit me.

I was going to die, and I couldn't do a damn thing about it.

Darkness blocked the overheard lights. Jack bent over me, looking into my eyes as my vision spotted again. Unconsciousness was a heartbeat away.

Jack's sadistic smile was the last thing I saw.

6
———

MAKE ME WHOLE

Kim

Aunt Lacey's silence needled me. "Do you think Sophie's dream is significant? In a bigger purpose sort of way?"

No answer.

Considering she heard the question before I asked it, zero feedback from Aunt Lacey was frustrating.

"What could they mean?" I prodded. "She says she doesn't know the man."

All the earlier questions, plus this nighttime excursion, had made Aunt Lacey's intrigue obvious, but why was she so interested? Besides the dream's repetitiveness, no other oddity sparked my weird-o-meter.

"What she sees is as real as she claims, Wiccum," Aunt Lacey finally spoke. "Though they are not dreams."

"What are they?"

"Visions."

"Visions while she sleeps?" Sounded like dreams to me.

"Astral projections...?" Her voice was soft before it trailed off in question. "Sophie's role is as vital as these visions. And this man... something else." I saw Aunt Lacey's head shake in my peripheral. "They could mean everything."

What does that mean? Attempting to decipher Aunt Lacey's usual mystique challenged me. Think. Ask the right questions, questions garner details, details produce answers. Nice and neat.

"Remind yourself that the realm of magic works beyond neat labels and, therefore, cannot be contained."

I managed not to huff out loud. I wanted to figure this out for Sophie. Blooming friendship, a universal pull, whatever it was, she was my kind of people. If we could get past these dreams, she could become a full member of the Coven and focus on the magic.

Aunt Lacey gasped. "Drive faster!"

"What?! Why?"

"Sophie. Drive!"

Pedal to the floor, my adrenaline pumped while I kept an eye out for cops. My sight sharpened as I navigated the sinuous downtown streets, afraid of what could rattle my always-collected coven leader and mentor.

As we rounded the last corner and pulled up to the curb outside of The Lush, Aunt Lacey had her door open before the car skidded to a stop. I ran after her and saw her stop in front of the door. It must have been locked. She stood back a step and lifted her hand in front of her. I heard the lock click before she pushed open the door. Her power was so mastered no spoken spell was required.

The scene we barged into rocked me with confusion. My hands tingled as shock overtook me.

Jack stood up in a drunken wobble. Blood dripped off his knuckles.

A body lay on the floor.

Sophie? No!

My hands flew to my mouth as I gasped at the gore of her face. Was she alive? She had to be. We still had so much to figure out, so much to work through.

She can't be on the floor dead. She can't be.

"Get to her and begin CPR," Aunt Lacey demanded.

I kept staring at Sophie's swollen face. Her dark hair shimmered with blood. Blood ran from her nose and cuts in her cheek. More blood splashed the front of her white shirt. Her eyes were mere slits, without a hint of life.

"Help her, Kim. Now!" Aunt Lacey's strong authority put me in gear.

I ran for Sophie. Jack took a few steps back as Aunt Lacey moved toward him. Her expression told me she would make things right.

Panic bloomed when I knelt next to Sophie, and my knees felt warm and wet.

I looked down.

A knife! A big knife impaled Sophie's side.

Any composure I'd gathered was scattered. The sight of the weapon triggered my gag reflex, forcing me to turn away and tongue-wrestle bile back down my throat.

Sitting back on my heels, I covered my face as a flash of heat rose up my neck.

How could this happen to her?

Tears hit my cheeks.

I can't do this.

Come on, Kim, she needs you.

I tried to pep-talk myself into getting a grip. Aunt Lacey was busy with Jack, saying something I couldn't hear over my blood pumping too loudly in my ears. All Sophie had was me, and I was losing it.

I turned back to my friend, wiped my face, and cleared my eyes. Mixed with the red stuff was the remnants of Sophie's last meal. Vomit I could handle, had handled far too much in my lifetime.

Don't! I fought back a vision of my mother, holding back her hair as she vomited, then blinked away more tears. The blood was better than that right now.

My thoughts raced to remember CPR procedures as I realized it had been a decade since I learned it for a babysitting course. I learned more watching hunky men on medical dramas than from that class.

"Focus," I heard Aunt Lacey's voice in my head, emboldening me. Telepathy wasn't an everyday occurrence, though I was happy for the redirection.

Aunt Lacey had a long history. One with tales of blood far worse than from a knife wound. If I planned to reach even a tenth of Aunt Lacey's strength, I had to remind myself of this.

Should I pull it out? It meant much more blood if I did. The thought of more had me in panic mode.

"Leave it," Aunt Lacey resolved telepathically.

Perfect.

Picturing a practice dummy, I worked through the steps. I pinched Sophie's nose, placed a finger on her chin, and gagged as the shift caused a grinding pop as her jaw relocated.

If Sophie's sallow colouring was evidence, I was running out of time. I watched Sophie's chest expand in my peripheral with my artificial respiration. Then I did it again.

Chest compressions were more difficult than I thought. I was unsure if I was doing it right and was afraid I'd break her ribs. The Bee Gee's 1977 hit *"Staying Alive"* sounded in my brain to keep the rhythm of my chest compressions. Staring the knife into submission, I prayed it didn't pop out like a grotesque New Year's party favour.

"Whatcha gunna do, grandma?" Jack was goading Aunt Lacey. "Go back to yur knittin', maybe you can stitch up your friend." He howled at his joke. "Add some booties. That body's gunna get cold real quick."

I refused to think of Sophie as just a body. Aunt Lacey could fix her. She had to, because what I was doing amounted to diddly-squat. After checking again, Sophie's heart still wasn't beating.

With the taste of blood and vomit on my lips, I kept up compressions until my elbows ached. I listened to Aunt Lacey speak without raising her voice. "You've earned your fate. Sophie is the last innocent soul you will impose your wrath upon. This cycle of torment ends at my hand."

"What the fuck you talkin' 'bout, you crazy ol' bitch?" Jack slurred with a laugh.

Ignorance about Aunt Lacey's capabilities would not keep Jack safe. Witnessing her power for the first time had left me awed. I'd been so amazed, it shaped my teachings ever since.

Jack would regret every word.

Without dignifying Jack's insults, Aunt Lacey shook her head, saying, "*Vulnero haud alius, tantum obscurum.*" The power in her words was far more inspiring than any motivational speaker I had sat through.

The instant Aunt Lacey finished the incantation, Jack changed. His taunting eyes unfocused, expression relaxed, and he lost his inebriated wobble.

Aunt Lacey turned to me. I was still pumping the inert muscle in Sophie's chest. Aunt Lacey waved me back.

"I'm not stopping. We need an ambulance."

A move of Aunt Lacey's hand spelled my arms away from Sophie. She recited a quick, "*Cesso*" at Sophie before I had control of my limbs again.

"Help me put her in the back of your car."

Stunned by Aunt Lacey's swift takeover, I saw no change in Sophie. She lay as broken as we found her.

Prodded to hurry when Aunt Lacey pulled her sleeves over her hands and grabbed Sophie's feet, I fumbled hoisting her up from her underarms, straining to get her outside.

"Wait! People will see us." I hissed as Aunt Lacey backed into the door to open it. She kept pulling, and I didn't want to drop Sophie.

We stepped outside. When a group of half-drunk chicks carrying their high heels passed without screaming or pulling out their cell cameras, I realized Aunt Lacey had hidden us under a spell. We hoisted Sophie into the backseat of my car.

Thank begeesus for stain-free leather seats. As soon as I thought it, I felt bad and mentally called myself out before the thought of my seats and my forever–stained, posh princess jeans triggered my vanity again.

To add to my overwhelming night, Aunt Lacey jumped in the driver's seat.

"You can drive?" All the times I carted her around, and she could drive?

Strapped in, tires squealing, Aunt Lacey proved she could handle a vehicle like a stuntman.

In the backseat, Sophie looked the same: knife where Jack left it, skin shaded with blue undertones. "What'd you do to her?"

"Her body rests, waiting until we can gather the others. Contact the Sect. We need to perform a healing." Her voice was strained.

"A healing?" She thought those of the Coven could heal someone? They may be the only Magics in this region, but the Sect Aunt Lacey led was tiny in comparison to the Mother Coven considering its members were all over the world. "What about the spell you did? *Cesso* means to stop or linger in Latin, right? Is that what's happening to Sophie?"

"In this case, delaying. Sophie's organs required sustenance for her soul to remain. You provided the sustenance, while I delayed further damage."

For all I knew, Sophie was long gone, but I believed in Aunt Lacey.

"What about Jack? The police might—"

"Someone will handle that," Aunt interrupted.

"A Covener? They need to know about the security tapes. Plus, Jack is still inside."

"Place your faith in your coven, Wiccum. Another will care for the details. No one will know of Sophie's involvement."

She blew through a red light without flinching.

"Sophie need not have any knowledge of your apprentice trials. They may remain your secret. However, she must survive in order to become your first assignment. Concentrate on my instructions and the need for swift action. Ask questions later when time calls for reflection."

In other words, someone in the know would be on it. It was relieving to know a professional could sanitize the scene, giving us the chance to do what was needed on our end. Sophie was more important, even more so than she being my future assignment.

The only thing stopping me from peeking into the backseat every thirty seconds was focusing on something else. Right now, it was calling the Coveners. The scent of blood lingering in the car made me so queasy I had to put my window down.

Grabbing my cell, I dialed Donovan. He may have joked about being the teacher's pet, but he was, for whatever reason. Aunt Lacey would expect me to call him first.

He answered on the second ring. "Hello?" I could only imagine what lay in Donovan's suspicions. A call after the bars closed landed in booty-call territory, and I would never expect him to take me up on the offer, if I lost my self-respect long enough to ask.

"Donovan, get to Aunt Lacey's as soon as you can."

"Why?" A female voice murmuring in the background explained his reluctance.

"Gross. Tell the vagina to jump off. We need you. I don't know if you remember my friend Sophie from the last meeting, but she needs healing. She was attacked and is in rough shape."

Donovan's laugh came without humour. "Aunt Lacey doesn't need my help. She can—"

"Now, Donovan!" Aunt Lacey demanded before he finished.

With a huff, he hung up. He never said no to Aunt Lacey.

Most members didn't answer, forcing me to hang up before hitting voicemail. A future in a leadership position would be non-existent if I began outing people on their answering machines.

Others were ecstatic I called them to help, even without details. For those with loved ones unaware of their coven status, the call put them in a personal hell. They had to fabricate a believable story for leaving in the middle of the night if they preferred to keep their coven involvement "in the broom closet."

When we arrived at Aunt Lacey's, I saw Donovan and two others waiting outside. "Give me a hand," I yelled.

Blake and Jared followed Donovan, wide-eyed when they saw Sophie in the backseat. Donovan took hold of her under the arms while I directed the burly Blake to grab her feet. I warned them about the knife.

Jared, a brick wall of a man and Blake's best friend, ran ahead to open and hold doors.

Sophie was laid out on the basement floor. Everyone gave her room, standing awkwardly and gawking at her. I would have liked a bigger crowd. A crisis of this magnitude was new for everyone, but when a request comes through from the Coven Leader, you fulfill your duty to the Coven and lend a hand.

Denise whispered to her bestie Jamie. Both surprised me by showing up, especially after what Sophie told me they said to her at her brother's concert. If Sophie died, I was going to go apeshit on them. Rachel, Deidra, and Gwen were frozen with shock. Louise's hands covered her mouth, her husband Henry's comforting arm embracing her shoulders. As a retired family practitioner, this was out of Henry's depth, more battle triage than, "Turn your head and cough." The sense of loss in his eyes tipped me off to the severity of Sophie's condition.

"Is she dead?" Donovan asked without peeling his eyes off her.

"No. Aunt Lacey did a spell to keep her from...becoming dead, I guess."

"What happened?" Gwen's thick voice asked.

"Our neighbour Jack attacked her in the bar where she works. I have no idea why. When we found her, she wasn't breathing."

After a moment of incredulous calm, Donovan looked straight at me with fury ablaze in his dark eyes. "Is *he* dead?"

His intensity tripped me up.

"No," Aunt Lacey said and hurried by us, saving me from trying to explain. "Wiccum," she focused me further, "I need you to remove the knife."

"What?" Please no.

"I'll do it," Donovan volunteered.

Deidra and Rachel moved to allow him ample room, the couple about as thrilled to see what he had to do as I was.

Donovan knelt at Sophie's side. He took hold of the thick knife handle, braced his other hand on her ribs, and yanked out the six-inch, serrated blade in one swift movement. A chorus of repulsion filled the basement as he tossed it aside. The mixed sounds of wet blood, tearing muscle and flesh, and the hollow scraping of metal on bone had spectators, myself included, giving an involuntary retch. I paced a few steps away, the guilt of not being strong enough bruised my confidence in a way I hoped the others were too distracted to see.

"Do you know CPR?" Aunt Lacey questioned Donovan.

"Yes."

"Can you handle what that means?"

Everyone heard her, each of their expressions looking as confused as mine.

He answered with a strained, "Yes."

"Good. When I tell you, start vigorous compressions. Be wary of breaking her ribs." Donovan nodded. "Everyone, encircle our fallen. Lay hands to use your combined powers to pull her through this."

Everyone surrounded Sophie, Aunt Lacey sitting with her hands bracketing Sophie's head on the carpet, without touching her. Adrenaline made my palms itch. Everything was happening too fast.

"I'm going to remove the stasis spell keeping her from death's progression."

Donovan nodded again, ready for his task.

Aunt Lacey bowed her head, reciting, "*Cesso haud magis.*" Blood spilled from Sophie's wounds and poured onto the carpet and Donovan. I bit down on my lips and sucked in a gulp of air, affixing my eyes on her face instead of the new surge of blood. Without the spell delaying her condition, the colour around her eyes and lips was turning odd shades of whitish-blue.

"Now," Aunt Lacey commanded.

Donovan pressed his lips to Sophie's and blew into her lungs. The knife wound sprayed blood across his legs. The taste of bile rose on my tongue, and I had to close my eyes against the gore. When I opened them again, Henry had pressed a handkerchief to the wound while Donovan administered another breath without a hiccup in procedure.

"Everyone, close your eyes and remember the young woman you met only days ago. Transmit your energies through her while you focus on that image and repeat after me." Aunt Lacey paused, waiting for everyone's eyes to close. "*Effrego ties ex caecus, solvo penitus vires. Resarcio somes, resarcio mens...*"

Voices shaky and frightened, we repeated every word in unison.

Time crawled as we ran through a bunch of spells and rituals, healing Sophie's internal injuries until her blood clotted and stopped colouring the carpet.

Donovan stopped CPR.

I kept waiting for her to wake up, to open her eyes, and blush with embarrassment as everyone fussed over her. But we kept chanting, and she remained the same. Across from me, Donovan watched Sophie with equal intensity. His exhaustion from the CPR left him looking faint, sweat beading his hairline, a smudge of Sophie's blood on his lips. Exhaustion I expected, but the emotion I found in his glassy eyes, had me dumbfounded. It was out of the scope of the Donovan I knew, a guy who treated women like walking, disposable sex dolls.

Taking a moment to rub a hand down each of his arms, lips in a flurry of unheard words, I saw a flare of light in his palms as they passed over his skin, just enough to catch my attention. Interest peaked, but unable to ask any questions, I continued to watch Donovan as he laid shaky hands on Sophie and closed his eyes. He chanted with everyone as we worked on her crushed throat, broken jaw, and extensive facial bruising.

A grin creased Aunt Lacey's laugh lines seconds before Sophie took a wisp of breath. Nothing like a movie gasp, but enough that we heard it. We all beamed without faltering from the chant.

Aunt Lacey grew quiet, her words diminishing to a whisper. Unable to hear if she'd stopped, though the rest of us had.

We waited.

Our leader settled back onto her heels. "Sophie's wounds are sensitive. Nonetheless, her soul is intact, her vessel recovering as she rests." She put out her hand for Jared to help her to her feet. "You are welcome to stay, leave, and return as you wish. Soon, Sophie will have the opportunity to thank you personally." Aunt Lacey gathered her skirt and took to the stairs.

That's it? A look around the room showed the same question on the faces of the other Coveners as we looked to each other seeking direction.

No surprise to anyone, Denise and Jamie left first. And while I appreciated the hugs from Deidra, Rachel, and Gwen and the sympathetic look from Louise before she helped her husband up from the floor, I found it difficult to process anything.

What do you do with the leftover adrenaline after watching someone you care about almost die? The familiar feeling of sitting bedside next to my mother crept up. I swatted it away and realized that's why I wasn't feeling as much as I should. My body was trembling, but my emotions settled on a plateau, saving me from worse visions of my mother.

I focused on Sophie, the pallor of her skin and her dark hair, so different from my mother's. That helped my thoughts remain in the room instead of in the past.

The stark contrast of all that blood on the beige carpet drew most of my attention, and I fell into a comfortable action-mode.

The Coveners had fixed Sophie's body, I could fix this mess. Cleaning I could handle far better than what had my hands shaking.

IN THE SPAN OF A BREATH

Kim

Treating Sophie was my first extensive healing. I assumed it was for the majority of others as well. As a general practitioner, Henry would be used to this waiting period, but I had no idea what experience he had with healing within the Sect. I was comforted by the drastic change in Sophie's appearance, and even Henry, with all his medical know-how, was in awe of how quickly she was healing and made mention of this before he left with his wife.

While I was busy gathering some things to clean up the mess, distracting myself from thoughts of my mother, Donovan asked for Aunt Lacey's yarn basket. He'd stuck around as well, though I didn't get why. By the time I got back to her, Aunt Lacey had changed Sophie into a white, cotton nightgown, made her comfortable with a fluffy pillow and blankets, and erased all signs of blood, making the bucket of cleaner in my hand useless. I didn't ask how she did it; this was just another thing she could do that amazed me.

Aunt Lacey continued to aid Sophie's healing by laying cloth saturated in pain-impeding ingredients upon Sophie's now-raw stab wound. As she finished, Donovan brought in a length of red yarn with intricate knots tied along it. I watched him sweep aside Sophie's hair to string it like a necklace. Before he could finish, he tore his hands away.

"What did you see?" Aunt Lacey asked him.

I looked between them as he glared at Sophie with a disgust equivalent to her sitting up and spitting in his face.

Instead of answering, he fled upstairs.

Did Donovan have a second sight? I dismissed the possibility. Palm readers read, they didn't see. What did Aunt Lacey mean?

I hated not knowing things.

Confused by Aunt Lacey's question and Donovan's exit—both without explanation—I watched as Aunt Lacey resumed dressing Sophie's wound. Judging by her pinched expression, whatever just happened, it was something big.

Now that Sophie was going to live, I couldn't help but think of what would have happened if we hadn't been on our way to get her from work. How quickly the night turned. "She dreams so violently. If she encounters the grey-eyed man, she could reopen her wound."

"Until she fully heals, Sophie will not dream." Of course, Aunt Lacey had already considered the possibility. "I have left it up to her body to take care of itself. She possesses the ability. This will draw it to the surface."

"How long will she be like this?"

"Two days at most."

"What about her dog? It's alone and probably needs to be walked and fed."

"What breed?" Donovan was suddenly perched on the edge of the couch behind us.

Aunt Lacey's gaze flicked to Donovan, I thought I saw tension in his docile expression. "Does she have family to care for it?" Aunt Lacey asked me.

"It's a pug," I answered Donovan, then turned back to Aunt

Lacey. "Her family will ask questions. He's like her four-legged offspring. Telling her family she took off without making overnight plans would send up a red flag. They can't see her like this."

"My place isn't set up for a dog," Donovan said.

I imagined Donovan's place as hazardous for human inhabitants.

"Mine is," I told them, "but if I leave him alone all day while I'm at work, I may as well just leave him in her apartment. And I want to be here when she wakes up."

The last thing Sophie would remember was being at The Lush. Being here for her when she woke wouldn't make up for not being there to help her fend off Jack, but it was all I could do.

"Bring it here," Aunt Lacey decided. "With both of you assisting, I gather the animal will adjust. While at Sophie's apartment, retrieve what it requires and provisions for when she wakes."

With Aunt Lacey sounding not-so-thrilled on the concept of pets in general, I prayed Bosco didn't ruin any of her things and cause her to shy from the whole institution.

Things got awkward as I grabbed my car keys. Picking up Bosco and coordinating an overnight bag was within my competency. I could make a llama red-carpet-ready. What I failed to understand was why Donovan volunteered to tag along.

I couldn't differentiate between the guy now in my passenger's seat and the guy I swore I had pegged over the last year. Why would he help with Bosco? Why help at all?

The ride was conversationally mute. I was thinking too hard about Donovan and the incongruity of his actions, and he sat so still it was as if he thought if he didn't talk, he might disappear.

When I unlocked the door with Sophie's keys from her purse Aunt Lacey had remembered to grab, Bosco barked until he realized we weren't Sophie. Silent and edgy, Bosco's body stilled, ears perked up, eyes wide, and usually silly expression tightened. I knelt, calling his name, and the moment of uncertainty passed as he ran to me, resuming his excited barking in between pants, tongue hanging out.

Donovan grunted. "Great guard dog. She needs a pit bull in this part of town."

After a few puppy kisses, I watched Donovan look around, running his fingers over the wall next to him and then the arm of the couch.

"It's not so bad," I said. "The building's clean, and we get dishwashers."

"You live here too?"

"Next door."

"Hmm." He didn't elaborate.

Focused on my task, I found Bosco's food, grabbed a baggy of treats, comfort toys, and packed them in a plastic bag. Donovan was no longer in the living room so I went in search, finding him in Sophie's bedroom.

"Anything worth stealing?"

"Just looking. I haven't touched much." He gave a devilish grin with dimples, making me swell with lust that I resented.

I reviewed my interactions with Donovan in the last few hours. My inability to reconcile the differences between who I thought he was and this new Donovan, plus what happened when he tried to tie the knotted yarn around Sophie's neck, grated on my nerves.

As I slid open Sophie's closet door, I couldn't help blurt out, "So what spell did you remove before healing Sophie?"

"I healed her. Like everyone else."

The pause before his answer was just long enough to reveal the lie.

Grabbing a duffel bag off the floor, I removed other empty bags from inside and looked at Donovan over my shoulder.

"Not like everyone else." I grabbed a shirt I'd seen Sophie wear, folded it, and put it in the bag. "I know what I saw. I didn't hear the reversal, you made sure no one would, but I know one when I see it. What could you possibly need to remove in order to help heal someone?"

"Guess you haven't learned that during your apprenticeship yet."

Now it was my turn to pause too long. Donovan opened a small, wooden box on Sophie's dresser, his distraction giving me enough time to freak out. How did he know I was in an active apprenticeship? Aunt Lacey wouldn't tell him, and I sure as hell didn't.

"Was that a part of yours?" I said instead, using the moment to try and get information out of him.

He made a grunting sound in his throat and, without bothering to look at me. "Yeah. Sure."

"We all start somewhere." This was meant to be a trite comment, but he didn't let it pass.

"For Magics like you, it starts and ends with a book."

"You saying you're more than a Kitchen Witch?" I watched him as he picked up a photo of Sophie and her brothers off of Sophie's nightstand. He lingered on the photo as I stood watching with my arms crossed.

Another moment passed before he put the frame down. His jaw flexed, his lips pursed, before he turned and came toward me. I flinched as he reached out, but it was only to reach past me to look in the closet.

"Why don't you run back to Aunt Lacey and ask her?"

I would do that if I didn't already know she would want me to find out on my own, as part of my teaching. Just because Donovan was a difficult subject, and the sight of him intimidated me, it didn't mean I was ready to back down.

Something was going on, and it needled me not to know.

He grabbed the sleeve of a hanging shirt, the one Sophie wore in the photo with her brothers.

"What are you doing? I can manage her clothing. It's my thing." I opted for a lighter topic, prepared to return to Donovan's secrets later.

His shoulders tensed, and he dropped the sleeve of the shirt he held. His dark eyes shifted to mine. I held my chin up and fought against melting beneath his gaze.

He looked like he was going to say something and changed his mind. "Like I said, just looking. A lot can be discovered about a chick by her room. It's *my* thing."

"You've probably seen enough of them." He didn't argue, so I pushed. "Like with the reversal spell before the healing, you have talents beyond the palm reading?"

He shook his head and turned away from me. "You don't need power for honed observational skills." The mattress groaned as Donovan made himself comfortable against Sophie's pillow.

"What does Sophie's room say?" I asked, humouring him and looking for any nugget of information I could gather about him. I reached back into the closet for clothing with feigned disinterest.

"She's...happily mediocre, even if only for now."

"What does that even mean?"

When he stretched his arms behind his head, hands interlocked, cradling his head with his elbows in the air, I had to look away again before he noticed my cheeks flush at the sight of his accentuated biceps.

"Her space is clean and organized, yet not sterile. Nice clothes," —he jutted his chin toward the open closet—"nothing expensive or bargain basement cheap, nor does she have a million pairs of shoes. Simple jewellery box,"—he looked toward the wooden box on the dresser—"some real, some costume, nothing too flashy, yet every piece has character. None I'd classify as boring."

Bosco jumped up beside him. "Then she gets a dog that possesses attitude, but lacks the physicality to utilize it." He scratched Bosco's head, making his ears waggle. "She's realistic. Wants the stuff she has to be special, but practical, considering her budget."

He picked the book up off of her side table, one without a cover. "She spots potential in most people and is intelligent, without making others feel inferior."

From what I knew, he was pretty close. Maybe this was amongst his secret abilities. Nah, Donovan wasn't that profound. I'd lay money on him showing off his ample experience in women's bedrooms.

"You could have picked up most of that when you read her palms. The rest is speculation." I refused to sound impressed.

In search of underwear, I moved toward the dresser. Donovan was on his feet and in my way. I didn't even hear the bed creak.

"You think I'm wrong?"

I pushed by him. "You don't know her. Judging Sophie by her room is shallow and ridiculous."

"Okay." This was not a moment of impasse, he was gathering momentum. "As an example of my observational skills and to prove you wrong for my own entertainment, I bet I know what your room looks like without ever seeing it."

"Please." I found Sophie's underwear drawer.

"Even her underwear is interesting," Donovan said over my shoulder, so I grabbed whatever I could and shoved the drawer closed.

"Scum bucket." Task complete, I flicked off the bedroom light, leaving him in the darkness.

"Fine, we'll move back to you." He followed close behind. "I'm offering a *serious* bet."

"Why? You can't tell if I'm lying." I faced off with him in the living room, irritated by the inane conversation.

He crossed his arms over his broad chest. "Lying is easy to spot. You'd drown at a poker table. If I'm wrong, until Sophie can take care of it herself, I'll be responsible for picking up the dog shit from Aunt Lacey's yard. Or vice versa, if I'm right."

Though the subject was infantile, my masochistic streak secretly loved he found assessing me enticing. I hadn't many chances to draw out a conversation like this with him. I conceded.

"Alrighty," he said with a smug grin and sanded his hands together. "Organization is your science. Every pair of socks matched, clothes folded and in assigned drawers, every shirt hung and freshly pressed, every girly figurine in its specified place. All surfaces are dusted and polished. Every picture hung at a perfect right angle. I bet you even have designer baskets, contents labelled."

I loved my label maker and was beginning to resent this game.

He continued. "Numerous gold and diamond rings inherited from a grandmother or two, complete with matching earrings, and possibly a necklace. And of course, the OCD perfection wouldn't be complete without a collection of creepy porcelain dolls. Probably a gift from your father. You were too afraid to hurt his feelings by putting them out of their misery, so you keep them in prime condition just in case he asks." He leaned in. "Which by the way, he never will. He has no idea what girls like and picked dolls because his mother used to have them. If you're not getting laid, that's a good reason. Ditch them."

He finished his assessment still equipped with that smug smile, dimples engaged, and watched my face, waiting for a reaction to confirm his evaluation.

"Wrong." I turned to retrieve Bosco's leash.

"Correct on every level, huh?"

"Nope, not at all. You should re-think your observational prowess." I knelt down and slipped Bosco's harness on.

His arrogant laugh as he revelled in triumph had my fingers clenching the leash. "Told you, Kitchen Witch, your poker face is pathetic."

Masking my irritation with a smile, I left Donovan to lock up and grab the bags, his smartass laugh ballooning my irritation. That he had me pegged while he was still much a mystery made me crazy, but I continued to deny him any satisfaction from confirming his victory.

Stupid game.

I was treated like a chauffeur the whole way back to Aunt Lacey's as Donovan talked to Bosco and held him on his lap like a doting father. Once we arrived, he took Bosco to the backyard, reminding me with a call through the kitchen not to go far, that he thought Bosco had a package for me.

I ignored him and went to the basement to check on Sophie, who looked more human now. Colour highlighted her cheeks, her pulse strong. Aunt Lacey promised she wasn't suffering, that her body needed time to reclaim its strength.

Persecution and chaos was what Magics had to look forward to if we tried to integrate into Blind society. No matter our abilities, those without a clue of Magics and their capabilities outnumbered us. If the Blind only knew our healing capabilities. Hospital waiting rooms would empty. No need for surgeons. No parent could resist banishing their child's suffering. Some days it was difficult to think someone could have done something to save my mother. If only Aunt Lacey had found me sooner.

"The backyard is safe for the animal," Aunt Lacey said, breaking my thread of reflection.

"The animal's name is Bosco. He's an adorable little thing."

"I'm sure he is," she replied. "Do you know when Sophie is due to work?"

"Oh shit." I slumped. "She works tonight."

"I will handle it." Aunt Lacey gave no details, and I was confident she had it covered.

I bit my lip. Wanting to leave it, I decided to ask anyway. "Why is Donovan here?"

"He cares for her," she answered, taking a seat on the couch.

"Excuse me?"

Aunt Lacey tilted her head driving home the implication.

Cared for her? He didn't even know her. I tried not to let my immense WTF reaction show as I looked down at my unconscious neighbour.

"He knows enough."

"You're shitting me, right?"

"I assure you, I am not. Unable to identify where these feelings originate, confused about what they mean, and what to do about them, he waffles in indecision. Much has occurred in the span of a breath. He will learn all too soon what lies within her that draws him in. It helps that the games he orchestrates have lost appeal, and Sophie is too strong-willed to be fooled."

Stunned and beyond hiding it, I couldn't grasp how this had developed. No build-up, here it is, accept it? If Donovan didn't understand any of this, then Aunt Lacey saw something, and knew more than she was saying.

Sophie was dreaming of one gorgeous man while another was awake and on her coat tails, though he's met her once. No evidence of special abilities besides the dream pinpointed Sophie as a Magic, but Aunt Lacey spoke of potential. Being unable to see as Aunt Lacey did was what kept me practicing my craft, in hopes of one day being stronger. But for now, nothing about this scenario made sense.

"No conclusions are set, Wiccum, not even mine." Answering my scrambled thoughts was another reminder of my lacking talents; I couldn't keep her out of my mind. "Sophie's choices will prove diffi-cult, as they would for any in her position. For now, Donovan is content with dwelling on the sidelines, while he sorts out his past and present worth. This blindsided him, like a sudden sickness. One he seeks to understand. Sophie may never know."

Sophie was my friend. Any attraction I felt for Donovan would go unreciprocated—not that I'd revealed my interest—but I wouldn't sit by and watch him use her either. He'd picked the wrong target.

"How's she doing?"

The sound of Donovan's voice made me jump and thrum with gratitude he didn't share the gift of telepathy, couldn't overhear my pining thoughts. Or so I hoped. Just in case, I frantically tried to think of the last movie I saw. I realized it was *The Little Mermaid* and felt my cheeks flush redder than my hair.

"Healing beautifully," Aunt Lacey answered. "Why don't you two rest? Her dressings won't need changing until tomorrow. The trials of the night have ended, and you've been through enough."

The adrenaline that left me energized after the healing was waning, and I suddenly felt just how late it was. "Can I sleep in the Victorian room?" I loved the dark wood, four-poster bed. It was much better than my own double, so I may as well take advantage and get some sleep on a majestic mattress, surrounded by fluffy pillows. The small staircase needed to get up into it made me want to squeal.

"Sleep where you wish." Aunt Lacey looked at Donovan. "You as well, as always." He returned a curt nod I had to stop myself from attempting to interpret.

"I can wash your jeans," he offered as I wondered how often he stayed over at Aunt Lacey's and why. "I'm doing mine anyway, since they're covered in her blood. Might stain, but they'll be clean." When I hesitated, he added, "I'll be up keeping Bosco company anyway."

I had a feeling about what he would be doing, and it had nothing to do with Bosco.

After changing into a spare nightgown, I left my jeans in the hall for Donovan to wash and climbed under the sheets, not so excited to spend the night alone in the big, empty bed.

———

After a few hours of restless sleep, my scrambled thoughts hadn't let me enjoy my luxury accommodations. I dressed in my clean, ruined jeans, which had been left folded outside the bedroom door, and wished I'd stopped at my apartment and grabbed an outfit. If only I hadn't let myself get roped into Donovan's stupid "I know what's in your bedroom" game.

I went to check on Sophie and stopped short when I reached the last step of the basement stairs. Donovan was sleeping on the couch next to where Sophie was still asleep on the floor. Wearing a pair of blue and white, plaid pyjama pants and a plain white t-shirt, Donovan was stretched out, belly down, head off the side ready to wake any second and lend a helping hand. Following his arm, I realized he already had: he was holding her hand. Was Sophie clutching his? Maybe she woke up in the night.

My preconceived notions about Donovan no longer stacked up, and I was suffocating under their weight. Unable to handle it, I escaped the room.

In search of fresh air, I shut the back door with too much force, wincing as the glass vibrated when the door recoiled.

Aunt Lacey spun to see who was treating her property so poorly.

"Sorry." To my surprise, she was playing with Bosco, smiling as he twirled around in circles with his tongue dangling out one side of his mouth. "I see you warmed up to him."

"I'm not one to condone the domestication of animals, however, he is such an odd creature. Loves immediately without the usual song and dance of introduction. Offers no protection, except over Sophie's heart, yet something about his personality proves irresistible."

"Donovan said the same thing, that Sophie should have a bigger dog to protect her." Something in my voice must have tipped off Aunt Lacey.

"His affection is not her doing, Kim. Sophie is very much unaware and has much healing to do aside from the horrendous attack. Harbouring such resentments will change nothing and only cloud your ability to bring her into the Coven. How do you suppose she can trust you otherwise?"

"I'm not some petty teenager. I don't hate her, or him, for that matter. It just doesn't make sense. He's known her all of ten minutes. A literal ten minutes. You don't have feelings for someone that quickly without being a tad touched or psychotic."

"Your assumptions are based on the meagre information you possess, my dear."

"If there's something I don't know, then great. At least that means this whole thing isn't as much of a dreadful rom-com TV special as it seems."

Aunt Lacey chuckled as Bosco chased after a stuffed frog she had tossed. "Matters of the heart are rarely so fantastical. Even with their power, Sophie and Donovan are human, slaves to human emotions outside Hollywood happy endings. Again, look beyond your boxes. They cage you far more than those you seek to package within them."

Open-minded was easy when you knew what to expect from certain people, certain personalities. I may see people in terms of the boxes they fit, but my boxes were rarely tested. Sophie and Donovan? I couldn't wrap my head around it.

I knew I had to suck it up and move on, so that's what I decided to do. If they ended up together, I'd deal with this new box like an adult and hide my eagerness to solve the mystery of Aunt Lacey's insinuations.

8

———————

ENOUGH TEACHING

Donovan

What was it about her? Sophie wasn't the most beautiful chick I'd ever seen, not even the most interesting.

I had to admit I was bullshitting myself about my lack of interest. Stacking her next to the inferior standard of women I was accustomed to, Sophie was more than just a blurred memory of body parts and unsatisfactory sex. She was a person. One I'd found intriguing from the moment I caught a hint of her snark and read her palm. Being in her room, looking over her things, things she spent every day with, I'd been envious of the inanimate objects.

I resisted the temptation to hold her hand again, in case she woke up and caught me. When I had last night, the result was indescribable, and resisting now had me aching.

Why did I even do it? Maybe to *will* my power through our hands, in hopes of facilitating more healing? Fuck, I don't know. What I got was a shit load more than anticipated. The result...something else. I didn't know what, but lethargy took over, a mental drain weighing heavily on me once the connection was made.

Energy was being siphoned from me? Was she doing something to me?

As I contemplated what stirred inside, Aunt Lacey appeared.

I couldn't look away from Sophie's face. "She's getting better."

"You made the difference, once you broke the Binding."

I turned to Aunt Lacey, searching for meaning.

"Your Binding. You think I was unaware you shackled your powers?" I turned back to Sophie as she went on. "No amount of Binding can quell your most innate gifts. You know this."

"Yeah, well, it took care of the rest."

"For a time."

"I'll re-establish it when I can."

"No, you won't."

I turned back to see soft eyes. She was amused. Maybe she knew for sure, maybe she didn't, she didn't say.

"You had an immense hand in her recovery. You felt it, could *see* it."

Again, I looked away. "You could have healed her yourself in seconds by touching her. You should've done it at the bar. Leaving it up to the Coven was irresponsible. Most of them are book-learned or still dormant." More like swimming in the kiddie end of the talent pool.

"It needed to be done by them. And by you. They may not be as talented, but they do have subtle gifts that attributed to her survival. You, your breath filling her lungs with magic, and your healing ability working through your hands, a gift I must say you have cast aside for far too long regardless of any Binding. Now that the cobwebs are shaken loose, you can return to your teachings."

"I've had enough teaching, thanks."

"I meant teaching others."

"That too."

"You may not see its significance, but you communicated with her essence. You are much stronger than you will allow. She will change this too."

"Is that so." This was no question, but a condescending remark she lifted a brow at.

With my elbows on my knees and my chin on my knuckles, I tried to buy what Aunt Lacey was hawking. Maybe she was right, and I had buried my powers for too long. I didn't need most of them anyway, nothing more than tricks, the prickle of power representing the piece of shit that made me. My inherited gift was a fucked-up reminder of where I came from and where I may still end up.

Never before had I been a tenth this doubtful. Normally my over-confidence was iron. I'd especially never been knocked off-kilter by a chick. A life of bachelorhood was the only thing that made sense given the poison my blood seeped. Getting laid by some random was easy. Not because I was the male ideal, but because those types of females gravitated toward me, easy targets serving a purpose. Sophie was no club bunny begging for a trip to a private stall.

After last night, I knew too much. And with all the knowledge I had gained about Sophie's past, about our...God, I knew dick-all about how to handle what I saw, yet every part of me ached to unravel her as she unravelled me.

Did she know? No. How could she?

"Will it make any difference to her?" I said aloud.

"She will be grateful to all who helped her. The rest is up to you. You will need to see if she reciprocates and bear the consequences if she does not."

"Do you see us together?" I braced for her answer, never looking away from Sophie's sleeping face.

Aunt Lacey's pause was discomforting. "Sort out your intentions first. A future is possible, if you make yourself worthy."

"Thanks. Your all-knowing wisdom has made me feel so much better."

She was never surprised by my sarcasm.

"You are right to believe she is nothing like the others you have bedded. You may find her personality too iron-willed. I cannot see you two together, as the choice has yet to be made, although I am certain it will be her choice. She may not be meant for you, Donovan."

So much for a straight answer.

"Are you going to tell me what happened last night?" she asked and waited.

I shrugged, content to act ignorant to her insinuation.

"Okay." She landed a hand on my shoulder before leaving the room.

As with everything else, she would wait for me to speak, humouring me by asking since she already knew, and I had no plan on repeating whatever she *read* from me.

One conversation with this stranger at my feet and one night lying next to her, and Sophie had turned me into a pussy, second-guessing everything I thought I had a handle on. I could make Sophie happy. At least, I thought I could. She wasn't exactly high-maintenance.

Look at me. A creepy stalker she doesn't even know, making her hold my hand, planning for her to give a damn about me, based on what?

"Fairy tales are for morons."

9

———

NEWFOUND PURPOSE

Voices were muffled by my water-logged ears. No, not water. Why can't I hear anything? When my ears did clear, I didn't understand what I heard.

"I can add some astragalus or maybe goldenseal?"

Kim?

"The worst has passed. Have faith in Sophie."

Aunt Lacey.

Silence lingered. My body was a lead cage as I tried to join the conversation, even though I was elated they'd found me in time.

"Where'd Donovan go?"

"He will return when he feels ready."

What's wrong with Donovan? The errant thought worried me as I fought unconsciousness.

"Here she comes."

Aunt Lacey's elegant voice radiated excitement as a tingle awakened my skin. Blinking to clear my blurry vision, I felt softness below me. Not the bar's hardwood floor.

Soft heat brushed my skin in the dim flicker of candlelight in Aunt Lacey's basement. I sat up too quickly when I saw Aunt Lacey perched next to me on the edge of the couch, but a sharp spasm in my gut had me cursing and laying back against the pillow.

"Rest, you're still healing. Let me take this." Aunt Lacey reached for my throat and I flinched. I remembered the last set of hands at my throat trying to squeeze the life from me. Aunt Lacey untied a red string from around my neck and held it gently as she left.

The memory of Jack's snarling face was fresh. My fingers found bandages hugging my torso, something bulging beneath them. "No way I imagined the honking knife in my side. Tell me that's not my intestines."

"Nope," Kim laughed and moved from the floor to where Aunt Lacey had been next to me, "just bandages and healing ingredients. How do you feel?" Her eyes narrowed with the question.

"Um...I'm not in pain. Not unless I move." My bones ached. "How long have I been out?"

"About two days."

"Two days!" Fuck, how could I let a man twice my age and plastered get the upper hand? Flashbacks of Jack over me had my heart hammering.

"Less than," Kim softened the blow. "You'll barely scar. I bet your throat doesn't even hurt."

I swallowed without pain. Remembering Jack's crushing hands, I'd be content to never have someone touch my throat again.

"Why was that string around my neck?"

"Knot magic for pain relief. Aunt Lacey will wrap the yarn around the oak out back, and you'll feel even better tomorrow."

I saw no correlation between string and pain management, but if it got me home quicker, I'd dress the tree myself. Home. "Shit... Bosco! I have to go." I scrambled to get up. Kim grabbed my shoulders to stop me, the shock of muscle spasms in my gut kept me down.

"Bosco's upstairs, probably snoring like an old man. Aunt Lacey's actually having fun with him and she's not a dog person. I'd bring him down, but you're not ready for his energy."

How they got into my apartment to get him didn't matter. My head was stuffed with scrambled thoughts.

Aunt Lacey returned and sat on the floor, handing me a large pillow to use to prop myself up. Adjusting myself, I cringed at the white nightgown I was wearing.

"I'll pretend neither of you saw me naked while dressing me in this creepy get-up and move on to details besides whether or not my bra and underwear match. What happened to Jack?"

Kim looked at Aunt Lacey.

"What do you remember?" Aunt Lacey asked, her expression teeming with secrets not hidden as well as she probably thought.

I recalled every hideous detail of Jack's vengeful attack and the confrontation leading to it. My hands shook with adrenaline as I pushed my emotions at arms' length to keep from breaking down. "And since you skirted the question, I'll ask again. What happened to Jack?"

"No need to worry, darling," Aunt Lacey's apathy was less than reassuring.

That they expected me to be content with "Don't worry" was insulting. "I *do* need to worry. Jack's a neighbour's husband. Plus, it happened at the bar. Do the police know?" My words felt acidic, so I rephrased. "Look, I'm unbelievably grateful for all you've done, but... I *need* to know. So, one of you spill before I ask Donovan."

Kim's eyes widened. "Why Donovan?"

"While I was waking up, I heard you talking about him being around." Kim visibly relaxed. "Now tell me what's what before I hunt him down."

"Jack's mind has become maniacal, unhinged," Aunt Lacey finally said.

I mimicked the narrowed look Aunt Lacey gave me. When I remained unsatisfied, she recapped them finding me near death and how they dealt with Jack's unapologetic, drunk ass.

I had a moment of internal "Wait a second, I died?" before

deflecting to the root of what Aunt Lacey said. Jack was alive, trapped in his own little hell in a psych ward.

Seemed generous.

"Does Theresa know?"

"She's aware of his state of mind. At the moment, she is distraught and blames herself. She will move on." The last part sounded more a promise than speculation and made me wonder if that too was part of her plan.

"Does anyone else know?"

"No, my child, you have nothing to fear," Aunt Lacey promised.

Was nobody knowing just as bad as everyone knowing? I couldn't decide.

I nodded, too uncomfortable to speak candidly.

Aunt Lacey offered to make tea. I didn't want any, but it would give me a few moments to speak privately with Kim.

"What now? What time is it? Being underground is crazy disorienting. How do you handle no windows?"

Kim laughed and looked at her watch. "It's Thursday, around six. Plus, this isn't my house so windows aren't on my honey-do list."

"And not up to code." My construction foreman father taught me enough to know.

Kim laughed again. "As to what's next, that's up to you. You don't work for a few days, since we called you in sick. Well, Aunt Lacey did using this wicked spell to disguise her voice. Unless you have plans, you should stay put."

"Only if you're staying, cuz being alone with her gives me the creeps. I'm an ungrateful dickbag for thinking that, but I can't help it."

She laughed. "Course, but Aunt Lacey's just trying to help. You'll get used to her."

A sombre realization hit when I thought of how she helped. "I haven't been dreaming."

"You said you wake up in a panic and have fallen out of your bed, so they're on hold."

After an anxiety-rattled moment, I successfully replaced Jack's greasy face with the grey-eyed man's. I could barely explain my eagerness to see him. With conversation in the dreams now an option, we could unravel the mystery of the park together, if I could remember to speak next time.

No matter how much I fought against it, I was curious about my healing. Kim explained in detail. I felt better knowing Henry, a medically-trained healer, was present. They went over and above to save me. Everyone, including Donovan.

"Wait," I stopped her. "Aunt Lacey could have healed me, but didn't, so the Coveners could bond with me? Nobody asked me if I wanted that."

"It's not some alien force, more a camaraderie thing. She wants you to join the Coven. Helping solidifies their predilection for you so they'll want the same thing. The healing itself makes them a part of your future, since they made it possible." She paused as I stared at her. "She really just wanted to save your life."

I let this settle in. Though I didn't know her well, I didn't get a malicious vibe from Aunt Lacey, and Kim seemed pretty confident in the woman's abilities and motives.

Resting against the pillow, I thought of what the Coven members went through to keep me alive. They, what? Waved their hands, and, poof, I was better? Maybe Henry did something doctor-like and made the biggest difference. However they managed it, how could I repay them?

Kim felt responsible for bringing me into this weirdness. I got that. A drunken asshat's attempt to murder me wasn't her fault. The attack had been earned and paid for by my own big mouth. Kim's weird world saved me.

My reflections built toward one of those pivotal moments that happen before making an important decision. This time, it was one easily made.

This coven stuff was terrifying, crazy as a spinster's feral cat collection, yet seductive. I wanted to know who the grey-eyed man was and discover these abilities everyone claimed I had. Despite having only participated in one meeting, unconscious for the other, and struggling with whether any of it could possibly be true, my resolve was set.

"I'll do it." My tone was so absolute, Kim's head shot up.

A palpable shift affected the room. Like a blast of air causing me to shiver, yet I felt no breeze. I set my resolve, shoving the strange feeling aside.

"Do what exactly?"

"You're not hallucinating, Kim. The Coven. I'll join."

"Really?" Kim's voice pitched.

"Hasn't getting me to join been the whole point? Or did I miss—" Kim stopped me with a squeezing embrace, unable to contain her excitement even when I winced in pain.

Like she timed it, Aunt Lacey returned with tea on a serving tray, Donovan behind her showing a hint of his dimples. Kim was still squeezing my ribcage as Aunt Lacey placed the tray on a side table. Then she laid her hand on my cheek and said, "Welcome."

Donovan's dark eyes looked happy yet subdued, standing with his arms crossed, keeping his distance. The look he gave me confused me more. Maybe something happened between him and Kim, and he was just happy because Kim was? I wondered if she would tell me and decided to let her come out with it on her own.

———

I remained at Aunt Lacey's until my shift, four days after the attack.

Before I left, I caught Donovan with his head in the fridge, happy to have a moment with him alone. He had been around the entirety of my stay, but was always busy somewhere else.

"Hey."

He twisted around with a can of pop in his hand, stared at me, extended the can, and said "Pop?"

Awkward.

"Um, no thanks. I'm headed out in a minute."

He let the fridge door shut, opened the can, and gulped a mouthful without looking away from me.

"Right, I'm actually glad to get the chance to say thank you without an audience. Kim told me how you helped me. The CPR and whatever else you did, so...thanks, Donovan. There's no way I can repay you, but I'm grateful."

"My pleasure." The look he gave me made my stomach flutter.

Kim scared the shit out of me as neither of us noticed her until she plopped my purse down on the kitchen island. This gave me the perfect excuse to look away from Donovan. He used the interruption to flee into the backyard.

"You ready?" she asked me.

I responded with a positive noise, but couldn't find my voice until we left the bubble of disorientation Donovan sucked me into.

Whatever it was in his eyes, I couldn't interpret it. Intrigue? Caution? Annoyance? Condescension? Flirtation? I had no clue and had difficulty shaking off the impact of it all the way home. Kim also seemed stuck in her own thoughts.

I prayed for a day when confusion didn't overshadow my good mood.

I dreaded returning to The Lush, anticipating the end of my shift before it started. Cringing as I opened the door, I was afraid my conscience would roar up and blurt out what happened to the nearest customer.

With uneasy steps, I walked inside. No suspicious glares. No screaming or running as FBI agents pounced. Nothing changed. No blood stains, no evidence of the attack at all.

The only hitch in my return was when Drew stormed in during happy hour and saw me slinging drinks behind the counter. While I poured a couple of beers from the tap for guys seated at the bar,

Drew got close enough for me to smell his fish and chips lunch as he looked me over.

"I thought you were sick?" His dickish tone flared an immediate reaction I decided I wouldn't work too hard to control.

"Were as in was. Do I look sick now?" I served the guys their beers over the bar top and pocketed the tip, ready for whatever Drew had to dish out.

I died and was brought back by a coven of witches. I may be the powerless undead, but I could swat away this taint-licker like a shit-caked fly.

"Could'a fooled me." He crossed his arms over his man-boobs. "What? Was there a convention for lazy bartenders? Or maybe a sale on shoes you just couldn't miss?"

"No. More like a trip to the labour board with a harassment claim against a sexist boss who makes insults like a twelve-year-old tween." My tone never wavered as I soaked up the condensation from around the ice bin with an already soaked towel.

"You little bitch. Like you've got the balls," he said loud enough the conversation between the two young men at the bar stopped.

An unimpressed laugh left my lips as I tossed the soaking towel on the bar and then looked at Drew with a hand on my hip. "Nope. Balls are those crowded acorns in your shrivelled little sack, burrowed somewhere beneath your gut. I've got a vagina. Granted, you probably haven't seen one in a decade, but this one happens to have a fall-back strategy." I leaned forward and cupped my hand around my mouth so the guys at the bar couldn't hear. "Next time you want to disrespect me, or any of your staff, in front of customers, or get the itch to check me out like employing me gives you the license to peruse me like merchandise, remember," I paused for effect, "I do your books."

His eyebrows rose, and I knew I had him.

"Yup, that's right. So, this vagina is content to work the job you hired it for, and you can behave yourself so I don't need to tell those oh-so-curious government folks about how you refuse workers proper breaks. Or how you buy off-the-truck booze. Or how you cook the books after I do them and write-off your trips to hooker alley as business meetings. Or—"

"Shut up," he seethed through clenched teeth.

I stopped, but only because he was exactly where I should have put him a long time ago.

It was my turn to cross my arms and look at the worm in front of me with the smug expression he enjoyed doling out whenever he was in a mood.

"Can I go back to work now, boss? Or would you prefer I take a walk to find more interested parties to converse with?"

Seeing Drew walk away in a huff, knowing that any one of the complaints I mentioned could land him with a huge fine or in jail for years, was a triumph that soared through my entire being.

My mouth may have landed me in hot water with Jack, but I couldn't work here one more day and take the abuse from Drew just because confrontation with an oppressive asshole was terrifying. I couldn't do it anymore. Maybe Jack's attack gave me the motivation to stand-up for myself, maybe I'd reached my limit, but if Drew pushed the boundaries I'd laid down, I was prepared to fulfill my promise and find a way to make him regret it.

The guys at the bar pretended not to be listening, but I refilled their bowl of complimentary mixed nuts and did a round of the floor to clear tables, riding out my shift with extra pep.

———

The weather had picked up during the days I slept, segueing into the Canadian summer I expected. This translated into thirsty customers, but left me a sweaty mess as I fast-walked home, then took my barking buddy out for a quick tree-watering.

Once back upstairs, still flying high from my win against Drew, but waning quickly from the emotional output, I closed the curtains, unplugged the phone, checked the pouch thing was still nestled under my pillow, and I was ready for the Sandman. For good luck, I added the silver necklace, surprised it had survived Jack. If the clarity in the dream *was* a placebo effect, I was happy to cater to it.

Cocooned in my duvet with a cuddly Bosco, the prospect of facing *him* after the absence of the dream was daunting. Twenty-five minutes of tossing and turning passed while I searched for answers only reconcilable if I could pass out.

———

A chill shot through my bones as wind and rain pelted me the moment I opened my eyes in the storm-torn park. In previous dreams, I'd been discombobulated by the dream world, my fear overwhelming. This round, I wasted no time weighing options or focusing on worst-case scenarios. I turned to seek him out, grounded to my body, engrossed in the moment within the park.

He approached from off in the distance and across the grass, the movement of his dark form difficult to focus on until he came closer. Waiting for lightning was unnecessary. The clouds thinned enough for the moon to seep through. Now that I looked upon the grey-eyed man, the storm abated, the wind was strong yet tolerable. The rain streaked across the sky without blinding me, though the floodwater was still rising.

Before I could talk, he grabbed my arm above the elbow. Whatever expression I adopted was enough for him to re-think the tactic and let go.

"Talk to me. Please!" he begged as water dripped down his face.

"I-I'm sorry?" My first words in this place, and they were an apology. Great start.

"Sorry?" he barked with a look of confusion and then stepped closer. "What did you do?"

"Nothing. I'm just standing here." Straightening my posture, I fought the impulse to cower away.

"No..." The word audible above the wind as his infuriated expression smoothed. He paced a few steps away, ran his hand over his short hair, and stood looking off in the distance.

I followed his gaze. All I could see was the path lined by trees disappearing into the darkness.

"No." He wheeled back and stepped toward me again. "No, I know you. I've seen you before. Here. Standing here."

I crossed my arms. "Yeah, you have, and each time's a peach of a visit, thanks." He only stared at me, so I added, "I'm only here when I'm asleep."

He settled back on his heels, retreating into his thoughts, his smoky eyes unfocused. When his gaze affixed on mine again, I didn't know what to say and stared back, waiting for him to work out whatever had him frazzled.

My gasp went ignored when he surged forward to place both hands on my arms, this time to better look at me, not intimidate. His grey eyes pinned me in place. I shifted between wanting to force him to back off and pulling him closer.

"Answer me truthfully. Am I dead?"

"What—? Shit, guy, I don't know what you are."

He let me go and spun away, his hands gripped in his hair. Afraid he would disappear, I started talking. "All I know is, one day I started dreaming of being here. For a long time, I couldn't see your face."

Retreating into his thoughts again, he bit at his thumbnail.

"How long have you been here?" I asked.

He glanced at me. "Just moments...I thought." He pressed his thumb and forefinger into his eyes, hand on his hip, before he swiped water away from his mouth and rubbed his jaw. "No. Longer. Much longer. I can't tell."

My heart ached at his mystified reaction to what, I thought, would be a simple question. Aimless movement had him taking a few steps one way only to shake his head and walk back to the same spot. Keeping his questions to himself wasn't getting us anywhere, and the water around us was only getting deeper.

He may not have noticed it, but I was freezing and panicked at the thought of the dream ending without more information.

"What's your name?" I blurted.

He stood with his hands on his hips, responding absently. "Caine Berisford."

"Okay, awesome. Caine, tell me the last thing you remember. What were you doing?"

His thick brows pinched in question as he checked into the conversation. "What? What are you talking about?"

"I can't find out why you're here, or what the fuck is going on, if I don't have info. Spill it before this rabbit hole yaks me up again."

My sudden crassness evoked a surprised expression. He hesitated before responding, "I was driving my brother Cole back from...someplace...in the rain." His eyes skittered around as he sifted through broken memories. "We were talking about an upcoming cage fight. He wanted me to come over to watch it. I told him I would if he cleaned up his pigsty of an apartment first."

He paused, fidgeting.

"With the rain," his voice dropped, "I think I lost control." His lips hung open, eyes wide before the crease between his brows softened and he looked at me sharply. "I think I killed him." The memory must have been repressed, guarding him from the pain. He gasped and dropped to his knees, his head in his hands.

"You don't know that." I tried to comfort him. "And if he did die, it sounds like an accident."

He spun on me so quickly I recoiled, stumbling backward into the water before he grabbed my arm. His savage eyes bore down as his hands moved to clasp my face. "You have to find out more! You have to find out what happened!"

10

BRAIN DAMAGE AND CATHETERS

I burst from sleep and scurried backward, still trying to get away from him, stopping when the back of my skull bounced off the headboard. A surge of despair consumed me as I sat frozen, replaying the dream. The grey-eyed man was no longer a mystery. His name was Caine Berisford. Caine was no predator. Caine needed help, needed it just as urgently as I did, if not more.

My pulsating veins caused my head to swim, my knees pulled to my chest as tears fell. I felt useless and helpless and heartbroken. I was unable to measure the hell he had endured, was still enduring in that park.

Was Caine dead? Did he kill his brother in some accident? Watching this stranger fall to tatters crippled me.

As I'd learned over the course of the last couple years dealing with my personal tragedies, I needed to transform this powerlessness into action before it drowned me. I shot up and whirled the curtains back to gauge the day. The sun shone without impeding cloud cover, an affront to the weather I'd left Caine in. The clock in the living room showed the actual time as late afternoon.

Tapping into the newfound strength I'd worked so hard to build,

I walked Bosco, showered, and readied myself in no time. Calling Kim, I had her come over to talk about the dream.

It pained me to relay Caine's last plea.

"What are you going to do? What if this turns dangerous?"

I was floored by Kim's warning. "Dangerous? What's dangerous about hitting up the library archives or searching the net?" I fired back while pacing with Bosco at my feet. "If there was an accident, there's info about it somewhere."

"All I'm saying is you may want to think about it before you set yourself up for disappointment. If Caine is a real person, he could be where he is for a reason."

"What's with the tail-tucking, Kim? You were the one encouraging me to find meaning behind the dream as soon as you heard about it. I was hoping you'd help me with this, and now...what? You're playing it safe? You're the only other person who knows everything, plus has knowledge of a world I can barely admit exists. I *need* you." The admission took a bigger chunk out of me than I anticipated. "Look, I don't think I'm describing his despair well enough."

"Soph, he could be—"

"He's not dead," I interrupted, then sat next to her, hoping to connect to the part of Kim that had belief in me. "He's not. Believe me, I know how whacked this all sounds. I realize the level of straitjacket I've reached, but he's alive. Caine's real and stuck in some personal purgatory. I need to get him out. Please, Kim."

If Kim walked away, I would be grovelling at her feet. No one but me had face-time with the guy. Caine was my responsibility, I had no clue what to do, and I needed Kim.

She grabbed my hands. I held tight, my fingers rigid with hope. "Believing he's trapped isn't a stretch, Soph. This is your dream. I can't tell you anything you don't know about them, and I can't pretend to know what it's like to stand in the flooded park with him. Just promise me you'll leave a little room to deal with Caine being dead, if that's the case. You may be dealing with his soul, and not Caine as a live, savable, person. Am I making sense?"

"Fine."

"Sophie, I mean it."

"I know. He could be worm food, and I'm only talking with his husk. I get it."

Kim's disbelief was visible. I couldn't blame her. The words meant nothing to me. I just needed her support. I'd deal with the rest if it turned out that way.

Kim exhaled, and compassion flooded back into her blue-green eyes. "Okay. You know his name. I'm not running all over town if we don't have to. Get on your computer, and I'll get on mine. If the accident happened how he said it did, there has to be proof."

I threw my arms around her. "Thank you so much."

She held me back. "Yeah, yeah. Thank me when we get your dream boy out of the park."

With his name, I figured a simple search might prove promising. It would have been easier to narrow down with a year, but we didn't get that far.

Kim grabbed her laptop from her place and searched as I typed his name into the search engine. A few sports records for the Governor Simcoe High School's Redcoats Lacrosse team used the name "Caine Berisford." No picture accompanied the article as proof it was him and not someone with the same name. Even with the impressive "Player of the Game" designation, no one thought to add a photo. No other entries revealed a Caine Berisford involved in any accident.

"First dead end. That's okay." Defeat was not about to win.

"Did you find anything?" Kim asked.

"Just a name drop with no picture and nothing about an accident."

"Me too."

"You know, if an accident ended in death, his family may have wanted it to stay out of the papers."

"True."

I checked social media sites and found nothing, the tapping of keys filling the air.

My attention kept slipping, wondering what Caine was doing at that exact moment. I knew he was still in the stormy park, alone, confused—all compounded by my sudden disappearance. Concentrating on the task was the only thing stopping me from curling into a ball like the basket case.

I tried to escape the memory of his face as it twisted, tormented at the thought of killing his brother. They must have been close.

I had a stroke of genius.

"Cole," I said.

"Cole? Did you find something?"

"No. Caine said his brother's name was Cole. If Cole was killed, his info would be out there, not Caine's." I heard Kim's fingers on the keys before I finished explaining my epiphany.

"Sophie..."

"What?" The sound of her voice was wrong. "What? What did you find?"

"Get over here." Her gaze was glued to the screen.

My racing heart braced for bad news. It stopped me from talking, yet somehow I managed to sit next to her and look at the screen.

"That's not him," I said, the words punchy. A picture of a young man with dirty blond hair, dark eyes, and candid smile was on Kim's laptop. Kim scrolled down to an article and read it aloud.

"A Summer Storm Claims a Life," she read the headline. "Late Tuesday evening during an aggressive downpour, nineteen-year-old Cole Berisford was killed in a tragic car accident off of Oakdale Avenue when the driver, and brother, twenty-one-year-old Caine, lost control of the vehicle."

Her eyes skimmed down the page, stating details as she went. "Slick roads...high speeds...down embankment into Centennial Park...airbags didn't deploy...Oh! Caine survived and is currently in critical condition at McMaster Children's Hospital in Hamilton."

"When?" I yanked the laptop my way and searched for a date. "I can't...Years," I whispered. "It's been years."

"Years?"

"Almost four." My eyes welled with tears as Kim pulled the laptop her way. She finished the article, details about Cole's services and donations, words faintly heard above my racing thoughts.

Tears spilled down my cheeks, my hand covered my mouth, fighting to retain composure as I trembled. Kim put her arm around my shoulders.

"I think I remember this," Kim said, her voice thick with emotion. "I wasn't living here then, but people talked about the crash, looking for donations. I didn't know..."

Like her, I had a vague recollection of a summer crash in the park, but over three years ago my life was a mess, and I didn't care about some nameless car crash victims. I was too consumed by my unravelling drama to peek outside at the rest of the world to find my balance and live again. Going back to school was a part of the effort to find answers. Working at the bar wasn't a move I would have normally taken, but it kept me around people so I didn't slip into depression again. To think, at the same time I was broken and struggling to get my shit together, Caine was facing a worse tragedy. At least my family was alive, and I was awake to fit the pieces back where they had been ripped out. Caine was still stuck in that park while life went on without him.

I didn't know him, but I knew he didn't deserve this.

At some point I would have to tell Caine he killed his brother. Accident or not, judging by his reaction to the possibility, this would level him. Plus, he could still be lying in a coma.

"We were looking for answers and now we know." I swiped at my tears. I hated crying, especially in front of others. After another composing moment, I looked to Kim, and stubborn tears escaped. "How am I supposed to tell him his brother's dead?"

"You're more equipped for this than I am, Soph. Nothing I say can make you feel better, but remember, he could still be in the coma. Probably is since you're adamant he's alive."

"He *is* alive."

"I hear ya. Maybe he needs to know what happened so he can move on."

"Sure," I mocked, "you hear about earthbound souls all the time, trapped in their body, searching for reason. Then commercials roll, and you hit the fridge for a midnight snack only to find an old jar of pickles you take a chance on because the bread is moldy."

Kim cracked a smile as I deflected with humour.

"This isn't normal, Kim. People are supposed to die, and that's it. Some ghost hunter rejects can contend with the stubborn bastards who want to stick around. Caine has no clue what's going on. He isn't haunting the park, just me."

Kim stayed quiet, allowing me to work it through another moment.

"I don't know that I want him to move on." Selfish as it was, it was honest. Unable to meet Kim's stare I focused on drying my eyes and trying not to snot down my face.

"Moving on doesn't always mean passing away. Maybe he just needs to know about the accident so he can move beyond denial, and his mind can heal. Even doctors with PhDs littering their office walls don't know shit about why people stay in comas for years and then suddenly wake up. It just happens." Again, she was being optimistic for my benefit but I could tell Kim meant it, even if I disagreed with her logic.

No. There was a reason he was still asleep, if that's what this was. Just because we didn't have answers, it didn't mean it was something supernatural, but there was a reason.

Regardless, if I could pull off the impossible and find a way to help Caine, then what? He'll open his pretty eyes like a male version of Sleeping Beauty and profess his undying affection?

Please.

He might wake up and resume his life as he should have years ago, with one less brother and a few missed birthdays.

Either way, no one else had contact, no one else could bear witness to his pain, and although I was the only person who could tell Caine what happened that night, it was a burden I was unprepared, mentally and emotionally, to fulfill.

"I'm assuming you want to go to the hospital to see him. Do you want to go now?"

I wiped my tear-smeared palms on my jeans. "We don't know if he's still there. Plus, if he is, what if his family's there, or if we need special permission? We can't randomly walk into his room with a story about my crazy dream."

"Okay," Kim twisted her lips in thought a moment. "If he is, we say we're...old friends who've been out of the country. How will they know the difference? We only have to confirm he's in a coma. All it needs is a pair of good actors." She smiled. "I'm sure you can squeeze out a few more tears that'll make any bitter, old nurse's heart melt. They'll express line you right to him."

This was an attempt to make me laugh, but all Kim got was my pitiful smile. She was trying.

"ETA's about an hour. If they give us the boot, we'll chalk it up to a failed experiment, and you can tell Caine he's well-protected by douchebags, but not yet taking the dirt nap. And if he's pissed, then I say leave him where he is."

Numb to Kim's jokes, I was uncertain of the right thing to do. I wiped my face again, feeling uber gross and in need of a tissue. "'Kay, let's do this."

I mentally braced myself. If excitement existed within me, it was hidden below overwhelming dread. Being alive didn't mean the guy was in any condition to wake up from a coma. If we got through the doors, and if my luck shifted out of the red zone, the most I had to look forward to was an unconscious body in a bed.

Trusting in positive outcomes wasn't my thing, and I knew better than to keep my expectations high.

I knew we could have called and maybe suckered some administrator to give us the information. But going another day without seeing him, really seeing him, now that I knew where he was, who he was? Not an option.

"Gas is on me," I told Kim before I backed out, "and we'll need to stop for flowers and probably a card." Kim tried to argue about the gas, but I didn't allow a sideways word about it. "You're doing me a huge favour, Kim. No one else would go to such lengths without thinking I was cuckoo bird insane." I paused, gathered my gumption. "I truly appreciate everything, and I know I can never repay you for this adventure, stalking a coma patient who manifests in my dreams, but someday, I promise, I *will* try."

Kim smiled without comment on my awkward delivery. "Okay, darlin'," Kim closed her laptop and stood, pulling me up with her, "let's get motoring. We'll pick up our infiltration props and get us some road snacks." We headed for the door. "See this as a good thing. If Coma Boy is still alive, you might get the chance to snag yourself a hottie."

Kim's laugh finally drew me in, alleviating the building tension in my gut. I understood Kim not wanting to endure my blubbering for the entire trip. I was sick of it myself.

———

Convenience store blue carnations were the best I could find. Had Caine been awake, I would never have bought them. Flowers are wasted money in my eyes—beauty snipped off in its prime, stuck in a vase to wither and die, how romantic!

Kim helped search the limited supply of cards on a tall, previously-spinning, now-broken rack. Most had comical pictures intended for birthdays. All wrong.

"They don't make cards that say, 'Sorry you killed your brother, hope the coma breaks before permanent brain damage sets in. P.S. I bet the catheter is a real treat'."

Kim laughed and kept searching. "How about this one?" She handed me one displaying a sunset-lit beach in sepia colours. Inside, it read: *My warmest thoughts are with you. Get well soon.* "You can always pen in something that doesn't include brain damage and catheters."

"What's a get-well card without brain damage and catheters?"

"One that might get you laid in this decade." She pushed me toward the counter. "Now, move it, Toots."

After paying the leering cashier who'd overheard our conversation, we were back on the road with our infiltration props, sour jujubes, multi-flavoured liquorice, and a couple bottles of pop to top off the sugar overload.

Road trips were fun, except when suffering from motion sickness. I grossed myself out with memories of countless car rides wilting in my seat. I was well-known for my fainting and puking spells. Motion sickness and excessive heat were my worse enemies, so I forced myself to look straight out the windshield and took in fresh summer air from the open window. When Kim asked me to check her phone's GPS to double-check the directions, I was sunk.

I attempted to navigate the app and thought better when my eyes crossed and my throat tightened. "Sorry Kim, but if I read that, you'll be scraping Orange-Crush-soaked jujubes out of your dashboard air vents. We're going to have to guess, or you'll have to pull over. You'll kick my ass if you don't."

After all Kim was doing to help me, I felt like a jackass. The term "dead weight" came to mind.

"Why didn't you say something? We could've picked up some Gravol, you know."

"It makes me dopey. No nurse would believe I was bereaved while 'on the nod,' drooling on myself. With the sugar fix and fresh air, I'll be fine. I usually am when I drive. I suck as a passenger."

"Do you want to drive? I don't mind switching places."

"Oh no, like I said, fresh air and sugar helps. I just can't read anything. Plus, I'm in the front seat. I'll let you know if I've gotta yak."

Probably to save me the embarrassment, Kim waved it off as a non-issue and concentrated on the road.

I used this opportunity—being stuck in a car together—to get to know Kim better as a distraction. I learned Kim had an older sister, Anita, by two and a half years. She was the only other person who knew about Kim's involvement in the Coven. Now Anita avoided her at family holiday gatherings and treated her like a leper. After her mom passed away from a long fight with breast cancer, Kim's dad had a rough go at life without his wife.

Knowing she watched her mother die, then found me dead and worked to save me, I felt doubly guilty. It was the first time I'd thought about how finding someone in that position would make them feel. I'd been too self-absorbed with surviving to ask. She acted unaffected, but it had to leave a mark.

Great budding psychiatrist I was.

Not remembering if I had, I thanked Kim for introducing me to the Coven, wanting her to know that I wouldn't join only to gain what I could and bolt. My curiosity led me to Aunt Lacey and her group of Coveners, and kept me asking questions, even though I was still skeptical about their abilities. Without Caine's presence in my dreams, I may not have been so gung-ho. However, since the stabbing, I'd known it was something I belonged to.

The Coven was to meet during the week on a non-Sunday coven meeting day. My nerves spiked when Kim alluded to its purpose as ceremonial to initiate me into the Coven as a full-fledged member, peaking my imagination at what that might entail. The regularly sched-uled meeting was tonight, but work would prevent me from attending. After days of being "sick" I couldn't skip out on a shift again so soon.

Instead of getting into details about the Initiation, we chatted about everything from family pets to crappy jobs, enjoying the journey.

"So, what's with Donovan? Is there something between you two?"

"Nah, me and Donovan never had a thing. Will never have a thing." Kim didn't look away from the road, tipping me off there was something she wasn't telling me.

Obviously, Kim didn't want to talk about herself and Donovan, so I made it about myself to salvage the conversation. "Not that I'm looking for a man, I mean he's incredibly scrumptious,"—Kim nodded at my understatement—"but I don't know him from the convenience store guy."

Kim gave a wry laugh. "Yeah, he enjoys being a mystery." Then she nonchalantly changed the subject.

Getting the distinct impression Kim was hiding or understating something about Donovan, I noted the deflection, and this time let it happen.

After arriving at the hospital and waiting in line to get a ticket to park, I sat frozen in my seat as Kim climbed out of the parked car. All my reservations about what I might walk into and how I should be handling this situation crashed onto my chest.

Noticing she was alone, Kim walked back to my opened window. "Are ya comin'?" Since I was too panicked to respond, Kim got back in the car to talk instead. "It's okay, Soph. We'll just wait until you're ready. He's not going anywhere." I looked at her sharply. "Sorry, but he's not."

I flopped my head back onto my headrest. Concentrating on Caine needing me to get my shit together was supposed to help.

Yeah, right.

I needed to get a grip and get my ass out of the stupid car. Resolved to see this plan through, I opened the door, jumped out, and shut it forcefully. I stalked toward the front entrance.

Kim caught up with me. "You forgot these." She handed me the flowers and card. "You haven't written anything in the card yet, either."

Focused on not turning back, I didn't respond and kept walking before my feet could retreat back to the car.

Sitting in the waiting room trying to think up something for the card was counterproductive. The area, as with most hospitals, was dreadful, full of uncomfortable, plastic, peeling chairs, humming vending machines, and a twenty-year-old, nineteen-inch TV with bad reception. Not to mention all the people wishing they were anywhere else instead of contracting everyone else's summer sickness.

I turned away from a pregnant mother and her snot-nosed little boy playing with a toy school bus and focused on the card, trying to think of something that would tell Caine who I was without prompting unwanted questions.

Shit! "He doesn't know my name."

"What?"

"I never told Caine my name. I asked him what *his* was, but I never told him mine!"

I was starting to crack.

"The card is just a prop, Soph. You could transcribe the song 'When I Touch Myself' inside, and it won't matter. Relax and write something trite."

I huffed, then put pen to paper.

Dear Caine,

I'm dreadfully sorry for the trials you have been forced to face and hope one day you escape the rain clouds to bask in the sun once again.

I'll speak to you very soon!!

Sophie Saterlee

With Kim's seal of approval, I licked and closed the envelope,

cringing at the taste, realizing someone would open it and read it for
Caine anyway.

Kim ordered me to stay put so she could do her best sweet-talking
at the admissions desk, with the flowers and card in hand. She
possessed the finesse to pull it off and didn't need my face betraying
the lie. After a few minutes, Kim donned a triumphant smile out of
sight of the admissions worker, and we made our way up upstairs.

As we exited the elevator onto the fourth floor, Kim wrapped her
arm around my rigid shoulders, granting me much needed support.
By the time we reached the door, I was faint, weak kneed, and tasting
jujube-and-Orange-Crush-flavoured bile.

"Here we are," Kim said in a sing-song voice. The door was
closed, and nurses and patients milled around in the halls. "You can
do this, Soph. You put drunk frat boys in their place at the bar. You've
come so far. I know you can do this."

I couldn't force a smile, not even for one of Kim's pep talks, and
she knew better than to wait for one as she edged me toward the door
and across the threshold.

11

FLUCTUATIONS

Caine's hospital room was alive with paintings done by children, which obscured the institutional, off-white walls. Flowers, cards, and photos were littered across available surfaces. A multi-coloured quilt was folded on a chair, mimicking the comforts of home.

I stood at the foot of a hospital bed, fixated on the man laying motionless beneath clean, white sheets. He filled the length of the bed, and tubes ran from his body to bags hung from poles at his sides. A machine beeped.

Those haunting, grey eyes were hidden from me beneath closed lids. Jet-black lashes rested like feathers against his pale cheeks. Most shocking was the breathing tube taped in place across the shadow of a few days growth on his chin. As his chest rose and fell in a way that looked too violent to be healthy, I took in the heartbreaking realities of a coma.

Beyond the tubes and his overall shroud of sickness, someone other than nurses and doctors was looking after him. His dark brown hair was wavy and longer than it had been in my dreams. Now it was tucked behind his ears. Not his usual style, judging by how clean-cut he was in the park. Drenched in a desolate, storm-ravaged park or lying helpless in a sterile hospital bed, Caine Berisford was striking.

Lightheadedness brought on by the sight of his current physical weakness impaired my balance. I collapsed into the chair behind me, a stream of tears soaking my cheeks. Kim knelt down, putting a consoling arm on mine, her other rubbing my back, and cleared her throat.

"Holy shit. He's real." I had believed it to be true, but seeing him was still a shock.

"Never doubted you, Soph." Kim swallowed so hard I heard it. "Do you want me to leave?"

I grabbed her arm, feeling her muscles tense in response. "Don't..." My voice cracked. "I don't want to be alone."

"Okay, okay. I won't." Wincing, Kim shook loose from my grip.

With my ally secured, I headed for the right side of Caine's bed. There was none of the anticipated awkwardness when I reached to hold his hand, which was bruised from an IV. Entangling my fingers with his, my grip went unreciprocated. His fingers hung limp and unmoving, so I held them closed around my own with my free hand, being sure not to knock off the device monitoring his heartbeat.

Another wave of tears fought to escape. A few fell before I could rein them in. What could I say? There was no proof coma victims heard their loved ones talking around them. Judging by the news article describing a benefit to help his family with funeral costs and for Caine while in his coma, he was loved.

In the dream, he'd known nothing about people around him, had no idea he was in a coma at all. Nothing I said here would make a difference since I would see him tonight, but I still felt the need to say something.

"It's nice to finally meet you in person. I was beginning to think I made you up." I giggled uneasily. "Your hair's long." I reached over and smoothed it back. Taking a long moment to look him over, even considering the machines all around, he seemed more at peace here than in my dream. I leaned down to whisper in his ear. "I promise I'll get you out of this bed. I promise I'll save you, Caine." Then I kissed him on the cheek.

Looking back at Kim, I found her occupying the chair I fell apart in, elbows to knees. The door swung open, and Kim and I exchanged a look as she burst to her feet.

A short lady with long, dark hair pulled back in a low ponytail entered, looked at Kim and then me still holding Caine's hand. "I'm sorry, who are you?"

I dropped Caine's hand and dried my tears, trying to salvage my make-up. It was probably smudged under my eyes.

"Sorry, ma'am." Kim extended a hand warmly and introduced us.

"I'm Caine's mother, Joyce. How do you ladies know my son?" Motherly instincts poured from Joyce as she moved to her son's side, adjacent to me. She looked like she was seconds from paging security.

Kim took the lead, justifying our presence with the contrived story she'd already used to get us this far, creasing her eyebrows with the appropriate sympathies for maximum effect. Kim's charismatic lies seemed to win Joyce over. Maybe that was Kim's talent. Regardless, it crumbled the woman's rough exterior enough for Joyce to absorb Kim's explanation.

"I wish I could say he's doing great," Joyce stated, gazing adoringly at her child. "If you had walked in here only months ago, you would have seen a different man. No tubes other than the ones for nourishment and hydration and such. Of course, he hasn't opened his eyes since the accident, but his brain function is normal. Doctors are stumped at why he's still in the coma." She smoothed his hair down on his left side as I had on the right. Again, he didn't react to the contact.

I struggled to retain control over my emotions and tried to catch a couple tears before they leapt from my eyes. Seeing the inert body before me after meeting the tortured man in the park was more than I was equipped for, no matter my schooling and life experiences that already included far too many tears. Joyce handed me a tissue from a small blue box on a counter next to a picture of what looked like Caine and Cole as children.

"Thank you." Wiping my tears and clearing my throat, I felt I should say more. "So, all this is recent?" Joyce's lips pursed as she nodded. "What happened?"

She gave a small shake to her head. "I wish I knew. For years it was the same, day in, day out. He looked like he was sleeping. And then maybe six months or so ago, little things would pop up. Bed sores, infections, then antibiotic-resistant infections, pneumonia...the doctors said it's expected since he's,"—she paused—"in what they think is Locked-in Syndrome. Being in this bed is destroying his body."

I couldn't imagine how his mother was dealing. A steady decline is what they told her, but with his brain trauma-free and since his wounds from the accident had healed, why couldn't he wake up? And this all started about six months ago? The timing of his decline and the beginning of my dream had to mean something.

"I'm sorry for your loss," Kim said when no one spoke. "We heard Cole didn't survive the accident."

"Thank you," Joyce replied, with a sad smile. Time had apparently smoothed the edges of her despair at Cole's absence. "At least I still have Caine. Sometimes I think he only holds on because he knows I'm too scared to let him go. Though time is now making the decision for the both of us."

My gaze flickered to their childhood picture again, Joyce's gaze following. "My boys were inseparable. Cole would never blame his brother for the accident, but I know my son. Caine will still blame himself. Best case scenario would be him not remembering anything, I'm afraid." Her wishful thinking was heartbreaking. "I just want another of his bear hugs again. He's so tall." Memories of her son in happier times made her expression glow.

They say you can tell a man's worth by how he treats his mother. And right now I believed it.

"After the accident, we didn't have enough room to fit all his visitors. People eventually stopped showing up as often." Joyce shrugged. "Many still send flowers, mostly to me. Most don't believe he'll come out of it. They'd never say that, but I see it on their faces."

Her features distorted as Joyce continued, "His girlfriend couldn't handle his condition, though she hardly tried."

"Girlfriend?" My voice was far too pointed.

"Tracey. I suppose they weren't together long enough for her to stand by him. She stopped showing up less than a month after the accident." Joyce shook her head. "She wasn't right for him anyway." She smoothed his hair again and pressed down the tape on his cheek. She grinned as she added, "He would have figured that out, given the opportunity."

Typical mother. No woman would ever be good enough for her son. I wondered what he would think about Tracey's decision and his mother's opinion of her.

I changed topics. "So, there's been no change until recently? Sorry, it just doesn't make sense." I had so many questions and no right to ask a doctor about his condition.

Joyce shrugged and rubbed Caine's arm. "If he can hold on and fight this latest bout of pneumonia, he still has a chance to fight the rest. They recorded heart rate fluctuations over the last few months, mostly from the night staff. The doctor thinks he's dreaming, which is a clear sign of heightened brain activity, something he never showed before, so I refuse to give up hope."

I clenched my teeth with a discreet glance at Kim, who gave me a "no-fucking-kidding" expression. We both knew what had caused the fluctuations.

Joyce looked tired as she spoke of her son's condition. "At one point, they even thought he was faking. Post-traumatic stress reaction due to psychological trauma from Cole's death." She gave an indignant gruff. "Hacks."

The theory was wrong, but I had learned about it and understood how they came to the conclusion. The academic part of me was curious how they tested the notion.

"I truly appreciate you girls visiting. It's been too long since he's had friends drop in, but the nurse is coming by any minute."

As tactful as the request was, I hated to leave. Caine was alive and real, and now I was forced to walk away.

"Please come back soon," Joyce pleaded. "I'm sure he appreciated the company. I'll make sure to put your names on the list for next time."

I assumed Joyce craved the interaction as she no doubt spent most days with her silent son.

Kim shook Joyce's hand again. "Soon, we promise."

I gave Joyce a quick, tight embrace that surprised us both. "I'm so sorry. I truly believe he'll wake up."

"Me too," Joyce responded in a soft, choked voice.

"Here." I grabbed the envelope containing my card, ripping it open. "I'll write my number inside, and if anything changes, you can call me. Is that okay?" I asked as I wrote.

"Yes, of course, I definitely will." Joyce hugged me again, with more vigour.

While we headed out, a stocky, middle-aged nurse came through the door with what looked like sponge bath supplies. At least Joyce wasn't just trying to get rid of us.

I gave Caine one last look of longing before we left, thinking again about how to tell him what he so desperately needed to hear.

We rode the elevator down without a word, but once we were in the car, we burst out in unison.

"He's real!"

"His heart rate jumps when he dreams of you!"

"His hair's not long in the dreams."

"He's freakin' hot, Soph. You suck at describing him."

"He has a girlfriend."

"Hardly."

"Last time he was in the real world, he did."

"Do you really think he'd want her after she dropped him like that?"

"I don't know him. Maybe she'll come back after he wakes up. He could forgive that. He was in a coma."

"Oh, come on, Soph, does he seem like that type of wank?"

"I've had one conversation with him. He might be exactly that type of wank."

Kim shrugged, and we stared at each other a moment before things got serious.

"I peeked at the file at the end of the bed," Kim told me. "It's not just pneumonia."

"What is it?"

"Systematic shutdown. His organs are failing, and these little issues are bigger than Joyce admitted. They're evidence his body is giving up."

I looked away from Kim to face the front windshield, seeing nothing as I tried to process this new information. "We need to hurry. If he's this bad after only six months, then..." I couldn't say he could die at any moment. I didn't need to. Both Kim and I knew it. Caine was on borrowed time the moment he went into the coma, and now he was losing the fight.

Kim only nodded and started the car. I chose to interpret this as she was on board to do whatever we could.

I was amazed by the information we'd acquired during our visit. We found what we needed, but leaving him stuck in that hospital bed was depressing.

Kim draped her arm on the steering wheel as we waited at a red light. "Obviously, you two are connected. I don't know how, but you're not the one dreaming of him. He's been comatose for years, and you've only seen him for months. Now, it could be because he's been sick and that was the catalyst for him dragging you into his dream, or realm, or whatever, but it's still him who started all this. Accidental? Maybe, but this one's on him."

"So, I just happened to be the one to get his rescue beacon? If so, it could have been anyone that picked up the dream to help him," I said, working it out as I spoke, "which would mean it's *not* a specific connection between us."

"No, I think you're wrong, Soph. I think he's been looking for help for a long time, and there's a reason he found you. A connection exists. I don't know why. Aunt Lacey thought you might be using astral projection without realizing it. He's stuck in the park by your apartment, so maybe when you're sleeping your essence is drawn in by his energy."

"If astral projection is anything like they talk about in the movies, it would still mean my essence found him, right? And that I was looking for him and not the other way around." The theory failed to make sense to me. I wasn't looking for any guy. I would have been content to stay away from that park from the first moment I saw the terrifying, shadowy mass.

"Fine, but my vote is still on there being a connection. Does it really matter?"

"What do you mean?"

"Exactly what I said. Why does it matter *why* you two've found each other? It should only matter that you have. Maybe you can bust him out and then, you never know what could happen."

Buying into Kim's optimism was tempting, but I strayed from relationships for a reason. Reminding myself of why, I bitch-slapped the notion out the window.

"The dreams started happening around the same time as when his health took a turn. I could believe that's why he reached out. Whatever romance novel you have rattling around in your brain, write it down and sell it, but I'm not buying it. He may wake up and reconnect with his girlfriend or not wake up at all, and I get to see him every night until his body shuts down completely. There's nothing romantic about any of that."

"Either way, you keep dreaming about him, and he doesn't realize he's doing it, so he won't stop. Especially if he finds out he might be dead soon."

"Kim!"

"What? I'm sorry, but it's true."

The dreams were relentless. Every time I slept, he would be there if I wanted him to be or not. But loneliness had plagued him for years, the least I could do was sacrifice sleep to keep him company. "I'll probably stick around for as long as he's reaching out."

"Then it's worth a try," Kim deduced as she changed lanes. "If he wakes up and goes on with his life, you can take comfort in the fact you helped him to do so."

"I guess." I looked at passing traffic. "I don't want to get emotionally invested."

"By the way you reacted in there, I'm thinking you're already emotionally invested."

I hated that she was right.

The rest of the ride was quiet as I tried to come up with plausible theories. I never intended to be invested in this man. He was just a nightmare I wanted to be rid of. Now, I was infatuated with solving this for him. Not so convinced by men in general, something about him gripped me. I didn't get it and doubted the sensation would translate into the real world.

Regardless, any expectations were unfair after what Caine had been through. Before getting ahead of myself, I still had to tell him about Cole and then figure out a way to wake him up.

Rush hour slowed our progress, and by the time we reached our building, I itched to escape Kim's car.

"I'll let Aunt Lacey know what happened and see what she thinks up. Call me tomorrow with an update?" she asked me before I exited the car outside our building; she was now on her way to Aunt Lacey's to set-up for the meeting.

"I will. Unless he's so mad he flips his lid and murders me in my sleep. If you don't hear from me, have the cops do a wellness check," I half-joked, hoping "death by dreams" was a myth.

"Remember to run fast and climb trees. If he can kill you, you can kill him."

"Hmm. Equal opportunity murder, great end to the day."

Home at last.

I was greeted by Bosco's familiar chorus of un-canine-like noises. "Sorry I left you again, buddy, but I've to get ready for work." I squatted so he could lick my cheeks. I managed to strap on his harness despite his continued hyperactivity.

Bosco pulled the heft of his fifteen pounds toward the nearest tree, shaded from the sun.

How can I say what Caine needs me to? "Yeah, man. This sucks totes monkey balls, but guess what...?" Not exactly appropriate.

12

A SAD REALITY

Caine

I wedged my body between a pair of trees, seeking shelter from the rain and wind. When was the last time I'd stood in sunlight or smelled anything other than the dank creek and the stench of my dirty clothes? What I wouldn't give for a bottle of Gucci.

A gust of wind assaulted me. I shut my eyes, wrapped my arms around my knees, and buried my face into my arms. .

"Would a goddamned break be too much to ask for?"

Didn't matter. I wasn't budging. I was waiting for *her*.

She'd broken up the monotony of hunting for Cole. She might be able to tell me why the fuck we were trapped here, maybe even how to escape this hell.

Even if she couldn't, I still wanted to see her.

Beautiful.

Breathtaking.

She didn't belong here, but fuck, neither did I.

"Caine!"

Cole's voice had me forgetting my sore body. I shot to my feet.

My throat was tight as I remembered him as I last saw him, seated in my passenger seat. Moments before the accident. Or whatever.

Shit. I needed her to pop up again. I needed answers.

"Caine! Where are you?"

I ran toward Cole's screams. No way was I leaving my little brother lost and alone out there in this storm.

The rain pummelled my body as I pushed my soggy shoes over the grass, bypassing trees that all looked the same.

He was out there.

Again, I heard my brother's voice. In all our lives, Cole had never sounded like that. I couldn't imagine the horrors I would run into when I finally found him.

Slipping on the slick grass, I hit a bend in the path and wiped out, sliding in the rain. Mud covered half my body. When Cole cried out again, I pushed to my feet and started sprinting, my lungs burning as I yelled for him to find me. My throat was thrashed, but I kept screaming.

Why didn't he sound closer?

Why couldn't I find him?

Back and forth searching where his voice was coming from by the far side of the creek I still couldn't find him. This didn't make sense. He had to be here.

I ripped through overgrown brush to get to the water and slid in the muck. I braced myself on a fallen branch before I fell in and looked up and down the creek.

Nothing.

I waited for him to call out again to track his voice. Again, nothing.

"Come on, Cole. Where are you?"

My side cramped so I squatted down, dropping my head in exhaustion.

I'd lost him again.

Water grazed my fingers. The creek was flooding. I backed off through the brush, ready to escape it, and then realized it was a good thing. Rising water meant *she* was back.

Splashing through the few inches of water under my shoes, I pushed as hard as I could to get back to her spot before she disappeared like Cole.

Rounding the bend, I caught a glimpse of dark hair. She stood right where she always did, squinting through the rain.

She didn't notice me at first, but when she did, her expression tensed and she took a step back, dark eyes widening, her body tense at seeing me.

I kept running, feeling a smile crease my cold cheeks. The failure of not finding Cole vanished in my excitement to see her.

"You're back!" I yelled with enthusiasm I hadn't felt in a long time. I picked her up off her feet and spun her around, hit with the scent of her fruity, flowery smell. The giggle in my ear was a reward I hadn't expected. "I was afraid I scared you off." I put her down, realizing I probably shouldn't have done that. "I'm sorry I was so upset. I'm not usually such an ass."

She wiped my muddy cheek print from her face and smiled right from her dark eyes. Damn, she was beautiful.

"No worries." She pushed hair off of her forehead that had plastered there when I spun her around. Oh, God. Did I spin her around? Hyperaware of her closeness, I couldn't stop myself from staring into her eyes.

She looked down, and I realized how high the water was.

"Follow me."

She hesitated when I went toward the trees. And why not? She didn't know me. After a moment she followed, having a hard time walking. Her bare toes rose above the water, and I thought to offer to carry her, but I'd already picked her up one too many times.

I started climbing up a low-hanging branch of a willow tree, clinging to the slick bark. Looking down I was surprised to find her right behind me. We kept climbing until I got to a spot I used to escape the water, where the branches were thick enough to sit on without sliding off.

"Not exactly a cushy loft, but it's better than the pool." Lame joke. She made me nervous.

She looked below us at the water. "I can't believe I left the pathway."

I sputtered a laugh. I couldn't imagine how weird this was for her.

"It's nice to have someone to talk to. You don't even know..." My sentence fell off as I stopped myself from getting sappy.

"I bet."

I was watching more than anything. Snap out of it, Caine. She won't be here long. "Did you find out any info? About me, or Cole, or how we can get out of here?"

"Oh, ah..." Her hesitance made me edgy. I pulled at my stretched sleeves as she shifted in her seat. Come out with it girlie, I gotta know. "Well, I met your mom."

Of everything I expected, that wasn't it. Mom. I pictured her face creased with worry. Why hadn't I thought of her before now?

She shivered all over and hugged her body as she explained the accident, my condition, and Cole's death. I didn't know what to say. Was she for real? A coma? And how could Cole be dead? I'd just heard him.

She wiped her face clear of water and hugged her body again, the movement reminding me she expected a response. Now, I struggled to look her in the eye.

My mom wouldn't know, but I'd never wanted to live off of machines. Why hadn't she pulled the plug? Cole knew. Machines? I was living off of machines? Who cared if my brain was fine? I'd rather be dead than stuck on machines for the rest of my life. And how much longer was that? Apparently not long.

"Guess I was a shitty host." Another lame joke, but I felt compelled to see her smile again. I'd always done better with laughs than this serious stuff.

I swore I saw her cheeks redden as I got the smile I was hedging for. "I needed to make sure you were real."

"Had your doubts?"

"Fucking right I did." Her profanity had me sputtering a laugh. "I needed to know I wasn't insane." I felt myself smiling. In her shoes, I would have thought I was losing it too. "Your hair's longer, and you had a bit of a beard."

"Long hair and a beard."

"Shut up." She laughed. "Beards are back. You're trendy by default."

"Wonderful." I laughed at the prospect and ran my fingers through my short hair, my hand coming away muddy.

She was smiling until a big raindrop made its way through the tree canopy and landed on the top of her head, trailing down her face.

As much as I enjoyed her expression, I kept thinking about laying in a bed somewhere, on machines, growing a beard, while I was still here. Was this even real?

If she was lying, she was a pro. I'd told my fair share and seen just as many in the faces of beautiful women like her. She was telling the truth, which meant I was wasting away in some hospital bed. If *that* was true, then that meant the flashes of the accident I saw while searching for Cole were true, too.

I dropped my head in my hands, her explanation triggering my memory beyond the flashes I got searching for Cole. I saw him. Cole in my passenger's seat, his voice clear and alive with excitement which made me ache for my brother. I don't know how the accident happened, but it did. The flooded creek drowned out his screams.

How could I have forgotten? How did I get out of the car? Was I ejected? All that time searching for him, and Cole was already dead. But his voice? I'd just heard him. How could he be dead if I had just heard him?

"I'm so sorry, Caine. I really didn't want to have to tell you that. Your mom said Cole would never have blamed you for the accident, and neither does she."

Oh, Mom. How could she forgive me? She buried her son, and it was my fault.

"I wish I could do something more. I know there's only so much time, but I have no clue how to get you out of here."

A hitch in her voice popped my head up. "Please don't cry. You've done more than I could ever expect from a stranger." I reached out and grabbed her hand. Hers was so much warmer than mine, even though she shivered. I blinked through blurry vision, hating myself for making her look so sad.

We looked at each other a moment. I was tortured by seeing her in this prison with me. I didn't want to look away from those sad eyes and cursed myself for taking her down with me. But if she was right, and my "real life" body was failing, it meant it would end soon for her too.

"Your mom told me about Tracey."

She said this so abruptly I was thrown off. Who was Tracey? A moment passed, and memories filtered back. Oops. "Did you speak to her too?"

"No." She hugged her arms around herself again, her toes curled in from the wind filtering through the willow. "She wasn't at the hospital. Your mom said she stopped coming soon after it looked like you weren't going to wake up."

More fidgeting. Her discomfort was as bad as my own as I used the nail of my forefinger to dig into the skin around my thumb.

I felt the need to explain. "We'd been mostly casual. My friends weren't a fan of her. Cole called her a stuck-up bitch to her face." I smiled and shrugged. Tracey didn't make herself easy to love. "I don't think my mom liked her very much either."

"Yeah, she hinted at something like that."

"I bet."

I laughed along with her this time, and the tension lifted again.

The creek receded so we exchanged the hard branch for the soggy ground.

When she started pulling at strands of grass and wrapping them around her fingers, I was afraid she might leave. I didn't know if she could, but I didn't need her wishing it. "Are you sure Cole's dead? And if he is, is it possible his, I don't know, spirit or whatever is still here and that's what I'm hearing? Body or not, I can't leave him here. There's got to be a way out."

"Maybe? I really don't know anything about spirits. As for getting out, my friend Kim I talked about, well, she sort of got me into this coven, and I thought maybe they'd be able to help you."

I was thankful her eyes stuck to the grass around her fingers because I'm pretty sure my surprise was all over my face. "You're in a coven?"

She looked up and nodded.

"So...you're a witch?" I tried to keep my voice level and non-judgmental.

"I'm not anything. They are, I guess. There's men too. I've only been to one real meeting. The leader knew about you in my dreams without me telling anyone. Then I got stabbed at work—"

"Stabbed?"

"I'm fine. They saved my life. I'd like for them to try and help you, if that's all right?"

I'm talking to a sort-of-witch who dreams about me while I'm in a coma, hooked up to machines, and growing out a beard. The fact she was stabbed and passed it off as nothing was the most absurd part. If I could believe the rest, then I could let a coven help me. "Whatever they can do, all the power to them. Can't hurt, right? Wait, can it?"

She shrugged. "I survived without side-effects. Your case is a tad more fucked up, but I wouldn't volunteer you otherwise."

What other choice did I have? I was still holding out hope that she was mistaken and Cole was somewhere alive, but incapacitated like I was. A flash of him drowning hit me, squeezing my chest too tight. I cleared my throat to release some pressure, but it didn't help.

She filled the emptiness. "You know, you're taking this a lot better than I expected. I was prepared for screaming or crying. Call me a liar, something. Even contemplated a death scenario. Every time you get upset, it snaps me out of the dream."

"Death scenario?"

"I don't know what you're capable of. Who knows what's possible here?"

I shook my head in amused disbelief. "I didn't realize that's why you left. You'd materialized one minute then evaporated the next."

"Not every time. I'm not complaining. Don't get me wrong, it completely freaked my shit when I couldn't see you. I just wish I was able to be here sooner."

Even when she knew it was my fault, she still tried to be nice by lessening the blow. I wondered if she was like that with everyone. "Me too. And I'm pretty sure we've never met before. I think I'd have remembered."

"Not to be cruel, but you didn't remember Tracey until I mentioned her."

"Yeah, well, Tracey forgot about me too, so I refuse to feel bad about it."

It was a sad reality.

She leaned over and looked at the sky. "It stopped raining."

We stepped out of the willow cove and gazed up. The clouds were attempting to lighten, yet were still too thick to see the sky.

"Finally." I exhaled in relief as the knot in my chest let go.

Taking a chance she might pull away, I held her hand, letting her warmth heat my palm. I wanted to suck up memories of her for when things got bad again. I had no clue what came next, but would do everything possible to make sure she was okay, even if it meant me being stuck here with Cole.

"Wait. What's your name?" I asked her.

"'Bout time you asked." She laughed and stopped me from apologizing. "Sophie Saterlee."

"Sophie," I said the name softly, thinking it suited her perfectly.

"I'll forgive you if you buy me a cookie when you wake up. A big one. Of course, then you'll owe me for getting you out of this, so add on a piece of apple pie, and we're golden."

I laughed. "A big cookie and pie. Sure you don't want to add ice cream?"

"*Mmm*, now you're talking."

The sound of her slice of happiness was a dream. The clouds above might still have been an angry, swirling mass, but the rain let up, and after everything, I needed this. I needed her. I felt my eyes well with tears and had to choke them back.

"What if I wake up and don't remember any of this?"

"It'd be better to forget the years you spent here."

I turned to her. "That'd mean you too. I don't want to forget the person who freed me."

"I'm pretty sure you won't get a vote on that, Caine." Her brows creased, those dark eyes sad. I wanted to hold her and make sure she was never sad again.

"I know, but if I did, I'd rather remember you, even if it included all the shit before."

In case, for whatever reason, I never saw her again and her coven couldn't help me, I wrapped my arms around her, something in me yearning to hold her. Affection was never my thing. I never felt the compulsion without an ulterior motive and fielded many complaints because of it. Now, I just wanted to hold Sophie and was ecstatic when she didn't shy away.

13

ENCUMBERED WITH INFORMATION

When I opened my eyes, I was lying in bed alone. With Caine's intoxicating embrace lingering on my skin, I swam in thoughts of him while trying to ignore the reminder of the void left without that brand of comfort for too long.

Caine was now aware of events leading up to last night. I'd succeeded in what I set out to accomplish. Yesterday's trepidation to enlighten Caine with the hideous truth had been filled with anxiety. Today brought hope Aunt Lacey and the Coven could save him. They had to. What's the point of having power if not to help people?

I was too euphoric to worry about fallout. I sprang out of bed to shower. Afterward, I dressed and pulled my hair back into a wet ponytail before calling Kim.

"Hey Soph, no wellness check needed, I see." Kim's voice was hesitant. "Did you escape or take him down before he got you first?"

"No need to take out his nuts, but we did climb a tree. I told him everything. He's okay."

"Define okay?"

I recounted the night. The excitement in my voice was addictive and, by the end, Kim was ready to get a move on. As in right now.

"Okay, okay. We'll head to Aunt Lacey's to formulate a plan. Bring Bosco. And relax before you give yourself a stroke."

On the way to NOTL, Kim wasn't herself. After her excitement on the phone, I expected her bouncy optimism to annoy me halfway out of the city. Instead, she sat in the seat next to me tense and silent. When I asked her if she was okay, she fluffed it off and focused on the road like we were driving through a snowstorm and not a clear, sunny day.

When we arrived at Aunt Lacey's, I still found it weird to walk into the house without knocking, but we did anyway. Kim had no aversion to it.

"Put Bosco in the backyard. He can entertain himself," Aunt Lacey called from the kitchen, before seeing we had Bosco with us.

Kim smiled at my "I'm weirded out" expression, but even that was tense. What was with her today?

After Bosco ignored me to alligator-whip his stuffed frog, I heard movement and saw a tall metal ladder leaning against the house at the far corner. At the top was Donovan, wearing only dark cargo shorts and a pair of gloves, cleaning out the gutters. Music from his earbuds floated all the way down to me. Big job for a huge house. The height of the ladder alone had me squeamish. His back glistened with sweat, reddened by the sun, the muscles flexing with each reach as he wrestled with clots of decayed leaves.

Why is he always here? And doing his Coven leader's gutters? My dirty mind went to dirty places. House boy with benefits? I didn't get that vibe from either of them, but what did I know?

He paused mid-reach and froze that way for a heartbeat, then looked straight down at me. I felt my eyes widen, his expression crunched before it smoothed and he pulled an earbud out of one ear.

"I thought I was being watched." A dimple creased in one of Donovan's cheek.

"Oh, I wasn't watching."

"No?" He positioned himself sideways on the ladder, looking far too comfortable so high up.

"Well, I saw you, obviously." I stumbled since he was right. I had been watching and was totally caught. "I was just making sure Bosco would be okay by himself."

He descended the ladder. Since he was coming down, I waited, not sure what to say but I didn't want to look like I was scurrying off.

At the bottom, he pulled off his gloves and bent down. Bosco came over to him immediately, barking, whining, and doing circles as Donovan roughed up his fur.

"Looks like he's dying of heartbreak already." He stood and flashed a set of dimples that made me ache.

I was ecstatic for my sunglasses because Donovan's sweaty chest had me ogling. He was as gorgeous without clothes on as with them, right down to his bare feet.

"Why are you cleaning gutters?" I deflected.

He pulled out the other earbud and let them hang around his neck. "Big party to get ready for. Aunt Lacey will tell you about it, but all the bigwigs will be here." He didn't look impressed.

"And they'll be checking out the gutters? Rockin' party."

"With that bunch, I wouldn't put it past them, but it's something to keep me busy."

"Okay then. You have fun." I smiled and went to find Kim.

I was less than a step away when Donavon said, "Wait," and I felt his hand on my arm.

When I looked at him, he flinched away, plush lips falling open, his dark eyes unfocused yet wide. What the fuck? "You okay?"

"Yeah." He blinked and swallowed. "Yeah, I was just wondering how you were doing? Your wounds, did they fully heal?"

Whatever that was, he wasn't going to tell me. "Almost back to normal, besides the scar."

"And the dream?" His discomfort in asking made me wonder why he asked at all.

"Still happening." He nodded. "Could be worse, I could be cleaning gutters."

He smiled, and this time I left without him stopping me.

In a fog of "what the fuck," I headed to the basement to find Kim and Aunt Lacey.

"Get lost?" Kim said as I sat beside her on the couch.

"Nope. Ran into Donovan cleaning gutters."

"Gutters?"

"Apparently a snazzy party requires clean gutters?"

"For certain," the gutter owner called before she reached the bottom of the stairs, her hands full. "Often chores of the domestic variety cure more than simple clutter." She smiled at me, her skirt swooshing round her legs as she came to us.

I couldn't argue. Cleaning exhausted the restlessness caused by my dream. Maybe he was exhausting his own restlessness.

"A party,"—Aunt Lacey sat to my left with something large and wrapped in deep green fabric in her lap—"entails balloons and games to entertain bored and hyperactive children to grant parents a break from their children's needs. This gathering holds purpose."

Kim gasped. "An Elders meet?"

"Elders and important Magics alike."

"The Sect?"

Aunt Lacey nodded, causing an echoing squeal from Kim, who grabbed my arm in excitement. I was thoroughly confused by this point. "This is no insignificant shindig. The Elders don't gather often, and we get to be there," Kim explained. "Wait, is something wrong? Why are you gathering now?"

Aunt Lacey put the large object in her hands on the wooden coffee table in front of us. "Whispers. Ones we hope to unveil as mere rumours during the meet, better done in person than with traditional forms of communication."

"Sounds like a bigger deal than what you're making it." When I realized I basically called her a liar, I flushed. "I mean, I don't know what kind of whispers you're talking about, but with all the money you clearly have, you can afford some type of device to screen a phone call or encrypt an email."

A slow smile stretched Aunt Lacey's lips. "Never fear an honest argument no matter who you question." Her smile receded. "Yes, the tools exist, and we utilize them regularly, yet on occasion, it proves worthwhile to look into the eyes of the ones you speak to without the filter of technology.

"Each of us is a cog in the machine we drive. This Coven, an intricate system, requires the young to educate the old, to learn from a modernized world not always within our comprehension. The opposite is also true. While the young will observe and socialize with greater Magics, my hope is to create an opportunity for the Coven's Seedlings to mingle and glimpse the inner workings of Coven leadership."

"Seedlings?"

"Those new to the Sect, to the power, and to the Mother Coven as a whole."

"Mother Coven?"

Aunt Lacey smiled. "You will learn much in your time with us. Just know there are many who will be there in times of need besides myself and your fellow Coveners. And since you are not yet a full member your Initiation will need to take place tonight."

"Oh. Okay. I was going to work on a paper, but it can wait, I guess, so that works." Asking me would have worked better but I refrained from saying so.

"As I knew." Aunt Lacey smiled. "While I understand you may work the night of the gathering, I was hoping you would tend bar for the party instead. You'll find libations are as much a way to loosen the lips of Magics as with the Blind, so you will have the chance to learn while earning more than a normal night's wage."

"I've never worked a private party before, but it's probably not much different."

"Splendid. Make a list of everything you'll need, and you will be set up in the kitchen. All the good conversations happen there anyway." Aunt Lacey winked.

I was brand new to the Coven. The fact I was invited, even as part of the staff, was actually pretty cool. I found myself excited as well as nervous.

"Now to discuss a most pressing matter." Aunt Lacey clapped her hands together before picking up the large, wrapped object from the table. "I believe the solution for Caine's sleeping curse lies within this."

She pulled off the fabric to reveal a book with a distressed, leather cover the colour of dull rust. An intricate symbol was stitched into the front with a mixture of symbols. The tanned parchment pages had bits of fabric and leaves protruding from its edges; the book was at least six inches thick. I was captivated by wondering what juicy secrets hid inside the mysterious volume, thinking I'd give anything for the chance to curl up on the couch and absorb every word.

"This is an heirloom from my mother. She was a medicine woman of sorts. The most revered in our tribe, the most powerful of her bloodline. In it is the Awakening Ritual to help Caine escape his sleeping curse."

"You called it that twice. Sleeping curse is a fancy way to say coma."

"Caine's free of his injuries and yet he remains disconnected from his body. His condition is no natural occurrence."

"If it's on purpose, who put him in this sleeping curse?"

"The one responsible remains to be revealed."

Obviously. Proof it was a curse and not a coma would have been nice. Caine was dragging me into his dreams for a reason. Maybe this magic stuff had something to do with it.

I also noticed Aunt Lacey used the term tribe and not family, and wondered where she originated from. She didn't look traditionally Aboriginal, though her accent hinted at foreign origins I was too uncultured to identify.

Aunt Lacey placed a hand atop the book's cover. "The words that helped heal you can be found here, as well as the herbs used to channel Caine in your sleeping state. You see, what's written upon the pages may just be words, markings of my kinsman handed down from generations of pure-born power and raw knowledge, however, spoken by powerful beings like yourself, these words carry limitless, creative potential."

"I don't have any power."

"Can you not feel it, Sophie? It runs through your veins as sure as your blood. A life source, a part of your old soul. From the moment Wiccum brought you here, I sensed it radiating from your bones."

Afraid to call this woman a liar a second time, I said nothing.

"Let me ask you something, Sophie. When the decision to enter the Coven was made, did you feel it?"

I remembered the slightest touch of a shiver. It could have been the central air or a back spasm. Random shudders sometimes just happened. I didn't think it meant anything.

"Is that important?" Kim asked.

"Time will tell." Aunt Lacey raised her eyebrows and returned her attention to the book. I wasn't fooled by her indifference. "As I said, this grimoire holds answers. Solving Caine's sleeping curse will require inner strength if you wish to free him."

"I thought the term grimoire was for, like, dark magic spell books." They existed only in fiction to me.

Aunt Lacey sighed. "Some consider all tools of magic to be instruments of evil, when in our world, it is the one performing the magic that determines intention."

"Either way, I'll do what I can. I know nothing about this stuff, I didn't even pass grade ten chem. But, I can follow directions." I left out I still burn Minute Rice.

"Spell casting will be done by the Coven. You need to be with Caine while this occurs. Sleep will bridge the connection, and the others will perform the Awakening Ritual while you are under."

"What am I supposed to do while I'm with Caine?"

"Create a circle with woven willow branches to surround the two of you and sit within. This element is a part of your essence so it will strengthen your connection, easing the process of releasing him." I repeated the instruction in my head, hoping I remembered. "Take the necklace, you're still wearing it I see," she smiled, "wrap it around your wrist to keep hold of it and allow the symbol to hang into your palm. Hold Caine's hands, and leave the rest to us."

"What will the necklace do?" Kim asked.

"The symbol represents balance and connectivity in life. This will strengthen the body, allowing us to capture him while his essence connects to Sophie's, creating the moment of extraction. The willow tree branches are symbolic of dreaming, intuition, and deep emotions which are also characteristics of the Maiden..." When she saw the confused look cross my face, she abandoned the explanation. "We all come full circle, Sophie."

Encumbered with information, I tried to stitch my direct responsibilities to my memory since Caine depended on my accuracy.

"And that's it? Seems too easy."

"The experience during the spell, while within the sleeping curse, manifests in different ways for each involved, yet the overall method remains the same."

My attention shifted to Kim. Her tense expression from the car was back. I wasn't sure what drew me to look at her, but my gut told me something wasn't right.

"Tonight, your Initiation will commence. While I am retrieving a few supplies beyond those I possess, I need you to go to the place your dream takes place for a willow branch and vines."

"Why do we need those?"

"I'll explain more tonight," she smiled. "Gather the willow elements, take your time, and return later tonight."

Excited a plan was in motion, I went to the yard to get Bosco.

"Heading out?" Donovan asked while picking up the debris from the gutters and shoving it into a bag.

"For a bit. We need things for my Initiation tonight."

"Yup." I hadn't realized Kim followed me out. "May as well get some extra. We'll probably need it for the Awakening Ritual too."

"Awakening Ritual?" Donovan asked.

"For Caine," she told him.

He straightened and speared me with a look. "Really?"

"Um...yeah? Aunt Lacey said it would work."

"Of course it'll work." Kim sounded irritated as she scooped Bosco up, handed him to me, and shuffled me along.

I gave Donovan a smile in place of goodbye.

"What was that all about?" I asked Kim once in the car.

"What?"

"You ran out of there like you were afraid you'd smack the shit out of Donovan if you didn't."

"*Pfft*. I always want to smack the shit out of Donovan."

So much for an answer.

———

After parking at the apartment, we took the railway tie steps down into the park. Bosco enjoyed the long walk, sniffing every tree on the way. I stopped where it all happened, half expecting Caine to run out from the willows. It felt surreal not to see him there. To me, this place was now his.

Thick, live branches proved too hard to break from the trunk, so we settled for a fallen specimen amid the grass. Finding enough strength to do so, Kim grappled a handful of long, pliant branches that feather-brushed the grass and gave them a swift yank. A few heaves, and we had an ample supply for both ceremonies.

"What else do I need? Broomstick? Lucky mole?" I joked while Kim wrapped the tendrils around her arm as Bosco tried to chomp onto the ends.

"Yes! Don't forget your lucky mole. The last inductee who did ended up tarred and feathered, running naked down the street. Hazing can be a bitch. And no Marilyn or Enrique mark either. Strictly ugly. I vote the nose or the eyelid."

"Not the chin?"

Kim screwed up her face. "Too obvious."

"Geez," I played along. "Them Magic folk are serious about their lucky moles."

We laughed and made a slow loop back to the railway ties. I was happy to get away from the ache caused by Caine's absence to enjoy the carefree banter.

"What was your Initiation into the Coven like?"

"The Initiation itself? Aunt Lacey may speak of the Coven's origins, and then you'll get your Coven name."

"I'm named? Like a new pet? You know cults strip their members of their birth names as a method of control to reconstruct their identity?"

"Not like a pet, don't insult Bosco. It's only used by the Coven."

I nodded, still not understanding for the need for an alternate name.

"What's yours?"

"Wiccum." I'd heard it before without realizing it was a strictly Coven name. "It loosely means 'from the village meadow'." My perplexed nod kept her talking. "In good weather Aunt Lacey found me laying in the grass, in this park actually, just relaxing and soaking up the sun. It's a slice of peace in this shitty part of town, keeps me from shaving my head and going on a killing spree every time work or life pushes me to the edge." This was said with another uncomfortable laugh. "Believe me, I thought she was a batshit-crazy old lady once too."

Imagining the perpetually-on-the-go Kim doing anything close to sunbathing was laughable. I envisioned her as the type who considered sitting still for an hour being lazy.

"How does she choose the name, or do I have to choose it?"

"She will, and will give a reason too, and then the rest of us will say if we agree with the name. People don't make a habit of arguing with Aunt Lacey, so whatever she decides will stick. Don't worry, they're usually pretty cool. Nothing like Henrietta or Bunion Millipedegnasher."

"I kind of like Bunion Millipedegnasher. Gives a certain visual."

"Moldy corns and spindly legs, yummy."

As we reached the railway tie staircase, Bosco panted his way to the top, pulling me to the street above. He looked like a pudgy, galloping horse. We put the collected greenery into a garbage bag back in my apartment, and since we were in no rush, I offered for Kim to stick around for food.

"Since my skills are as honed as a college freshman's, pierogies and onions is my only specialty."

Her eyes flashed with scepticism. "Fine with me, if I can take a peek at your cupboards. Bet I can give the meal some kick."

Kim browsed the contents of my cupboards—also reminiscent of a college freshman's—and gathered spices from the rack she bought me, scoffing at all the ones she had to open. My offer of a quick, semi-edible meal evolved into a culinary masterpiece. The dinner was so appetizing, it evoked a moment of inspiration to become a five-star chef and take on Gordon Ramsey, an aspiration that lasted as long as a New Year's weight loss resolution.

Even though the meal was the grandest thing to come out of my kitchen, Kim felt no need to stand on ceremony. We ate with our plates on our laps, paying no attention to the diagnostic show on the early signs of Parkinson's disease as we discussed the Initiation.

"So how serious is Aunt Lacey about the whole devotion thing?" I asked Kim after she mentioned I'd be required to devote myself to the Coven.

She froze mid-chew and stared at me. "You're already planning on ways to back out."

"I didn't say that."

"Then what are you saying? Because you can't complete the Initiation and then—"

"Relax your slacks, Kim. I'm not backing out. Shit. I just...what am I supposed to do each week? I'll have to miss some meetings for work, obviously, but when I attend after all this is over with Caine, I'll be cooling my heels, dodging Denise, and driving myself batty trying to understand Donovan while everyone's doing witchy things, including you."

"Firstly," Kim put her plate on the coffee table and turned my way, "you were invited to a gathering with the Coven Elders."

"As the help." Denise will love that.

"Only because you're new, and she's creating a way to make sure you're there. These aren't PTA members, these are elite Magics with unbelievable talent and wisdom. You wouldn't be allowed to know they exist if Aunt Lacey wasn't certain you had a role in the Coven."

"So, this devotion thing is taken pretty seriously, huh?"

The look I got was like an impatient parent scolding their child.

"Sophie, the devotion is more than your devotion to the Coven. It's to yourself as well."

"Oh, I'm quite devoted to myself. Me, myself, and I have been together since conception, and a divorce would be quite bloody."

"I'm not joking."

"I see that," I muttered.

"You'll learn things that elevate your ability to function day-to-day. Tricks of the trade at first, and if there's true magic within you, then a hell of a lot more. You have to remain loyal to your values or you end up like Denise who thinks she's better than every Blind person thinking the worst they have to fear are shady politicians. Plus, you could be recruited to the other side."

"Do they have lemon tarts?" There was that look again. "I'm sorry. I just don't know how to take all of this."

"I get that, Sophie, I really do. But try taking it seriously. Something's not right if the Elders are coming. Talk of evil sounds hokey, but if you knew the histories of some Magics, evil would come to mind. And Aunt Lacey's devotion is for the Coven and its secrets, but also for you and the person you are aside from the power. The person you are to your family and your friends. For some, it's easy to forget."

I didn't expect all that.

"Hmm. Maybe I should learn that thinking thing. Seems handy."

Kim's answer was a smile with a pointed eyebrow as she popped a whole pierogi into her mouth as we went back to eating and watching TV.

While some humour was needed after Kim's intense warning, she did get me thinking and reminded me to contact my friends regarding plans, hoping they hadn't written me off since my last response. Not only did I want to retain my sense of self, I needed to remember those around me. I could be absentminded when it came to my childhood friends. I refused to be the crazy cat lady with twelve balls of fur in an apartment filled with overflowing litter boxes and a pet cemetery in the deep freeze.

Nah, I'd stick with pugs.

14

———

TEACHER'S PET

The basement glowed with candlelight and dim sconces. Seeing Aunt Lacey and the others waiting in a circle made that feeling of being the new kid on the block wash over me all over again. The last time some of these people saw me, I'd been beaten bloody and skewered by a big-ass knife. My nervousness flared, making me feel faint. They were staring at me, and all I wanted was to sit down before I fell down.

The circle had swelled in numbers since the last time, causing the furniture to be pushed to the walls. In the center were some of the willow branches Kim and I had brought; now they were arranged in an oblong shape comprised of rocks, branches, herbs, and flowers. Aunt Lacey's thick grimoire sat on the carpet in front of her. She was dressed in a heavy ceremonial robe in earthy colours with a glint of gold symbols embroidered and beaded down the middle and around the edges, ones I had seen before but couldn't remember where. Sprigs of baby's breath were entwined in her hair. Her smile was the most radiant thing she wore.

"Please enter the sacred circle and stand in the middle, Initiate," Aunt Lacey instructed.

Anxiousness made my muscles too tight as I walked through the middle of the circle and stood within what looked like a nest. Raising her hands to gain the group's attention, Aunt Lacey found no resistance as the room had been crickets since I walked in.

"On this night, we gather to induct Sophie Olivia Saterlee into our circle. She has shown great resilience and strength that will solidify this Coven, bringing it into its next phase as a whole with the universal mind and the collective energies of this plane and into the next."

Aunt Lacey believed I had pent-up talent waiting to emerge, when really I felt nothing but scared shitless I might projectile vomit all over her priceless grimoire.

This was not some self-deprecating denial. I saw no future, read no auras or palms or even tarot cards. Other than my connection with Caine, nothing pinged me as remotely interesting. For all I knew, Caine initiated the entire event, and it would end the moment he woke up.

If he awoke, I reminded my paper-thin optimism.

"Now, I apologize. Normally an initiate would have more time to gather the basics of the Coven and its practices before joining. However, due to pressing circumstances, the process has been accelerated to fit your needs."

I nodded, wishing I was sitting, and inhaled deep into my belly to counteract light-headedness. I focused on my soon-to-be Coven leader, and was jarred into participating when Aunt Lacey asked for my devotion.

Even after Kim's explanation, I felt a part of me twinge at the word "devotion." I struggled with the sensation of being a starving peasant kneeling at the feet of an old-world king. Pledging myself to any person or establishment waved red flags, which caused my hesitation to span too long.

"Is devotion required for membership?" The spark of discomfort filled the room, giving me the impression questioning this was against the norm.

"How about I rephrase?" Aunt Lacey's smile never left her eyes. "Do you promise to follow the ethics of use when considering teachings given by those within the Coven, respecting your Coveners and the Elders who reign over those who practice under their names, and refraining from going outside of the Coven with inter-Coven conflict?"

I paused a moment longer as I absorbed her definition.

"You remain your own, Sophie. Master of your own decisions and choices, ones taken seriously by those who wish only to guide you to discover and excel at whatever drives your soul."

With the terms laid out in full, the tension that had knotted my shoulders erased. My voice was confident as I said, "Yes, I can make that promise."

Aunt Lacey's smile reached her lips, and she continued on with my comfort level intact.

"Now, with the ring of this bell,"—she picked up a brass bell with light filigree etched into the metal and rang it a few times—"I purify those within our sacred circle and banish negativity, while inviting positive energies to surround us in this rite. To further purify those within, I will lead you in a traditional smudging."

Having never done a smudging before, Kim had had to explain this to me earlier. Thankfully, there was no memory work. Cup the smoke toward the body part you want to cleanse and state why. Easy peasy. With the scent of sweet grass smoke filling the air, I knew what to do when Aunt Lacey began with me. After she circled around me, allowing the smoke to cover every inch of me, she then stood in front of me.

I cupped the smoke toward my closed eyes, stating, "I cleanse myself in order to see my path clearly." Then I cupped the smoke over my head. "And cleanse my thoughts to understand why the path was laid before me." Last, I cupped the smoke to my chest. "And clearing my heart of past regrets, bitterness, and open myself to receive the love of others and give as received."

Saying this in front of the group was made easier by knowing everyone else would follow. After myself, Aunt Lacey stopped at each member and did the same with them, each cleansing different parts of themselves. Their ears to better understand and hear the wisdom of others, their mouths to better teach those in need and speak only truths, and so on. Every person left a little for the rest of us to better understand them and their hopes for this night and others.

With the large number of Coveners in the group, this took a while. I tried to remember each of them, knowing I couldn't remember them all. Notable was Donovan who didn't say anything as he completed the smudging. It wasn't required to state anything out loud though, as the Initiate, I felt it was important, and everyone else followed suit. Donovan did not feel the compulsion to state anything, though I watched as he cupped the smoke over his face, his ears, and his stomach wondering what each represented for him.

Kim's smudging comprised the need to teach others and to be open-minded to accept others as they are and not as perceived, which surprised me. I hoped to talk to her more about it sometime later.

Aunt Lacey turned to what I learned was the east. "With purified hearts we move forward to Call the Quarters in order to guard and protect our sacred circle."

Kim had outlined this part as well, though the complicated inner workings of the Elementals attached to each element of earth, air, fire, and water were more than I could retain in the short time I had to memorize everything. My part was rather easy: all I needed to do was follow along and repeat when necessary, so I did. Turning when needed and calling out with the others was the lengthiest part of the ceremony.

Once back in our beginning stance, we were able to sit. I refrained from groaning, but not everyone did, and it was clear their feet and knees needed the rest.

Kim poured a dark liquid from a gleaming decanter into a chalice Aunt Lacey held, careful not to waste a drop. Then my new leader directed us through a Blessing Libation as Kim continued to add herbs to the drink. Once ended, Aunt Lacey took a drink first to establish trust before handing it to myself to sip. It solidified that trust between me and my leader before handing the chalice off to round the group, to create a full circle.

The sweet taste of red wine and the herbal mix lingered on my lips as Aunt Lacey had another question Kim never mentioned.

"Who vouches for this Initiate?"

Kim surprised me by stating, "I do and take full responsibility if my choice brings dishonour to the Mother Coven." She was the one who brought me in, but I would hate for Kim to face consequences if I screwed this up. She loved the Coven. And I had a history of fucking things up.

"As the one responsible for this Initiate as she navigates the basics of the craft and the way of the Coven, will you show her the path? Will you pledge yourself as Sophie's mentor in our ways?"

"Yes, I will."

Aunt Lacey then turned to me. "Do you, Initiate, accept Covener Wiccum as your mentor?"

"Yes," I said, without question.

"Then it is so."

I exchanged a look with Kim that I hoped exuded excitement though probably looked more frayed as I couldn't help wonder what would happen to Kim if I failed as a student.

"As your Coveners before, you will now be given a Coven name, one used by only the rest of the flock to identify yourself as one of their kin in the craft. As witnessed by them, the collective universe, and our ancestors past yet present, I hereby assign you, Sophie Olivia Saterlee, the Coven name 'Salix.'" The others suddenly sounded restless, but I wasn't sure why. I kept my gaze forward and tried to ignore them.

Aunt Lacey spoke above their mumblings. "In its Latin form, Salix represents the willow tree. A tree with great strength, coupled with its rapid growth and healing abilities, it is unmatched by others. Within its branches it holds a cure that is widely used as a reliever of pain and it is a symbol of flexibility, intuition, and deep dreaming."

She came forward, placed a wreath of thin willow on my head, knelt in front of my nest, and placed her hands on my shoulders, looking deep into my eyes.

"In the short amount of time we have had the privilege to know you, much has occurred both unfortunate and miraculous. I feel that with your chosen path in life to help those in need, alleviating worry and distributing wisdom without judgment, I cannot ignore the many qualities of the willow ever present within you." She looked to the circle, with her hands still on my shoulders. "Does anyone object to this name or the reasons given?"

I stole a glimpse of Kim's face. She was smiling and, in unison with the rest of the Coveners, replied, "We acknowledge thee as Salix."

With their seal of approval, my Coven name was Salix.

All I could think of was the short, quirky character Willow from *Buffy the Vampire Slayer*, also a witch. I dreaded the comparison, even if I was a closet fan. Could be worse. I may not have agreed I was healing people, even if I was in school to try and get there someday, or that my strength somehow mirrored that of a sapling let alone a willow, but Aunt Lacey was confident no other name would do.

"Salix, I now introduce you to the Coven once again. With their true names."

Aunt Lacey motioned for Kim to begin, and she did, stating her Coven name as "Wiccum," which I already knew. Each member offered their names, each weirder than the next. Some I was relieved were not my chosen name, though I had no idea what most of them meant. Some piqued my curiosity, Donovan's included as he said his name was Wend. He said it with a dash of mystery, one of his cheeks dimpled, and his dark eyes gazing at me intently, further piquing my interest.

I hadn't the opportunity to put much thought into it as we were on our feet again, this time Saying Farewell to the Quarters, the process much the same as Call the Quarters, but in reverse to send the Elementals back to their stations so as not to allow them to run amuck. Before we started, Kim had explained it was the responsible way to handle them. Although I couldn't see them, I wasn't about to question what might be invisibly watching if it meant bad things for me by not giving them a proper send off. While lengthy, it was taken seriously by all of those who participated.

Free of the Elementals, Aunt Lacey asked me to join the circle, then said, "To end the ceremony, let's do an affirmation." Everyone held hands, Kim to my left and another friendly Convener named Jared to my right. His big hand made mine looks like a child's, as he held tight and swung our clasped hands into the circle with everyone else's and said, "Merry meet,"—swung them back—"merry part,"—and swung them back in—"and merry meet again." Then everyone clapped to release the energy, and it was time to celebrate.

Uninhibited and engulfed in the exhilaration of the event, the group erupted in clapping and congratulatory sentiments.

Kim jumped on me, wrapping me up in a huge hug. She squealed in my ear, bouncing on the balls of her feet while still attached to me. "I can't believe you did it, I never thought you'd go this far."

"Me neither." I tried to look content with the decision as my ass started to tingle with pins and needles.

Right as she released her grip, Donovan snuck in for his chance. While reciprocating, I noticed the flinch he tried to disguise as his embrace lingered. I pulled away and smiled in appreciation. He snapped out of whatever held him in the moment before melting back into the crowd. Kim gave me a strange once-over I pretended not to notice.

Kim had warned me the ceremony would be long, however it was far lengthier and intensive than I'd prepared for. Three hours later, and I was grateful to stretch my legs.

"Let's eat," Kim said. "Louise made my favourite pasta salad, and I want to get some before everyone downs it."

According to Kim, Louise's cooking was legendary in the Coven. She was accused facetiously of adding "a little something" to trick the taste buds, but she insisted it was all created with love and needed no enchanted additions to be delicious.

"Actually,"—Aunt Lacey's hand was on my shoulder—"I was hoping to have a moment with our new initiate."

I looked at Kim, hoping for some insight.

"Do you need me to stay?" she asked our leader.

"No, please, enjoy some eats. Sophie will be along shortly."

When Kim left, Aunt Lacey led me to the little wooden table in the back of the room. The basement emptied, leaving us alone.

"How did you feel about the ceremony?" she asked me.

"Good." I didn't know what else to say.

"Would you mind me sharing a part of my history with you, Salix? I promise there's a reason beyond my need to share."

This was the first time I'd been addressed directly by my Coven name. "I imagine it's not wise of me to say no, so sure. I'd like to know."

Aunt Lacey smiled, but it dropped after a few seconds, as did mine.

"First, you must understand my time was much different from yours, more years ago than I enjoy counting. No technology or long-range communication existed. Everything we possessed was hand-crafted and taken from our land to use in its entirety, never wasteful. Our Elders were considered so at a young age compared to today's standards, most passing away in their fiftieth year.

"My mother was our tribe's medicine woman, as I mentioned earlier today, as was her mother and grandmother, with healing which came from within, through their hands. The others were unaware of our full strength, for their fear would have been our downfall. We would surely have been killed."

I was taken aback by the turn the story had taken, apparently enough for Aunt Lacey to react.

"People were not as open-minded then, when it came to the unknown. Fear and chaos often ensued in the name of protection and pride." Aunt Lacey laughed sadly at this and paused before speaking again.

"The compulsion to marry or bear children never drove me. Not only was the likelihood of infant death or death during childbirth frightfully high, the men in the tribe were barbaric, having no use for women who were not skilled hunters, cooks, or healers. Since I was of a long line of healers, they insisted I procreate to ensure the blood-line. I refused. To my parents lasting guilt, they were unable to save me from the man who stole my innocence." Aunt Lacey's gaze held mine as I willed my immediate anger to settle. "Making quick work of my mother's gifts prevented fertilization, leaving me healed yet forever scarred."

Aunt Lacey was a trailblazer, even in her youth, and it had cost her. I thought it brave to stand for a life as a spinster rather than marry an imbecile. She had grit before it was a woman's right to complain.

"The tribe assumed I was plagued by sterility and allowed my mother to choose my husband. She selected a kind-hearted weapon maker who had disfigurement from birth that affected his feet, leaving them clubbed and unsuitable in the eyes of others for mating. Yet, he was tender of heart. My mother convinced the Elders our power stemmed through our hands, so if clubbed-foot children were born, the healing line would be protected. We parented four children, one boy and three girls. None suffered their father's deformity, and we preserved our magic's potential, its development and potency as a well-kept secret from others in the tribe.

"Our family became formidable, my grandmother and mother two of the most valued Elders in times of crisis. We could call upon the spirits for aid, strike fear in our enemies without bearing arms, see aspects of the future, and became so in tune with our essence, time held no dominion over us. We stopped aging."

She paused, allowing me to soak in the magnitude of such an idea. If I could believe Aunt Lacey's family stopped aging, it was easier to see why some people joined the Coven. Donovan fit into the category of someone seeking an extended life span. I wondered if the prospect would be so attractive if he spent those years old and withered, his beauty worn and faded. I doubted it. He was gorgeous. Gorgeous people don't like being anything but their gorgeous selves.

"Four generations of healers lived at once, my children the youngest. Only our family could practice and fight off the years, until Nya, a woman outside our bloodline, adopted the craft. My son Gareth, the first male in our bloodline with the gift, wed her, and in time they became two of the most powerful beings we ever encountered."

A smile showed off her white, oddly imperfect teeth. She beamed at me with tear-glazed eyes.

"Their love strengthened their bond, causing an otherworldly extension of their abilities. We didn't know what to make of it. Both were content to live humbly, never wanting without cause, never taking without true need. Even in their eventual death."

Aunt Lacey's expression was tortured. I watched as she sucked back the sadness like swatting a bee and slapped on a smile, leaving me the only one with tears in my eyes.

"I tell you this not to gain your pity, but to bring you understanding of what I tell you next." She hesitated. "You are a vessel."

"A vessel."

"Yes."

"Meaning?"

"Meaning my son and his bride became disillusioned with immortality, grieving the loves they lost to natural aging, and took their own lives to be free of the pain they could never quell. Psychologists today would label it depression and other names I find offensive, but those labels help to give definition to the sadness they felt. All I was told before my son and his wife gave themselves to the Witch-burners was not to fret, that their essences would live on in others."

"The Witchburners?" I was appalled.

She nodded. "Gareth and Nya were the only true witches our small town ever exterminated, though my loves gave themselves over the Witchburners who went on to extinguish far more souls across the world in the name of the crusade."

"So, wait a second…what does this have to do with…" The reason for the story clicked. "No." I shook my head, sat back in the chair, and crossed my arms. "You can't know that."

"Unfortunately, I can. The moment I saw you, I knew you were Nya's vessel."

I shot up from my chair. "That's some hardcore bullshit you're slinging right there. I'm not some dead chick your son pulled a Romeo and Juliet with because they couldn't deal." I contemplated taking off but paced instead.

Remaining in her seat, Aunt Lacey watched me pace until my curiosity required answers.

"How do you know? How can you tell I'm this Nya girl?"

"Not Nya as in the person or the personality attached to her. Only her essence, which made itself known to me at our first meeting, is contained within you. It is only able to be absorbed by another already ripe with power."

"I don't have any power."

"Caged, yet still it exists."

Following advice to put a pouch of herbs under my pillow was a far cry from believing I had power or an essence or whatever floating around in me. I felt no different now than I did my whole life. It was a crock of shit, and I just went through a whole ceremony to trap myself in this group with a woman I was destined to disappoint because I'm nothing like her long-lost family.

"Never." It was Aunt Lacey's turn to jump to her feet. She stopped me with a hand on my shoulder. "You could never disappoint any more than they did." She heard me? I knew she shouldn't know certain things, but she heard my exact words? I was stunned for a moment as she went on. "Pain is dealt with in many ways. Years were eaten up without understanding of this. You, too, will come to terms with the truth I have given you, and I have no expectations for this to be soon, though I do have something which may ease the process."

Reaching into a pocket in her dress, Aunt Lacey handed me a heavy, but small package. Handmade, organic, grey paper gave way to reveal a box. The box was also grey and was made of stone or resin and carved with filigree, adorned with the same symbol as the necklace she had already given me.

"It's beautiful."

"It is. Though nothing compared to your gift inside, Salix."

"Why are you giving me a gift?"

"Each member has a gift for you. Something to assist in your learning. This is my gift to you."

The box was gorgeous, but Aunt Lacey was right, it was nothing compared to what I found inside.

I gasped, closing the lid. "I can't accept this."

She smiled. "You will." Aunt Lacey sat again.

"I'm not saying I don't want it," I slid into the chair and put the box on the table between us, "but it's...*way*...too much. Like crazy-way-too much."

Aunt Lacey placed her hands on mine, attempting to hand back the box, and insisted. "Please, Salix, accept it with grace. I have had it in my possession for too long without the ability to wear it. It represents you so perfectly, and it was Nya's. She would be honoured."

"Nya's?"

She nodded. "Wear it and question me after."

After trying once again to get her to reconsider, it became clear there was no getting out of accepting the most beautiful, unearned gift I had ever received.

Nestled inside the box was a stunning ring that shone even in the dim lighting of the underground room. Small beams of light glistened off of every facet, the piece hands-down worth more than I make in six months at the bar. I was unfamiliar with the teardrop-shaped gem, an earthy brown-grey with slight transparency.

"What is it?"

"A smoky quartz surrounded by fifteen small diamonds set on a white gold band. A few hundred years old or so."

"A few hundred years old! And you're giving it to me?"

"I already told you, Salix, it's yours. The smoky quartz is pure. It can endow you with so much."

"I don't see how. A ring is a ring no matter how beautiful."

"The smoky quartz protects from negative energies and allows your perceptions to break through their bonds. A greater power lays dormant within you, and the quartz is a catalyst to uncover that." I dropped my gaze back to the ring. "Besides, diamonds are your birthstone, and every girl deserves diamonds."

I chuckled, hearing the awkwardness of it in my own ears. She insisted I was a vessel to this Nya's power, this ring somehow a symbol of such power. Fallacies are dangerous. On faith, they lead people down directionless paths. This might be another.

I removed the ring from its resin confines, then placed the ring on my left middle finger with ease.

As soon as the ring was in place, a strong shiver made me gasp and tense. My hands balled into fists, the muscles in my back zinging with pain before being released just as quickly. It reminded me of the shiver I'd felt, and Kim questioned, after deciding to join the Coven. All of Aunt Lacey's talk of connection, and whatever I thought was just babble made sense, the truth of what she'd told me so real I was beginning to wave the white flag, giving up on resisting the notion.

"Told you." Aunt Lacey grinned.

My hands shook as I looked at the ring and watched the light play off the diamonds. How could I be a vessel? I believed her, but a part of me didn't want to. What would this mean for my life?

"Your life is your own. Being a vessel means nothing more than what you wish it to. No one other than who you choose needs to know. And one day, if you wish, I can tell you more about the woman who released her power into the world so another could benefit from the life she deemed too damned to continue living it."

Sadness enveloped me. Even if this all turned out to be bullshit, the woman in front of me was harbouring a deep scar. These people had been her family, and they chose to leave her behind to seek solace in death. I understood this in the sense of why people chose to rid themselves of that pain, but I wasn't about to pretend I knew how it felt to lose a son and his wife. That pain was Aunt Lacey's to bear alone.

"You should join the others and celebrate," she told me, yet she looked to have no intention of following me upstairs. "Enjoy tonight and all it represents. You have earned every moment of it."

I disagreed, but no one with an ounce of compassion could argue, so I left her alone.

15

——————

NO NEED TO GO POSTAL

Once I slipped through the crowd in the kitchen and made it to the backyard, I unscrewed my smile, finally making it to Bosco. He ran to me, making canine squeals and wagging his tail. I scooped him up and nuzzled him as he squirmed and licked at my cheeks, catching air in his excitement. He was oblivious of the Initiation and me being a vessel, he just wanted me. His innocence was comforting.

I was close to losing my composure right then.

The events of the last few weeks clogged my thoughts, making me sit in the grass before my knees buckled and I risked dropping Bosco. My tears evoked an anger I hated as I'd cried far too much lately. I'd never been an emotional person. But you can only endure so much before breaking down and needing to cry it out, before beginning to rebuild the barricade, readying for whatever came next.

There was always something.

With my eyes closed, I held Bosco in my lap, attempting to stave off a complete breakdown. I refused to go back inside rosy cheeked with my eye make-up everywhere. To have those strangers surrounding me with sympathy, I couldn't do it.

A hand grasped my right shoulder. The sudden contact made me jump and gasp in shock, readying to take a backswing. The hand was immediately followed by a smooth voice that asked, "Can I join you?"

Donovan didn't acknowledge my overreaction. His eyes were clouded with nervousness and caution.

I hadn't even heard the door slide open.

"Sure," I told him even though I would rather be alone. "I'm just visiting with Bosco. I don't usually leave him alone outside for so long." Donovan's presence wasn't helping my galloping heart rate.

He sat on the grass next to me, extending a hand to scratch Bosco's head. "Bossman seems all right. At least it's warm tonight. The summer's been so wet, I'm surprised whenever we actually see the sun."

"A definite change from last summer."

Great. Straight to weather.

Now that we got the forecast out of the way, I wondered what he really wanted. Since he didn't offer an explanation, I asked my own questions. "How'd you get into palm reading? No offense, but you don't look the type."

Half-smiling, he laughed. "What do I look like I should be doing?"

"Um...Maybe going to concerts or scoping bars for chicks with your friends."

"Those things are fun too, I suppose. For people who don't know me, it's an unusual ability and apparently even more so for a guy like me, whatever that means. Really, this is my norm. Other Magics don't question it." To my surprise, Bosco moved onto Donovan's lap. He smiled at this and ran a hand down his fur. "It's a family thing. They usually are."

His expression turned shameful, though he didn't elaborate. I wished my family history was so colourful. Imagine living the life he must have with his family taking him under their wing. What was shameful about that? Though it hadn't worked out for Nya and Gareth.

"How'd you meet up with Aunt Lacey and the rest of them?"

He paused, looking reluctant to answer. "Doing private readings for extra cash. I still do, sometimes. One day Aunt Lacey came in for a reading. I could tell immediately she was someone different, not a bored housewife looking to find out if her husband was drilling his secretary, or the neighbour, or the babysitter. Which of course they always were. If you have to ask, it's already happening. I spent a lot of time explaining I was a palm reader, not a fortune teller." I had to agree. "The sneaky old woman with an ulterior motive made her claim and offered to take me in. I was resistant. She was special, but I figured anyone else in the Sect would be a bunch of Harry Potter wannabes."

I refrained from sliding in a "What's wrong with that?" thinking of the books on my shelf at home.

"Most members are open-minded and believe in individuality as well as the 'collective mind,'" his expression and intonation matching Aunt Lacey's. "Though not everyone in there has the same beliefs, we come together in common practice." Sharp, dark eyes looked my way. "She really does mean well in bringing you here."

"I'm sure Kim does."

"I meant Aunt Lacey."

"Oh. Kim actually asked me to be here." He looked at me oddly. "What?"

"Nothing."

That pissed me off. "I don't know you at all, but you're a shitty liar." He cocked his head in surprise. "If you can't control your facial expressions, you should've thought twice about lying to me."

"Jesus." His eyes widened with the word. He was clearly taken aback by me calling him out, yet also seemed amused, unable to hide his smirk. "Normally Aunt Lacey does the recruiting. As far as I know, she asked Kim to bring you in."

"Then why the mentorship thing during the Initiation?"

He shrugged. "No idea, never seen it happen before."

Why wouldn't Kim mention that? How would Aunt Lacey even know about me before I came to the meeting that night?

"Didn't mean to get anyone in trouble," he said. "Aunt Lacey's the big cheese, so she brings in all of the newbie Seedlings. It's just how it is."

I saw this as an opportune moment, hoping his lying face would reveal more. "What do you know about Nya and Gareth?"

"She talked to you about them?"

I nodded.

"Why?"

"You first. Tell me what you know."

Donovan went on about the basics Aunt Lacey told me, punctuated by their deaths and releasing their powers. "She doesn't normally talk...why would she tell you about them?"

Instead of speaking, I held up my hand and showed him the ring.

After a moment he said, "That explains a lot."

"Does it? Because all I can think of are questions I'm pretty sure I don't want the answers to."

"I'm not going to pretend it's not a big deal, because it is. Especially to her. She's been waiting a few lifetimes for them to resurface."

"I'm not her. Nya." I snapped. "Just her power, or essence, or whatever. I'm not her."

"Okay." He raised his hands in defeat.

"What else have you heard?" My question stopped his hand in the middle of petting Bosco's fur. Now he looked scared, attempting to hide behind a charming grin I refused to react to.

"Really, it's no big deal. No need to go postal."

"Fatal flaw, kid. Don't call someone crazy when they have a right to be mad. I just found out some pretty steep shit, I can't handle more surprises. Out with it." My stern gaze pinned him as I tried to ignore the stunning sight of him in the light and shadows of the backyard. "No fucking way am I walking back in there without knowing what the rumour mill has on me. Would you stand for that?"

"I don't give a shit about them. Rumours are all they have.

Though not one of those Seedlings knows a damn thing, so don't go all Charles Manson on them." I shot him a look that said how ridiculous that was. "Aunt Lacey came to some conclusion last night, but hasn't said what. It has something to do with that guy you're dreaming about. They're all excited to do the Awakening Ritual. Usually, this dream guy of yours would be a goner."

"What? Why?"

"The sleeping curse has been rooted too long. If you can pull off the Awakening Ritual..." he hesitated, "it'd be a first."

My mouth dropped, and he clarified, "*One* of the firsts. They're unsure, actually. The ritual's been done, obviously, but never perfected or properly documented. Not everyone makes it out all right. So, if he wakes up normal and doesn't pull you into his dream state instead? You get a gold star. Though Nya's power has got to give you an advantage."

Rage clenched my fists as heated anger made me dizzy, paralyzing my tongue. My eyesight wavered as a surge of pain rolled inside my skull. I pressed my fingers into my eyelids to reduce the pressure, but it only faintly helped. When I could speak, the words came out in a rush. "Why would she assume I could do this if it's possible only a few have? I can't do shit other than dream. You have family talent. Every other person in that house has more power than I do. I've done *nothing* to make her assume I can do this."

"Wow, babe." Donovan placed his hand on my arm, but then he jerked it back with a hiss. I noticed, but wasn't in the mood to be calmed.

Donovan kept his distance as I paced. "Why does it matter? Aunt Lacey has faith in you and wouldn't have suggested this if she didn't know you could pull it off."

Even though they'd kept the truth from me, I'd like to believe Donovan was right. "Wait, being pulled into Caine's dream state. That's possible?"

Opening his mouth then closing it, Donovan had only a palm-up shrug to offer.

"That's fucked! All this talk of Aunt Lacey having my best interests at heart and the Coven bonding, it's all bullshit." I stopped and faced him. "I have people. People who give a shit if they never see me again."

Donovan pushed his hands into his pockets. "Of course someone like you has people who would care."

I continued to seethe as I paced. "Even if I was a loner hermit who practiced taxidermy on roadkill, I should get all the facts first. I kind of like living. My life's not the greatest, but it's been far worse, and I'm working on it. The park where Caine is? Is a nightmare. My nightmare. I'm not spending the rest of my life there!"

"And you won't. Let's go inside and get something to drink. I'll sneak some whiskey in your Coke. Just don't mention I'm the supplier."

I huffed. "Please. I'm a bartender. Guaranteed I can make it better than you."

"Perfect. Fix me up one while you're at it."

I didn't answer him and paced a couple more steps. I didn't know where to go with this information.

"Firstly, babe, I have no patience for their bitching. The fact they look down at alcohol at the meetings is mind-boggling. Secondly, I'm sure they were just trying to boost your confidence. And, like I told you the first time we met,"—he put his hands on my forearm to stop my slow pacing, flinched and grunted, then dropped them—"you *do* have power. Flabby like a two-cheeseburger-a-day habit, but it's there. Find your calm before you fuck this up for everyone."

I looked up at his fierce gaze and couldn't decide if he was on my side or shutting me up because he was on theirs. Oddly enough, this time his stare failed to make me squeamish. He was looking at me with a soothing yet somehow flirtatious glare that coated my anger and popped the balloon of my fury.

"Better?" he asked me.

I shook my head. "I didn't know magic was real until this Coven shit dropped in my lap. Now, I'm expected to catch up overnight, and

I don't know what I'm doing. I'll do this because I said I would try out the whole Coven thing and because Caine needs me to. But I'm warning you right now, I appreciate you filling me in on my own mortality, but I'm having a *big* talk with Kim and Aunt Lacey if I make it through. Tricking me into this is bullshit, and I'm not in the habit of letting anyone make decisions for me anymore."

"Anymore?"

I didn't answer him, ignoring the Freudian slip. Instead, I chewed my lip until it tasted like I'd licked a brass handle.

What would my family think had happened to me? That I'd fallen asleep and never woke up? Would my parents sit next to my bed like Caine's mother, unaware of the futility of hoping I would wake up? I needed to give them solace in the event of that possibility. But how? Trust Kim to let them know? Not bloody likely.

My laugh was part sinister, part hopelessness, completely out of context for Donovan who stood with his hands still in his pockets, not inching for the door or attempting to console me, just letting me work it out until my pacing slowed.

"Are you sure he's worth all this?"

"Excuse me?"

"Going through with the Awakening Ritual. You don't know him or what he was like before his coma. What if you save him, and he becomes the next Mussolini or something?"

"What the fuck are you talking about?"

He ran a hand through his hair before he went on, "I get you're dreaming about him, I'm sure that means something, but what if you're sucked into the dream? What if you don't come out of this?"

I crossed my arms. "What happened to not having anything to worry about?"

"No." He huffed in frustration. "You probably don't. I will try everything to prevent it, I won't let you die or spend your life in some nightmare with..."

"Caine."

"I don't give a fuck about his name! Sorry, I just don't. But you,

you can't get caught in there with him. If he ends up dying, we don't know what'll happen to you in there. You could die too. Or be stuck there alone."

"I'm not fighting you on that fact, Donovan. I don't plan on screwing the pooch here."

"But why? Why are you so gung-ho for this guy? This isn't about you being a hero. You want him to yourself. You want him to look at you like you're the only one he sees. You're setting yourself up for disappointment again."

"Again?"

He took a step closer. "Are you doing this for the right reasons?"

"What? You want him for yourself? He *is* very pretty." I was thoroughly pissed off at his assumptions. Again? Please. He knew nothing about me.

His nostrils flared in response. I don't know what his point was, but I definitely missed it.

"Look it, Donovan, you're getting real pissed, real fast, and I don't get what the hell your problem is."

"Not a clue?"

"No! Fine. Yes, I know this is lampshade insane, but it doesn't change anything. Someone has to help Caine, and *apparently* Aunt Lacey thinks it's worth a shot. Would you sit back and do nothing?"

"Nah, I'd do the same thing. I think." Uncertainty clouded his tone. "I'd save you in a heartbeat." This caused me squirmy discomfort again. "I'm not sure I could pull it off, but we'll see if Aunt Lacey's right about you."

We looked at one another. I felt like he was searching for some type of reaction I wasn't giving him.

Since I wanted to know and wanted even more to move to another subject, I asked, "Are you only here so you can become immortal?" I realized how ridiculous it sounded.

He looked shocked. "I told you, this is a part of me."

"Fine, but here, with Aunt Lacey? You could be anywhere, or on your own, and yet you chose here. Clearly you're not friends with any of them. I don't get it."

He looked at me a long moment. "Does immortality sound seductive? You'd be lying if you said it didn't. Is it why I stay? No. Aunt Lacey was one of the only people to believe in me in desperate times. I stay for her. I'm loyal to her." His sincerity made me feel like a shmuck. "If it's loyalty that holds you to coma-guy, I'd understand, though you don't know him enough to be loyal. I don't want to see you wasted on someone undeserving." He had taken another half-step closer and was now looking down on me, barely any space between us.

"You know him less than I do. How could you possibly label him undeserving?"

"I know about you, and believe me, you're too good for him."

Hyper-aware of his closeness, I felt myself being drawn to him without understanding why. He was making one assumption after another, but I knew he wanted me, that maybe his scornful words came from that place, and Donovan hadn't the skill to express his affections.

Another look into his eyes, and I was certain. I spoke in a softened voice, trying not to make my words cut, yet needing to be direct and assertive. "You think you can knock some sense into me and I'll, what? Stay here and work on my immortality with you?"

"I already told you I expect you to save him. That doesn't mean you have to be his when he comes to."

"His? What cave did you crawl out of?"

"You know what I mean. With him. You're special and you don't even know how much yet." I shook my head. "I can teach you. I can make this work."

"Are you shitting me?"

"This isn't just me wanting you, it's," he paused in his struggle to articulate his thoughts, "it's the way it's supposed to be. You're a smart, compassionate, and an especially talented—"

"Supposed to be?" I threw up my hands and stepped back from

him. "Look it, buddy. I have too much fucking with my head as it is. If you're trying to be Mr. Hilarious, you're not the least bit funny, and if not?" I didn't know how to finish that. "I just have too much to worry about right now."

I made a swift sidestep around him to escape into the house, knocking into him as I tried to pass. Donovan's hand shot out and grabbed my wrist. I spun, ready to make him regret it, feeling him flinch as he usually does, but he didn't pull away. Instead, he held firm, his eyes unfocused as he stared off across the backyard. A moment hung until his dark eyes shifted to mine and he said in a low, soft voice, "Dear heart," as if he had called me this a thousand times.

Not only was I tripped up by the intensity with which he spoke, but by the way his body adopted a comfortable confidence on the opposite spectrum of his usual cockiness. I was flushed with a familiarity, one I ached to respond to. How? I didn't know, but there was no fight in me when, in late-night-romance-movie-fashion, Donovan took firm hold of me, arms surrounding me, bringing me up against his body and pressing his lips against mine.

His fierce determination thoroughly shocked me. I backed off and he let me go as a part of me roared up and regained a split-second of clarity against whatever this was.

His eyes popped open, his lips wet from the kiss. The sight of this, and something else I couldn't grasp, had me bursting with unexpected passion magnified to a degree I was unaccustomed to.

This time I was on him with a shot of desperation, too overcome to resist.

Everything in me wanted more. His soft lips, his wet tongue moving with precision, his hands over every part of me.

Donovan's strong fingers moved firmly up my spine and tangled themselves into the back of my hair as mine wandered, beyond my control, in the same passionate motions. They explored the contours of the muscles of his back as our bodies ground against each other. The enticing bulge in his jeans swelled and hardened.

I couldn't tear myself away or stop myself from positioning my hips so that bulge could rub against the right spot and send a jolt of shocking pleasure straight to my nipples.

Carnal and insane, it didn't matter. I didn't want to stop. I wanted to throw down in the grass and follow through with what my body ached for. The strain in his jeans promised a worthwhile adventure, and if the wetness saturating my panties was any indication, my body was giving me the thumbs up to take what he offered.

Head clouded in a lust-filled fog, Donovan's lips never left mine as he reached into my jeans and found the source of my aching. His fingers slid inside with ease. I pulled away from his lips in a gasp, pressing my hips forward, wanting more.

Opening my eyes, I was face-to-face with Donovan's flushed expression. A squeak pulled me back to my surroundings. It came from Bosco playing with a toy, reminding me of my purpose in the backyard. Any other time I would have revelled in the warm night air to the singing sounds of the jittery cicadas. However, I was now acting on my most animalistic impulses with a near-stranger. I pulled myself away, an action made more difficult by his fingers still buried inside of me. I pressed against the stone of the wall, not remembering when I'd been moved against it.

Snapping out of it as well, Donovan leaned the weight of his presence over me. Both his hands now rested on the wall at my sides. My eyes closed again. I dropped my head between us, placing my fingers over my lips, and tried to douse the fire within. I managed with extreme difficulty considering he was still pressed against the pulsating need of my core.

With my palm against his chest, and with gentle pressure, he leaned away. His chest muscles flexed beneath my palm. I dropped my hand, still unable to force myself to move as I tried to ignore the tantalizing smell emanating from him. My head reeled as the tingle in my lips refused to fade.

To make matters worse, I caught movement in my peripheral vision and looked to see Kim's shocked expression as she stood outside the back door, in full view of our compromising position against the wall.

She must have seen enough. Kim didn't speak and hurried back inside and shoved the sliding door closed behind her.

Donovan's head spun to the door, then back to me when Kim ran off, his hands up in defence. "Promise, I had no idea she was there."

He'd been as preoccupied as I was. We'd thought of no one but ourselves.

At that moment, I wanted nothing more than to kick him in the crotch, but I knew the infantile behaviour was unjustified.

My clarity restored, I realized I should have recognized Kim's demeanour around Donovan before as one of affection. It was one-sided, hers only. Now, after everything Kim had done for me—even if she did lie, whether it was for Aunt Lacey or not—I was throwing in her face the fact Donovan wasn't into her. To lash out at Donovan would mean I deserved the same.

Why had I done that? I don't hook up with randoms, not ones like Donovan who were used to having chicks hanging off of them. I didn't want to be seen as just another one of those women.

"It might not've changed anything," he finally said. "I don't even know where that came from or why it happened, but it had to be done."

"Why?" Having trouble speaking, I felt disconnected from my body as I remembered he called me "Dear heart" before everything got out of hand. Why did he call me that?

"I needed you to know I'm serious. What I was saying wasn't making an impact, and I can't see you and this guy together without knowing I'd made some type of move. Apparently, I was right." He smiled and crossed his arms smugly, reverting to the cockiness I was accustomed to.

"You took me by surprise."

"Please." He snorted. "I know what a kiss is. You *let* me kiss you and then you kissed me back. Plus, you didn't stop me when things got intense. I didn't plan on that part, but there was some meat on that one." He smirked as I shot him an unimpressed sneer. "At least now I know for sure there's something between us."

"Donovan," I snapped then continued slowly so he would listen, "that *won't* happen again."

"Sure it won't."

He was far too confident.

He grinned, resolve swimming in his eyes. I wanted to slap the happiness off his face. Picturing myself with Donovan wasn't a stretch, but he didn't exude long-term relationship-kind-of-guy. He was more the type you use to piss off your parents in your teens. I was too old for that type of rebellion.

Once we rejoined the Coveners in the kitchen, I did my best to stay clear of Kim, unable to take her searing criticism, no matter how warranted, while I ignored my wet panties. When she left the kitchen, instead of forcing Donovan to go wash his hands, I insisted he give up the goods on his whiskey stash.

16

MY THUNDERING HEART BLOOMED

Under the ruse of needing cleaner, Donovan directed me to the cupboard under the sink where I found a mickey of whiskey wedged behind a fire extinguisher.

We retreated outside, clinking glasses before enjoying our drinks. As much as being alone with Donovan carried the risk of a panty-dipping replay, it was worth it to get away from people. Especially Kim. Information overload had me craving isolation. Donovan seemed to read this and didn't strain to create conversation as we sipped our drinks under a ceiling of stars.

My thoughts were chaotic. Ignoring them was difficult. Thankfully, my headache had disappeared. I needed to draw some strength from this peace.

Beyond his devilish looks and brash attitude, I had to admit I felt at ease with Donovan. If this Coven thing didn't work out, and I survived, I decided I would find a way to keep in contact with him.

The alcohol may have helped my stress levels, but I also drank in the peaceful atmosphere.

I really needed this.

Later, with our glasses empty, Kim came out back, demanding to know what we were up to.

"Playing hacky sack," Donovan responded.

I laughed.

"Wonderful," she answered him, and then asked me. "You ready to go?"

Donovan cocked an eyebrow at me in question, his fingers laced behind his head.

"I'm coming." I did my damnedest not to reveal my irritation, clenching my jaw until a zing of pain shot through my teeth.

"Why're you all flushed?" she asked me. "Have you been drinking?"

"Yes. I don't care about being the teacher's pet."

She didn't miss the dig, but her blue-green gaze slid to Donovan.

"Don't look at me," he said. "This teacher's pet didn't funnel it down her throat."

Instead of answering, Kim spun back into the house. Donovan gave a gruff laugh as I grabbed Bosco before we both went in.

"What's this?" I eyed the wrapped presents and gift bags at the front door suspiciously.

Aunt Lacey leaned in. "These are the official welcoming gifts I mentioned, given to a new initiate for securing a place within the fold and attaining your Coven name."

I turned to Kim. "Right. Did you forget this part too?"

She raised an eyebrow. "You don't like free shit? Seems like you're cool with giving it."

No way she missed the hurt her comment caused, but I didn't have a moment to process it before Aunt Lacey pulled me into a strong embrace.

"You deserve every gift," Aunt Lacey said a matter-of-factly. "You're a part of us now. These will equip you with the introductory tools to assist your success." Her tone softened, "And those that chose a more personal gift have done so with love."

I knew she meant the ring, but I was seething and doing my best to shake off Kim's attitude, so I refrained from speaking at all.

Donovan hugged me, hard arms pressing me to him, not playing it shy as the Coveners came into the room to say good-bye. He flinched, then lingered as he seemed to do. I turned my head to evade a kiss, just in case he tried. Instead, he whispered in my ear, "Forget the jealous bitch and enjoy the goods. You deserve 'em all."

As my cheeks warmed from his contact, I returned a thoughtful smile and watched as he disappeared behind the other Coveners. I was left with the urge to chase after him and say something more.

When the door closed us outside, we loaded my gifts into Kim's trunk. I stopped before getting into the passenger seat. "I can find another ride, Kim. That's not me being a bitch. I'm a big girl. I can find my way home safely and save us the awkward as fuck drive home." I realized I should have asked this before filling her trunk with my stuff.

"Shut up and get in." She slammed her door shut.

I contemplated calling a cab, but decided if she wanted to hash it out or write me off, it would happen now and not in a week when she couldn't ignore me anymore.

We drove in brutal discomfort. I would have been happy for it to continue all the way home and start over tomorrow, but Kim noticed the ring.

"Who gave you that? I didn't see you open any gifts."

"I didn't ask for this...I..." My hands waved in front of me as I struggled to articulate my thoughts, but of course the ring didn't budge, because it fit perfectly, as Aunt Lacey knew it would.

I recounted the important parts of the Nya/Gareth story and me being Nya's vessel. Half-way through, Kim was white-knuckling the steering wheel.

"Guess that makes sense."

"Are you fucking kidding me?"

"No," she snapped and glanced at me. "Most of the Coveners have been working for years to gain Aunt Lacey's attention. You show up, and she's all about you. And you don't even want it. They don't know how to take it, and so far have been cordial, but when they hear about this..."

"That applies to you too?"

"Soph, I brought you into this. I wanted you to succeed, still do. Even with this vessel talk, Aunt Lacey isn't telling us everything, which scares me because it's not like her."

I made a throaty protest. "It's exactly like her."

"Meaning?"

"Don't play it like that, Kim. I know the Awakening Ritual is a Hail Mary. I'll be lucky if it doesn't kill me, and both you and Aunt Lacey let me believe it was some easy peasy spell."

"If I thought—"

"Oh, you thought it and kept it to yourself. I wondered why you were acting weird after she mentioned the spell and then on the way here."

Her non-answer spoke for her.

"Right." I wanted to be done with it, but I wasn't. "Following orders is fine, but if it involves my life, and you plan on us staying friends, keeping shit from me is not the way to go. I've got trust issues you know nothing about. This doesn't help."

"I'm sorry. I wanted to tell you, but you have to understand Aunt Lacey knows things I don't. What if I told you, and it changed something that should have happened, and *that* killed you? I got all stuck in my head and didn't want to screw things up with the ritual."

"She can't dictate what you do, but if she knows more than she's saying, she's putting people at risk. It's not okay for her to decide what I can and can't handle. I'm not doing it."

"And you shouldn't have to, Soph. None of us should. You just met her, so your experiences with her haven't been the greatest, but she did heal you—"

"No, the Coveners did."

"She kept you alive until they could. My point is she cares about whether you live or die. She hasn't showed her best side, but she has unshakable faith in you. I didn't get it, but if you're strong enough to be a vessel... The ring and her telling you all that history, something I've never been told, says more than anything else she could communicate."

"I didn't want to take the ring!" I was so frustrated by the damn thing. I wanted to rip it off.

Kim grabbed my arms before I could. "I know. Relax. It's not about the ring, but everyone's noticed that she's spoken about a 'power' within you a thousand times. You'd think a vessel would show signs of inherent gifts. More than dreams."

We agreed on something.

"I thought I was going to a tea leaf party, not becoming Aunt Lacey's Jedi apprentice or daughter-in-law substitute."

Kim sputtered a laugh. I thought back over previous conversations with Aunt Lacey, trying to see in her what Kim saw so clearly. She doted on her Coveners, but her mysteriousness was off-putting.

"Are we gonna talk about what I walked in on in the backyard?" Kim asked.

Trying to talk my way out of having the conversation was a waste of time. "It was nothing at first. Talked about the ring and stuff Aunt Lacey told me. Then he turned it to saying Caine wasn't good enough for me, because I was 'special,'" I added with actual air quotes, "and when I got fed up hearing it, I tried to go back inside, and things got weird, and he kissed me." I didn't know what to make of the "Dear heart" comment so I didn't mention it.

"Right," she exaggerated as she turned a corner. "I call bullshit."

"Excuse me?"

"Come on, Soph. You want me to be honest with you and then you blow me off with that lame horseshit? He wasn't mauling you against your will. What I saw was more than just kissing, and you weren't stopping him."

Fair enough. "I didn't realize you were interested until I saw your face."

"That's not what this is about."

"Sure about that?"

Wrenching the wheel, Kim pulled onto to the gravel shoulder. Bosco hit the door and yelped, then shook himself and panted in the backseat.

"Was that necessary?"

Kim ignored my question and faced me. "Getting involved with Donovan is stupid."

I blinked. "Calling me stupid isn't helping."

"Don't twist my words."

"Clearly, like with Aunt Lacey, I know him differently than you do."

"You don't know him at all!"

"Look, Kim. Neither of us realized you were there. It's not like we had you in mind at the time. This wasn't a malicious dig. I'll save those for Denise."

"I don't get how it got to there so quick. I didn't think you were like that."

"Are you trying to slut-shame me? Not my best decision, but I'm an adult and have nothing to be sorry for."

"No, but that's how Donovan sees all women. Don't be surprised if he treats you like a leper now. I don't want to see you hurt."

"We hung out afterward. Plus, I didn't say I was looking for a repeat."

She scoffed. "Please."

"And I'll forgive you 'cuz I believe you want to warn me, but leave this alone. You weren't there for our conversations. He's been more honest with me than *you* in the last twenty-four hours. And, sure, maybe he needed to get it out of his system, but I can't explain where it came from in me. I still don't get it. He said he *had* to do it 'cuz 'it's how it's supposed to be' or something. What the shit does that mean?"

"He took advantage of you."

I shook my head. "I gave him the green light, Kim."

"Absolutely, but you were overwhelmed. Freaked about what

would happen with Caine, and like the asshole he is, Donovan used it like some type of game. I'm not saying you aren't special, and for more than your vagina, but why would he be like that? He doesn't know you."

"No kidding," I gushed an agreement. "He was positive I was making a mistake with Caine. I had to stop him, but then the kiss happened and, well, you saw what else. So yes, the vagina works perfectly well."

"And has a mind of its own."

"The bitch just does what it wants sometimes."

Kim shook her head, a smile creeping into her expression. I couldn't help but add one of my own, granting some levity as Kim got back on the road.

Still, something sat rotten in my gut as she wound around the back streets to St. Catharines. Since we were laying everything on the table, I refused to waste the opportunity.

"You know, Donovan also told me Aunt Lacey recruited me, not you. How's that possible?"

Kim's jaw flexed. "I don't know why he told you that. I swear the guy's up to something, but he's right. I was with Aunt Lacey visiting a Covener and stopped by the apartment to get something before driving her home. She saw you across the street, walking Bosco, and told me I needed to bring you into the Coven. Thought you'd never go without some persuasion, which I get sounds shifty, but she knew the Coven would be a great fit for you and that she wasn't the right person to make the pitch."

I made a sound of disbelief, which hurried Kim's pace.

"It *was* true I thought you'd come because of the tea leaf reader you know and all that, but really, it came from Aunt Lacey first."

Though my instincts to trust him were now proven twice, I was unprepared for Donovan's claims to be true, ill-equipped for the wrench in my chest. I knew without his intervention I would have never known anything. The context of the lie made no difference, only the fact it had occurred.

"Please, Soph, don't be upset. If she says to bring someone in, she means it. I had no reason to question her. Regardless of that shit, you're an awesome friend. I was *not* pretending any of that whatsoever. Everything I've done with you was my choice. I'd never lie about that." Kim's conviction was solid.

"I believe that part," I told her to ease her guilt. Aunt Lacey was Jon of 'Bon Jovi', calling all the shots. I regretted the thought of holding back with Kim, for fear she'd relay everything to our leader.

"So, Donovan *was* telling the truth," I said to myself.

"Maybe about Aunt Lacey, but he's wrong about Caine. I wouldn't question that."

"Did you tell her about me and Donovan?" I knew before Kim shook her head that she hadn't, but I had to ask.

"You okay?" Kim asked.

The pause before my answer was long enough for Kim to shift in her seat. "The Coven, including Donovan, helped me and will do what they can to help Caine. How can I be upset about that?"

"But us. We're good?"

"We're good." As good as I was going to get.

Kim dropped the conversation. Pushing me for more would only cause the opposite effect, and she was smart enough to see it.

Kim helped me get the presents out of the car and into the elevator. We got out on the sixth floor, and I steeled myself. My cousin, Serena, stood at the end of the hall outside my apartment. When she saw us, she started walking toward us in her strappy heels.

"Shitmonkeys," I muttered as she approached with quick steps.

"Need some help?" She grabbed a wrapped gift.

"Oh, they're mine actually," Kim told her.

Serena's blonde brows screwed up as she looked at the tag. "Did you change your name to Sophie?"

"Well, that one..." Kim stammered.

"Who's Gwen? And why's she welcoming you to the Coven?"

"Um...."

"You're sunk, girl. Explain."

Without a way of walking from this without insulting my cousin by lying, I told her to grab what Kim carried, and we left Kim behind to enter my apartment.

"I thought Kim was cool," Serena said as she put down the gifts, then took what looked like a jeweled dagger from the bag and held it up. "What the fuck did she get you into? And it better be some geeky book club, or I'm beating her ass and shaving her head."

The next half hour was filled with me talking as if I was paying per second, explaining everything from the dream, the Coven, to even the ring and vessel explanation.

"Maybe we should call your mom."

"Serena."

She opened her mouth to say something, maybe thinking I'd finally snapped, overwhelmed as I had been and looking for an adult to handle things. I didn't blame her, so I told her about Jack's attack. This got a bigger reaction, and I had to stand in front of the door to stop her from going after him. I may have a mouth on me, but Serena's bite was just as big as her bark, if not bigger. She only stopped when I explained he was taken care of and would never be coming home.

Serena crossed her arms. "Is this some mafia shit wrapped in shiny, new-agey, magic fetish silk?"

I lifted my shirt and showed her the scar slashing my waistline.

She gasped. "That wasn't there before."

"No, it wasn't."

She bent to look closer and ran her fingers over my side until satisfied I wouldn't fake a scar for some stupid story. "Are you telling Aunt Lu?"

"Yeah, right. Telling my mom about any of this would only freak her out. Which means you shut your mouth about it."

"You're telling me witchy stuff is all real, and you expect me to sit on info like that?"

"I'm not giving you a choice. I'm pretty sure I wasn't supposed to tell you at all, and my Coven Leader, who just happens to know everything before I tell her, will know. Considering I'm supposedly this special vessel, it probably means a longer leash, but I'm not testing it by advertising. She may not take me out, but you're no one to her."

I doubted Aunt Lacey would hurt Serena, but she needed a big enough threat to keep her mouth shut. Serena was impulsive, but she wasn't moronic.

It worked.

For the next thirty minutes, as we opened the gifts, I fielded questions about "witchy stuff." All about stereotypical Hollywood crap, but it was all she knew. Most I had no answers for.

I was surprised Denise got me anything, and cradled the dark granite mortar and pestle from her in my lap as Serena's expression questioned what I'd use it for. I had no clue and wouldn't be crushing weed in it as Serena suggested. The gifts that followed grew more and more bizarre: a silver ceremonial knife set with red jewels on ivory handles, decorative bowls, vials filled with ingredients I didn't know what to do with. Other gifts included colourful candles, incense, oils, stones and gems, herbs, divination pendulums (another item I was confused by), and a multitude of books outlining spell work and rituals. These would be most helpful considering my inexperience.

Where did they buy this stuff? St. Catharines' downtown district or the mall was too mainstream to take the chance on a store for witchcraft essentials.

A thick book from Donovan covered palm reading along with gag gifts including the movies *Practical Magic* and the *Harry Potter* box set along with a black, pointed witch hat and plastic wand. Serena put it on, and we laughed as my thoughts went to kissing Donovan in Aunt Lacey's backyard. My thoughts about him ended there before my cheeks flushed. It was the only thing I refrained from telling Serena. I wasn't sure why, but I couldn't make myself repeat it until I understand how it had happened.

Kim had given me a beautiful spell book heavily decorated with a faded mixture of earth tones stained into the leather, with the same triquetra symbol from Aunt Lacey's necklace. Thick, empty pages begged to be filled. It was accompanied by a smaller version with the same likeness but lined pages. The card explained the larger one was to begin my own tome, the smaller one for dreams or general journal use. A spell in the back made it so everyone but me reading it saw blank pages.

I wished I'd had one in grade school when Adam read mine and told our mother I'd tried smoking with Serena and a few of our friends. My disgust and asthma flare-up was all the punishment I'd needed.

Kim's thoughtfulness shouldn't have surprised me. I wasn't one to share with the group.

When all the presents were opened, my bounty of odd items lay out on the coffee table and floor. Serena got quiet. Her blue eyes unfocused as her inner thoughts monopolized her attention. I waited, but it had been a long night, and I was wilting.

"Why were you waiting for me?" I asked her.

"What?"

"It's late, you're in club clothes, and were waiting for me to come home. Why were you here?"

She snapped back into herself. "Aunt Lu's been calling, but couldn't get a hold of you. I figured you were working, but I was out and stopped by The Lush. You weren't there, so I tried here and was waiting a bit before heading home."

"What'd my mom want?"

"Trip to Grandma Lizzie's tomorrow."

"Really? On a workday?"

"Yup. Aunt Lu has an early morning appointment with Dr. Konnor so she's taking a day off. Since she still has planning to do with Gram's for the family reunion she's trying to get us all together. I'm off, so I'm down for the drive. Adam's been hooked too, so you're not getting out of it. Plus, if what you're saying is true, you won't be sleeping anyway."

As much as I wanted to focus on Caine and what needed to

happen for the Awakening Ritual, I didn't need to be at Aunt Lacey's until later in the day for the gathering. Seeing Grandma Lizzie would lift my spirits to get me through it. I missed her.

Having taken in all she could for one night, Serena headed home, leaving me and Bosco to ourselves.

———

Frustration had me rolling around in bed so much Bosco opted for the floor.

What was wrong with me?

Recent events had me edgy and I couldn't deal. I needed something, anything to relieve this tension, to feel something other than my powerlessness and the fear of the consequences if I royally fucked the dog. The peaceful drink with Donovan was what I needed then, but now the emptiness created an itch I couldn't reach. I wanted to strip my skin off to get to it.

Unexpectedly, my fingers landed below my waistband. With no significant other, and since I refused to take home a random from the bar, orgasms were few and far between. As far as coping mechanisms went, this was safe enough.

When my fingers made contact, I captured a moan in the back of my throat and bit into my bottom lip. The sensation developing confirmed this was exactly what I needed.

Wetness gathered at my fingertips, coated them as I pushed inside and teased the heat within. My knees fell open, hips angling so I could reach deeper. Thoughts of Donovan doing the same pushed behind my closed eyelids.

A thrill slid down my inner thighs. I raked my nails along my skin to quell the toe-curling tingle that crept up to my nipples, which were now hardening in anticipation. Unable to endure the ache, I grazed my hands against the flushed skin of my exposed stomach and continued upwards in search of relief. My thumb and index finger pinched and rolled one hardened nipple and then the other. The slick fingers at my core quickened their pace, building a slow burn that raced forward with an urgency I rarely felt when alone.

Uncontrollable gasps fell from my lips. I was beyond caring what the neighbour kids might hear. Instead, I clawed at the sheets as sweat broke out over my entire body. I added pressure in just the right place to push me over the edge.

The delicious orgasm hit hard, shooting through me and had me tensed, then trembling. Curling into myself, I drew out every sensation while aftershocks rocked my oversensitive nerve endings. Relief swam through my limbs.

Imperfect, but effective.

Thoroughly exhausted, itch scratched, I threw my twisted sheets over gelatin limbs and passed out more relaxed than any masseuse could manage.

Orgasm or not, escaping the dream haunting me was impossible.

Raindrops splashed my face. My toes were tingly with numbness before I opened my eyes. I was standing in water up to my ankles.

"Sophie!"

I looked up to see Caine coming out of the willows in front of me, waving, water dripping off him as I stood shivering and squinting through the darkness. I'd taken no more than a few steps forward, and then he was running to me through the rising water. As he came close, I thought he was going to pull me into another bear hug. Instead, he grabbed my hand and hoisted me onto his back.

"Hold on!" he yelled over the roar of the rain, and I did, clinging to his strong shoulders.

Once we got to the willows, he pushed me higher so I could grab onto a low-hanging branch. We both climbed to where we sat the last time I was here. Out of reach of the water, he swiped his hand through his dripping hair and licked water from his lips.

"I thought the storm stopped?"

He nodded. "It came back when you left."

The disappointment in his slate eyes was heartbreaking. He'd thought the rain ended for good, and so did I. Apparently not.

"Sorry," I said.

"It's fine."

It wasn't, and we both knew it.

I scrambled for something to say. Asking how his day went was not an option. I hadn't seen his mother again, so no news there.

"The Coven's going to try an Awakening Ritual to counteract the coma." I didn't call it a sleeping curse as Aunt Lacey had. Worrying him didn't make sense. He had enough to deal with. If someone put him in the sleeping curse, it could be dealt with once he woke up.

"How does that work?"

"Not entirely sure." I also didn't tell him about the danger, for fear he may not want to try. After how strongly I'd laid into Kim about honesty, I felt like a hypocrite. "I'm not sure when either. Now I'm a full Coven member, so I'm sure soon."

"A full member?" He shifted on his wood seat.

I looked down. Water still pooled beneath us; rain still fell as well.

"Yeah." I explained what that meant and rehashed the Initiation, admitting how I was oblivious to most of what Aunt Lacey said and talked about the weird gifts I had received. By the end of it, he was smiling again, and his slate eyes softened to the smokiness I preferred.

When he looked above us, my gaze followed. I wondered what he was looking at, I could only see the branches of the willow. When he looked down at me again, his beaming smile caught me off guard. He then looked down, my gaze following his again to see the dark water had receded back into the creek. And then I realized what he was so happy about.

The rain had stopped.

"It's you." He shook his head, not in disbelief, but in more of a "well, I'll be damned" gesture. He thought I had something to do with the rain stopping, but it wasn't me.

He came closer, grabbing onto a branch higher and standing next to me on a branch lower, holding my hand, his thumb caressing the back of my hand. "Why do you come here?" he asked softly. I couldn't help but stare at his lips.

"I don't. Remember?"

"What if the spell doesn't work? Will you stop visiting me?"

Damn. The water may have stopped falling, but now it was gathering in my eyes. "I won't leave you alone."

The muscles of his jaw flexed under his skin. "Promise?"

"Promise."

My thundering heart bloomed life into the parts of me the cold grasped. Whether it was from his words or his closeness, my thoughts were far from my freezing toes.

"Caine!"

The scream was masculine and guttural.

"Cole." The name fell from Caine's lips, and he scrambled down the tree.

"Wait! It's not him, Caine!" I called after him as I tried to follow as quickly as I could. He ignored me and took off running.

The mossy bark was slick, and my foot slipped. Gravity took over as I yelped, and my arms flew out to stop my fall. Sparks flew in my vision as the back of my head smacked off a branch.

That was nothing compared to the feeling of landing in the grass on my back.

———

Propelled awake, I was blind in the darkness as my spine screamed. The wind was knocked out of me. Minutes passed as I lay in bed trying to chase a sense of calm. My head spun, making me nauseous. A hammer still pounded at the back of my skull. I barely made it to the toilet before I spilled last night's dinner into the bowl.

My muscles ached from retching until I had nothing left. Laying on the cold tiles of my bathroom floor, I grabbed my head, surprised I didn't feel a lump or wetness from blood.

How could hurting myself in a dream affect me while awake?

I couldn't think straight, but I didn't remember another time when something in the dream had affected me physically.

My guts lurched. I was glad it was already empty because, when I sat up, I lost my balance and hit the side of the tub. I clutched the edge of the porcelain as heat punched through my pores and peppered my skin. Bosco was worried, whining at my side, but I couldn't soothe myself let alone him.

One downside to living alone were times like this, when having someone around to take care of me would have been a bonus. Hold my hair, fetch a cold cloth, or make a clear decision if I needed an ambulance or not since my thoughts were as fuzzy as my vision.

For a long time, I sat slumped against the side of tub. Head pounding, guts twisting, I remembered having this feeling when Jack attacked me before everything went lights out. Another memory I was desperate to chase away.

So consumed with ignoring the smell of vomit in my sinuses, I was shocked and blinded when the light flicked on and Kim's voice invaded my bathroom.

"Shit! What happened?"

I groaned as I covered my eyes with a heavy limb.

"Sophie?" She was right next to me now. I heard toilet paper rip, then rustle, then a flush. The sudden blast of water zinged my brain with pain I couldn't compress with my hands tight enough to make it subside.

"How'd you get in?" I managed.

"I got a loaner key from the super. He's an idiot, but he gave it to me. Aunt Lacey called and said you needed me. What happened?"

I told her as best I could, sticking to important details that put me on the floor. I was exhausted by the end, and Kim snapped into action while I talked. She got me water to rinse my mouth, a washcloth for my face, and helped me to my couch.

"Seems like a concussion to me." It took me a moment to realize Kim wasn't talking to me, but to someone on her phone. "No, I've got some. I'll call back if I need to."

After that, Kim disappeared for only a few moments, and then was clapping in my face to wake me up. "No sleeping. I'll get you fixed up, but you have to stay awake."

With the ringing in my ears, staying awake shouldn't have been an issue, but I felt drained and had to wrestle my eyelids open.

With my face over a pot of water filled with some herbs Kim had mixed into it, I held a towel over my head to keep the steam in. I inhaled deeply and groaned as my sinuses screamed.

"Yeah, Aunt Lacey said if it burns, it's working."

"Great."

After twenty minutes of this, the nausea subsided, and my temples stopped throbbing, now a low beat in comparison to the jackhammer before. I sunk back into my couch and sighed in relief. When I opened my eyes and looked to Kim, who was waiting for a sign if her steam-mix worked, the room swayed a bit, but it didn't tilt. More buoyant than seesaw.

"I feel high."

Kim laughed. "You look high."

"You can have the rest. I share with friends."

My hand touched my face before I realized I'd reached for it. It was damp from the steam.

"Oh geez, you *are* high." She tossed me a clean washcloth, and I managed to wipe my face, noting how I couldn't feel it and yet it felt refreshing, confused that both could be possible.

Bile still felt like acid in the back of my throat as the rest of me floated. Since getting high was never my thing, the experience was a mix of pleasure and anxiousness about my body and mind being not quite within my control. For years now, I'd worked to regain that control, clinging to what made me the person I was without it being dictated by anyone else. Back then it was a man, one I pushed out of my thoughts, yet not before the image of his face popped into view and made me choke on my own breath.

"You okay?" Kim looked at me with concern in her blue-green stare.

"I-I..." I couldn't finish because I didn't know what to say. Kim didn't know, no one really knew, and now that control I'd fought for was slipping.

I flexed my fingers. They felt foreign as I moved to stand. I stumbled a bit, and Kim rushed to steady me, sloshing her tea over the sides of her cup.

She was asking me questions, but my ears were ringing again. My eyes squinted against a pressure within them. My numb fingers grasped my hair until it hurt, the pain grounding me to my body for a split second, but it wasn't enough. On my feet again, I grabbed the lip of the window as my head spun. My view overlooking the park across the street was a blur of green.

Kim's voice was in my ears, noise without words, her worried pitch the only thing I could interpret as something else took over.

My chest burned, skin crawled, eyes ached. I closed my eyes and pressed my fingers into them. It worked for the moment, but I still had to squint.

"Sophie, are you okay? This isn't the steam-mix."

"It's not okay." I may have said out loud, but I wasn't sure.

Kim grabbed my arm in some gesture of assistance, but her touch overloaded me. I couldn't handle her in my space, couldn't handle her help, and needed to get away. My fight or flight response was in full flight mode, and I bolted for the kitchen.

"Sophie!"

"Stay there!" She needed to stay away. I didn't know what this was. Maybe the steam-mix, but why the panic? Why was my chest burning? What was happening to my skin, my eyes? This was more than a panic attack, all the symptoms making me lose more and more of my control. I didn't want Kim within ten feet of me. If I had the strength to make her disappear, I would have.

The counter was cold against my hands as I leaned into it. I turned in search of Kim, seeing her form through my messed-up sight. She was still too close, but stayed where she was, asking questions I couldn't understand as my hearing had fizzed out.

Get your shit together, I told myself over and over. Closing my eyes again, I worked to control myself before I passed out. After a few moments, the sensation on my skin, the pain in my chest, it all subsided, leaving me with the numbed-out side-effects of the steam-mix.

Giving it another few beats, I opened my eyes, ecstatic my sight was normal. The excitement in Kim's eyes reached across the small space. She took a step toward me.

"Don't move!" I snapped. "Just stand there a second." I wasn't ready to share my personal space.

"It's okay, Soph. It's gone. Whatever that was, it's over."

Exhausted, I sunk to my ass on the tile floor.

Kim surged forward.

"Can you not take direction? Hold on a *fucking* second!" I barked. She listened. "Sit back down." I tried to sound less harsh, but failed.

My trembling hands and drumming heart settled. Kim stayed away, far more obedient than Bosco ever was.

Once I got my thoughts in order, I resigned myself to the fact that the steam-mix effects would take time to subside and I couldn't sit here on my kitchen floor all day. I stood, noting the room remained stable, and joined Kim, who was seated on the couch with Bosco on her lap.

Exhaustion hit me again. "I need to sit."

She kept Bosco from coming over to me as I slumped into the couch and curled my legs up.

"That wasn't supposed to happen," Kim said.

"I don't know what that was."

"Aunt Lacey does."

"How nice of her to know everything."

A few quiet moments passed.

"Are you going to talk about it? I know it was more than you freaking out."

"Ask your boss." I didn't have the energy for conversation.

"She said it was the first stages of your power and to let it take shape. But there was a catalyst. Not the steam-mix, it wouldn't affect you like that. Something you were thinking set you off."

Another image of the face I didn't want to see popped up. I squirmed and fought against any lingering memories that accompanied the face, replacing them with other faces that evoked different feelings altogether. Mainly Caine and Donovan's. I still wasn't myself and I wasn't getting into this now.

She must have known, because Kim gave up, grabbing me a bottle of water instead. I should have probably felt bad for shutting her out, but I didn't. She wasn't the only one and she wouldn't be the last.

17

———

SILENT WAR

Serena shook me and her hand in front of my face. "Yo, Soph. What the fuck's wrong with you?"

I looked at her through the haze, captivated by her ice-blue eyes. So beautiful, the complete opposite of mine.

Her forehead creased.

"Did I say that out loud?" I asked.

Kim nodded, her arms crossed, brows pointed in worry.

"Are you high?" Serena questioned me, then turned to Kim and asked her the same. She started yelling.

"Stop," I finally managed. "Serena. Stop. I'm...yeah...I'm high, but it's not Kim's fault. Actually, I guess it is." I giggled. Serena got in Kim's face.

More yelling.

I grabbed for Serena's shirt, clinging to the hem with numb fingers.

"I fell, Serena. I fell."

"What?" she moved back to me.

"The dream," I explained. She didn't understand. "Caine. The dream. I fell from a tree."

"So?"

I sighed, trying to focus enough to finish what I was saying, but I couldn't. Kim finished for me. I tried to touch my nose as you do while playing charades and missed, poking myself in the eye.

Kim sat next to me. "She has a concussion. I gave her a steam-mix for the symptoms, but there's obvious aftereffects."

I peeked at my cousin through my good eye. "I get why you do this now."

She rolled her eyes and muttered, "Fucking light-weight." I shot her a sloppy middle finger as I leaned in the armrest, the beaten-up fabric on my skin blissful. "So, what now? Your mom'll be here in, like, two hours to go to Grandma Lizzie's. Will this wear off by then?"

"You tell me, mentor," I said to Kim.

Kim sighed. "It will, but then Sophie will be in pain again, and won't be going anywhere. We need to get to Aunt Lacey's, so she can fix this."

"Road trip! Let's go, Bosco."

I got up too fast and wobbled as I tried to get Bosco's leash on. Serena pulled the leash from my hand and did it herself. Then she and Kim argued for another five minutes about Serena calling an ambulance. When Kim explained why the hospital wasn't necessary, the argument shifted to Serena coming along to Aunt Lacey's. I knew my cousin, no way Kim was winning this one, so I walked out of the apartment and leaned against the wall, waiting for the elevator as they hashed it out.

As I predicted, Serena won and sat in the backseat with Bosco as I laid my head against the window.

As Kim drove to Aunt Lacey's, the steam-mix began wearing off. The feeling in my fingers and body came alive, forcing my environment back into focus and stealing me away from the numbness. The sense of panic and skin-crawling returned, not as strong as in my apartment, but enough for Kim to ask me if I was okay. I lied and said I was fine. This time I breathed through it and leaned back into the closed window until it dissipated. The success over whatever the sensation was, was small, but in some ways a victory. I didn't want to feel that way ever again.

In front of Aunt Lacey's, the sound of a lawnmower drove a spike of pain, the first one post-steam-mix, right through my temples. Donovan turned it off when he noticed Serena helping me up the front path.

"You fixed it," Kim said from the car.

"Fixed what?" I asked.

She only pointed, so Serena helped me back to the car. We bent to match Kim's line of sight.

"You fixed the crack in my passenger window. Two weeks after I bought this car, a rock flew off a truck tire next to me and cracked it. And you fixed it."

"I didn't do that!" I looked at her, to Serena, behind me at Donovan, then back at Kim. "I didn't, I swear!"

Kim laughed. "It's not a bad thing, Soph. You did it without realizing. I knew something was off. Did you feel your powers again?"

"Powers?" Serena questioned.

"You felt your powers?" Donovan came in close. Too close for Serena.

"Hello,"—she got between us—"who are you, bro?"

"Who are you?" he snapped back.

"I don't know what I felt." I took a step toward the door to get them out of my space. "Right now, I feel fucking exhausted."

Kim was giddy. "You have no idea how happy I am I never paid to fix the stupid thing."

"Kim, get off it. I didn't fix the window."

"Yes, you did," she muttered.

"How's the head?" Donovan asked.

"Damn, you a landscaper and a doctor?" Serena snapped.

"She doesn't need a doctor," he said.

"Who does she need? You? Don't think so, son. Walk off."

"Serena," I said.

"She needs Aunt Lacey," Kim chimed in.

"Yes, she does," Aunt Lacey's voice came from the front door. She was leaning against the doorframe. "Come, Sophie dear."

Aunt Lacey held out her hand, rings on each finger glinting in the sun, her smile inviting, but setting off a gut feeling that rooted my feet.

"What's happening?" Serena asked me, but I didn't know and couldn't answer.

When I didn't move, Aunt Lacey walked toward me. "You are correct to listen to your intuition. A touch from me heals you. However, the price for accelerating nature's rather tedious process is fleeting discomfort."

She held out her hand again, and again, I hesitated.

"You've survived worse," Donovan said, exchanging a look with me that gave me strength.

He was right, so I slipped my hand into Aunt Lacey's. Her other arm went around me for a hug I didn't understand until the discomfort hit, and her hold was the only thing keeping me on my feet. From the neighbours' perspective, it would look like a simple embrace, but the skin-crawling sensation was back, only now it was all directed at my head, blinding me with a finger-like kneading biting into the squishy bits between my ears.

When Aunt Lacey pulled back, her hands steadied my shoulders. A blink and I felt fine. Serena wasn't happy. She questioned what happened, Kim trying to hold her back. Donovan had moved closer, I'm guessing in case Aunt Lacey couldn't hold my weight. The gesture surprised me. It brought back thoughts I didn't want creeping up, of how often I needed small gestures like that, and how I'd been repeatedly let down.

I was taken aback by the compassion within Aunt Lacey's eyes when she touched my arm and said, "While my gifts are plenty, they cannot heal all aspects of us. Those you must fight alone." Though no one else knew what she was talking about, I did, and I fought not to break down right there on the lawn with relief that someone else knew. The secret ate me alive whenever I let it float to the surface, and it was out for Aunt Lacey to see, without me having to say it.

"Sophie?" Serena questioned.

"I'm fine." I wasn't, as evident by the thickness of my voice, but I was better now than I had been two minutes ago. "Shit." Only then did it occur to me that my cousin was at my Coven Leader's house, having just seen her perform magic on me. "Um..."

Aunt Lacey gave a small laugh. "I'm not about to burn you at the stake for sharing this secret with family, my dear Salix. This family," she jutted her chin toward Serena. "Though others—"

"I won't."

"I know you won't. And it seems you have an engagement to get to?"

Of course she knew about going to my grandmother's. Since we still had some time left, I said I'd prep the bar for the party so I wouldn't have to later, forcing Serena to help me to make it go faster.

"Good." My Coven Leader put her arm around my elbow and walked me inside. "Because you have a busy night ahead and need your wits about you if you hope to serve the Magics we have visiting."

Inside the foyer, I stopped her as something else hit me as important. "Can I die in the dream?" She didn't answer right away. "I fell out of a tree. What if I had broken my neck?"

She patted my arm. "Then tonight would have been a gathering of much grief."

While I stood in shock, Aunt Lacey yelled for Donovan to finish the frontyard, but to leave the backyard. He looked confused as she left him to work.

Confirmation that the dream itself could kill me took me for a loop. If I could've sat and processed it for longer than a few minutes, I would have. But I had to set up and get going. The chores consumed my worry, converting it to thoughts of whether or not we had enough wine glasses for the night.

Taking inventory of the provisions Aunt Lacey bought, it was like she expected five hundred people. As I understood it, she estimated a third of that would show up, but she still insisted we had just enough glasses to last the night.

Setting up my area in the kitchen, I prepared everything a bartender needed. My fingers were wrinkled from all the lime, lemons, oranges, and pineapples I'd sliced. Serena washed her hands and complained about her nail polish chipping. For helping, I promised to get her Kim's recipe for the steam-mix.

"Damn straight. Though you have to partake."

"Sure. Next time I get a concussion, I'm in."

"Nope. By my birthday or I'm keeping Bosco. You've been warned, chicka."

Aunt Lacey was in the back playing with Bosco, his tongue hanging outside his mouth as he ran around playing fetch.

"You can leave him." Donovan was at my side, making me flinch. "You're coming back later anyway, and Aunt Lacey still needs to prepare things for the party."

"Ah, yeah. Thanks."

"Are you for real?" Serena said as she dried her hands with a dish towel.

"Clearly," Donovan said.

Before they could get into it, I hurried Serena out the door, and we were on the road back to St. Catharines. Serena and Kim may have started out rocky, but they found a commonality in bitching about Donovan. I tuned them out, but could only take it so long before I told them to shut up and hit Kim with a hard stare I hoped she remembered from our talk on the side of the road.

"Plus, he looks familiar."

"No, he doesn't, Serena."

"He does," she insisted, and I returned to ignoring her.

When we got to the apartment, my mom and Adam were already waiting in the side parking lot. Kim only stopped to let us out before she went to run errands for the party.

Serena resumed talk of Donovan in the car and wouldn't let up.

My defending him piqued my mother's assumptions I was dating him.

"Think I got a shot at grandkids with this one?" My mom asked me.

I snort-laughed. "I'll leave the placenta to Adam. He's probably got a few out there he doesn't know about yet."

"Please," he scoffed without looking up from his phone. "Can't get pregnant doing anal."

"Adam!" My mom scolded him as he laughed at his success in disgusting her.

"Hailey looked far too prudish for ass play," Serena said.

"Serena!" My mother scolded her with equal result.

"Yeah right. If she turns up pregnant, it ain't mine."

Adam was still glued to his phone. I used the opportunity to switch the topic away from Donovan. "She's gone already? What was wrong with this one?"

"Too demanding."

"Of what?" Serena asked.

"My time."

Guess she stepped over a well-defined boundary.

"I can see how spending time with your girlfriend can be so annoying. That skunt!" I laughed at Serena's interpretation of his girl traumas as my mother shook her head, seeing her chances for grand-kids dwindling.

———

At the end of a forty-five-minute drive through the country to Dunnville, Hunter, Serena's older brother by three years, answered the door. He and Serena's mother Karen lived in the upstairs portion of the old, renovated home. Grandma Lizzie resided in the rest of the house.

Hunter's long, frizzy hair stuck up in all directions as he scratched his goatee and said, "Hey." We followed him inside.

The guys went upstairs as I ran to the washroom, wishing I'd forgone the chocolate milk on the drive up.

I found Grandma Lizzie in the kitchen with Serena and my mom. I gave her a hug from behind before she could turn around. She pulled free and gave me an unmistakable once-over, shock in her expression.

I had never received such an unenthusiastic welcome from my grandma in all my life. Usually, I got a loving hug plus a kiss on the cheek. This time, Grandma Lizzie did everything to prevent us from touching.

"You okay?" I asked her.

She recovered quickly. "Of course, sweetie. Did you change your hair?"

"Nope, just growing it out."

I tried not to read the reaction as a sign of Alzheimer's taking root the way it had with my Grandmother's father.

My Great-Grandfather would wander town to feed the horses, having not owned any for more than thirty-five years. Also, being well over six feet, rail thin, and forgetting to wear a belt, was a sad affair. I had fond memories of him playing the harmonica and the spoons while my Great-Grandmother sang in a shaky, fervent voice with her eyes closed.

My Great-Grandparents always seemed old to me. Grandma Lizzie was different. Always clear-minded and good-hearted, she was the type of woman that made me strive to be better. A person who treated others as their equal, often stating, "God loves us all, no matter our ilk, colour, or religion." I may not embrace the exact philosophy—religion was never my thing—but the moral lesson remained. Grandma Lizzie's love and grace was passed down from her mother, and to see that replaced with the slow, unravelling confusion of dementia would be heartbreaking.

I tried to shake off my concern, despite the cool welcome.

We updated each other on our lives since the last visit, and my mom and she chatted about plans for the upcoming family reunion as my mom took notes, negotiating a date next month. My mom boasted about her promotion and her new man, Brian, who seemed to be working out. Everyone chatted around the table as normal as anything.

Throughout the visit, I kept catching my grandma's lingering stare. I realized her initial reaction to me wasn't a symptom of losing her mind. She was examining me. I didn't know what she was looking for, but no one else seemed to notice.

Adam and Hunter came down asking for food, which they usually did instead of making something themselves. Grandma Lizzie was animated about offering cucumber sandwiches and asked me to help her pick a good cucumber from the garden. Suspicion flared as I followed her outside.

Colour bloomed, hugging the fence line with fresh tomatoes, yellow beans, and cucumber, leaving space for later season watermelon and pumpkins. Fragrant mint clung to the summer breeze, the smell a constant reminder of Grandma Lizzie's proudly tended garden.

I reached through sticky, velvety leaves to find a good-sized cucumber tucked behind plastic lambs filled with colourful peppers, sitting with their little feet curled beneath them. I'd seen them in pictures taken before my mother was born, now they had a few layers of touch-up paint to bring them into the next decade.

"What have you been doing, Sophie?"

"Oh, you know, like I said, working mostly." I stood and turned with my prize to see Grandma Lizzie's stern expression.

"You've been practicing."

"Practicing what?"

"You're a witch." She glowered at me.

I stared at her, astounded at how she knew. Unless...

"You're one too." I saw a flicker in her eyes. "How could you tell?"

Grandma Lizzie scoffed. "I am nothing of the sort and I can see it all over you. Don't you know what you're doing?"

"I have no idea what I'm doing! It started out of nowhere and scares the hell out of me."

"As it should! You're dealing with the Devil when you give yourself over to those senses. You need to stop this right now, girl. Put it out of your mind or Sophie, I swear to you, it will take you over and convert you into a vessel of evil."

The word vessel stuck with me. Could she know about that too? Still in shock, I burst with questions. "Why didn't anyone say anything? Is it just you? Does Mom or Aunt Karen know?"

"Sophie, leave this alone. I thought I got the Word into you soon enough, but you never had eyes for God. I tell you right now, using these powers will put you nowhere good, just crazy, locked in an institution or dead." Then she muttered something. I thought it was, "Damn you, Olive." The name meant nothing to me. "Evil. Pure evil. Your soul is at risk."

"I-I never said it was amazing, Gram. I said I was terrified by it, but evil? I don't think—"

"Your terror should be enough. Tell me. Tell me who's guiding you." She grabbed my arm with sudden force, making me jump. "Some new man? A friend? Do *not* listen to them, Sophie. Do *not* fall into their Devil's trap!"

I ripped my arm away and stepped back, heart filled with resentment. I wished I had never admitted anything, that I'd kept my mouth shut and denied her accusation.

"Where's my cucumber?" Adam called from the back door.

Staring each other down in a silent war, I had to break away from my grandmother's damning gaze before I burst into tears. On the way by, I slapped the cucumber against Adam's chest, a vegetable that had cost me more than my time.

Nothing would be the same between me and the woman in the backyard ever again. Every childhood memory spent in this town, summers at bible camp, tennis lessons, was tainted. Those memories were now coloured with desperation, a ruse to drown out the essence of our blood in some deprogramming scheme.

Inside, I went to the bathroom to compose myself before I screamed at my mother for stuff she probably had no clue about, before hitchhiking home. I was so upset that it took longer than it should to calm down. One conclusion I made, was that after years of my grandmother's devout faith, she never rid herself of whatever led her to know I discovered these powers.

The rest of the visit was tense. I couldn't wait to take off, mentioning working a private party and needing time to get ready a few times. Enough that Serena bristled at my impatience.

A barrage of biting questions carried the minutes too slowly hour to hour. I wanted to ask Kim or Aunt Lacey about what happened, hoping they, or even Donovan, had answers. How would I fix this? The problem was not information, it was personal. A spell, if one existed, to force my grandmother to embrace her heritage was unauthentic, and a false love was more hurtful than enduring her hate.

———

"What's wrong, my Dolly?" My mother asked on the ride home.

"Nothing, just tired," I told her, then thought she might be able to answer something. "Do you know who Olive is? Someone Gram knows?"

Her brows peaked above her sunglasses. "Surprises me she'd mention her."

"She turn her nose up at the collection plate in church?" Serena joked.

"Olive's your grandma's sister," my mother answered.

"Sister? Since when did she have a sister? Why doesn't she talk about her?"

"Or said her name until now?" Serena added and pushed herself forward from the back seat.

"Well," Lu hesitated. "Olive is your grandmother's younger sister. It's where your middle name originated, actually. Olivia was more modern than Olive, though my mother was still pissed about it. Back in the seventies, maybe earlier, the family had Olive committed."

Serena was astonished. "What the shit? So much for family?"

"No one talks about it. Your grandma's never explained it to me."

"Is she still alive?" I was twisted in my seat. Even Adam's attention was piqued.

"I have no idea." My mom's eyes flitted to me while she drove. "Though I'm not sure we would've heard about Olive's death when her life was a mystery. I do know we look like her. Though Olive was free-spirited like you two back there." She looked to Serena and Adam in the rear-view mirror. "Something of a handful, but maybe her behaviour could be chalked up to her mental instability."

"Where is she? What institution?"

"Why?"

Not providing an answer made my mother nervous.

"Don't you go sticking your nose into this, Sophie Olivia. I know you're doing the psychiatry schooling and all that, but this is way over your head. Don't go bugging some crazy, old relative to cure your curiosity."

"I'm not trying to cure her, Mom. What's the harm in verifying she's still alive? For all you know, she was put there for no reason."

"They wouldn't have kept her this long if she was sane." I had to agree. "I'm sure they have their own doctors with their own mandated assessments and, when Olive is ready, she'll be released. Even if she already was, she'd have no reason to speak to the family who committed her. Please don't do this. Your grandmother's an old woman. Dredging up bad memories would only hurt her."

I kept quiet after that. My grandmother had no problem hurting me or committing her own sister. As soon as I could, I planned to search for Olive and get to the core of the story and whatever else my family was hiding, regardless of who it hurt. The only thing I found insane was how easily everyone kept secrets. All those family reunions, and no one even whispered Olive's name or anything about powers. I felt disgusted.

———

I hugged my mom goodbye in the driveway, Adam throwing a "Later, hookers" out the window as Serena shot him the finger. My mom and brother were out of earshot before Serena started asking questions about my mood back in Dunnville. I told her.

"Seriously?"

I gave her a look she couldn't misinterpret.

"That's fucked," Serena said. "Though makes sense if she committed her own sister. Every family has skeletons, but ours are gettin' piled up. This magic stuff, insane people, I wonder what else we don't know."

I had a feeling this was only the beginning.

When Serena asked to attend the party at Aunt Lacey's, I had to shut her down. I didn't know who would be there, and she had to be a member anyway.

"How do you become a member?"

"You don't."

"Now you're shutting me out? I'm not cool enough to hang with the in crowd."

"I'm not cool enough. Why do you think I'm slinging drinks?" She didn't buy it. "I don't know enough about what's going on in the Coven. Let me get through…" I hadn't told her about the Awakening Ritual and didn't want to scare her. "Just hold up. If everything goes good, I'll talk to Aunt Lacey. Just be happy I was allowed to tell you about it."

She had no choice but to leave it alone. Serena started to walk home, but stopped after a few steps and spun back to me. "The Butterfly Lounge!"

"The what?"

"That piss-ant Donovan. I knew I recognized him. I've seen him at The Butterfly Lounge with different chickies finding a private bathroom a few times."

The Butterfly Lounge was an upscale club in Niagara Falls. I had never been.

"I'm sure he looks like lots of guys."

"With those dimples? Please, girl. They stand out." She pointed a finger at me. "Don't go trying to change a moth into a butterfly. The whole bad boy thing never works out. He'll be all charming and then, one day, you'll have the clap, and he'll blame it on you and disappear."

"I'm not trying to do anything."

Her head tilted. "Who you trying to play? You left him in charge of Bosco."

I understood what she meant. Under normal circumstances, I wouldn't trust anyone to look after him, but when Donovan asked, no red flags waved so I agreed. I may not always have had the best judgement with men, but this wasn't a test. When I told Donovan what happened with us in the backyard wouldn't happen again, I meant it.

18

A LOT HARDER THAN MATH

Back at Aunt Lacey's, Bosco was alive and well. At least I knew I could trust Donovan with the task, though he may read more into what it meant. I wouldn't let it happen often.

"Salix, I owe many apologies." Aunt Lacey came up behind me as I was looking at Donovan and Bosco in the yard.

Donovan came in saying, "Hi," and then crossed the kitchen to the bathroom.

"Yes, you do." I surprised myself once we were alone. I wasn't sure what had compelled her to apologize, but I let her speak.

"I'm sorry for not allowing you to know certain information I, at the time, deemed unneeded to pass on. I did have my reasons, however, I forget we have not known each other long and explicit trust is for those who have more shared experiences to draw from. I also know that this conversation is not enough to rectify any of that, though I do promise to be more upfront with you on matters concerning yourself, when able."

It was the most I was going to get.

"Unfortunately, at this time it is." Responding to my unsaid thoughts was creepy. She laughed, probably hearing just what I thought of her little trick.

"Do you, at least, trust me to guide you when considering your abilities? To empower you to thrive with what I know is deep within you?"

I thought back to my grandmother's speech about staying away from these powers and decided I didn't believe her threats or warnings about the Devil being attached to them. "Yes."

She smiled. "Perfect." She stepped outside, gathering her skirt in one hand as she bent and plucked a dandelion. She then handed me the dandelion and said, "Make it grow."

I took the weed. "That's a lot harder than math, and I failed math."

"You erased all signs of the crack in Kim's window." I cringed at the confirmation. "Soon you will look at this test as a mere trick. You need to feel the power and contain it within yourself to be used as you wish. The steam-mix allowed buried thoughts to come forward. I know you would rather leave these buried, but I am more interested in the feelings they evoked, not so much the content. Find the part of you willing to fight as well as feel, and you will discover your power."

Watching Aunt Lacey scoop up Bosco and leave me alone in the backyard, I was shocked by her instruction. Growing a weed was a ridiculous accomplishment even if I succeeded. I felt defeat and aggravation as I sat in the grass a few minutes without a clue of what to do.

"The make it grow test, huh?"

"Seriously, Donovan, this house is enormous. Find a room and entertain your penis like a normal little boy."

He shot me a cocky smile, unfazed by my attitude. "I prefer entertaining my penis to be a couple's effort." Thinking about what Serena told me about Donovan didn't help matters, not that his playboy status should matter at all since I wasn't planning on hooking up with him. "Besides, you're going to need my help to pass this test with your attitude."

"Sorry, I don't need a palm reader."

He walked over, squatted down in front of me, and looked at me meaningfully. "I know you know I can do more than read palms." He took the dandelion. Without looking away from me, I felt a hint of energy prickle my skin and crawl within me. I watched the dandelion grow, doubling its original size, now resembling a gerbera daisy.

I stared at him, trying to figure him out, as he sat down and crossed his legs. "Why sit in the meetings reading palms, surrounded by eyelash-batters, when you're capable of this?"

"They don't need to know the extent of my power."

"Why not?"

"As you pointed out, I already have batting lashes far too interested in the readings. Can you imagine if they knew more?"

"Hmm."

"What?"

"I would've figured an ego like yours would crave *more* attention, not less."

He captured me with his dark stare. "Then I guess you don't know me very well."

I looked away, "I guess I don't."

Donovan plucked another dandelion. "You have to do it before Aunt Lacey will let you leave this yard, so unless you wanna camp-out while the rest of us are partying, get to it."

I snatched the dandelion. "Any pointers, Master Green-thumb?"

"Yes. Call me that from now on. But drop Green-thumb. No need to get formal."

I smirked. "You can master yourself behind the rosebushes. Watch out for dog shit."

"What, no helping hand?" His dimpled leer disappeared when I shot him a disapproving look. "Fine. You already know what the power feels like. When it begins, keep calm and clamp down on it. If you freak out, it'll overwhelm you, and you'll lose control. Instead, force it through your hand and into the dandelion by imagining the flower growing."

When Donovan made the weed grow, he didn't look like he had to think about it. Closing my eyes, I felt Donovan's stare. I attempted to ignore him and remember what the dandelion looked like after he made it grow. I pictured the stem extending upward, the flower expanding in size and in beauty, no longer a mere weed.

I thought back to what Aunt Lacey told me to do, to find the part of me willing to fight as well as feel. Considering I didn't want to feel anything close to what she alluded to, I wrestled with giving up. I didn't need to do this just because she told me to, but I did tell her I trusted her to foster my gifts, which is what this was supposed to do.

Reminding myself what it felt like to feel like a failure, removing the content from the equation, as Aunt Lacey suggested, an uncomfortable presence expanded in my chest. When my skin started to crawl, my heart raced, but I shifted to thinking about the dandelion and making it grow.

More than fifteen minutes passed before I finally heard Donovan say something.

I peeked at the flower. It was bigger, bigger than even he made it. A peek was all I got before the feeling, the...the magic began to take over.

"Hold it in, babe. Push it down to where it came from." He instructed as I strained to recover my dominance. "Imagine it drowning. It can't win. Don't let it."

I tried to obey him, his voice muzzled as the sensation overpowered my senses, the discomfort in my body surpassing what I'd felt at my apartment. The struggle dragged on, but slowly, I gained a foothold and the built-up pressure dissipated, leaving my head spinning and my breath punchy, like I'd sprinted for my life.

When I opened my eyes, I was faced with Donovan's tight expression, but he was now standing a few feet away from me. I looked at the dandelion. What I found wasn't the picture of perfection I expected. Instead, the flower hung blackened and lifeless, crisping into ash as I dropped it. Then I looked to the grass encircling us and gasped, seeing every blade as blackened as the flower.

I scrambled to my feet and away from the blackened area around me.

How could I have done that?

Donovan tried to explain. "Our power is capable of exquisite things, like growing or healing, but as you see, it's equally capable of tremendous harm."

"I wasn't trying to kill it."

"While ridding yourself of the power, you robbed the dandelion of the power you put into it. Then it degraded until it had no life left. You were touching the grass, so it too was depleted."

Why didn't someone warn me? I could have sucked the life out of Donovan by accident or even Kim, back at my apartment, if I'd let her get close enough.

"Do it again."

My gaze popped up from the ashes to his. "What? No." I attempted to leave.

"Sophie..." He grabbed my arm, then flinched away with a grunt.

The flinch was what kept me in the backyard. "Why do you do that?"

He ignored me. "If you don't keep going, you'll never get over it. You need to identify the point of no return. It only comes with familiarity, or you'll use unintentionally and kill someone."

"I didn't have the power to kill someone until you had me training in the first place!"

"Boohoo! It's out now. The window proves you could use it without knowing, and I don't think you could bear the guilt if you killed someone."

He leaned down to the grass. "Watch," he said and made sure I was before he laid his hand on the ground. I felt the prickle of the magic again. Fresh, green grass grew from the ground I had scorched. I was so impressed, I knelt down and ran my fingers over it. It was real and erased all signs of the damage I had done.

"See?" He knelt next to me. "Here is a safe place to practice." He sat and crossed his legs. "Try again."

The next two hours brought false starts since I was leery of losing control. When I finally convinced myself to let go, I was overwhelmed, but this time it was far too much. Even greater than the other two times, it resulted in a shockwave released from my body.

"Holy shit," I heard Donovan say as I tried to hold myself up from falling over into the grass. The shockwave exhausted me. "No wonder you're having trouble keeping that at bay."

Kim came running into the backyard, Aunt Lacey behind her.

"I'm okay," I assured them, hoping it was true.

Donovan turned to Aunt Lacey. "I had no idea."

"She's getting closer," Aunt Lacey measured. "Salix, let go of your fear of failure. If you believe disappointment is inevitable, success is impossible."

"You sound like a fortune cookie. It can't be that easy."

"I never claimed easy. Keep working." She left as quickly as she came.

Kim lingered.

"She can't concentrate with you supervising," Donovan said without facing her.

I nodded her way, and she left with a torn expression.

"You don't need to be such a douche-nozzle, Donovan."

Donovan's tough exterior melted as I pleaded for him to act like an adult. Instead of promising good behaviour or laughing, he ignored me and continued with training. After another forty minutes I was ready to give up.

"Perfecting this isn't just a personal triumph. You need to get this before moving onto something more challenging." He forced a smile. It seemed that it pained him to watch me fail. I saw this with every failed attempt and wanted to succeed just to erase that look.

Okay, I thought. Make it grow, but don't destroy it. I closed my eyes for the nth time to trigger a response. After doing it so many times, this came easily. The issue was control and knowing how much to conjure before overloading myself. It was like an internal chemistry set with volatile ingredients I had to mix when the recipe was in a foreign language.

An energy simmered deep inside me. On the cusp of unbearable, I stopped feeding it fuel, allowing it to resonate at that level.

"Open your eyes," Donovan directed in a low, soft voice.

When I did, I saw the dandelion was now the size of my hand. Its petals thickened, brightened, and multiplied. I felt my power within me now in a new way. Buzzing like always, yet altered into a low, constant hum, no longer erratic energy wreaking chaos.

I laughed in exhausted relief. My head still ached with the effort. "Finally."

"It's beautiful."

I looked up to thank him, maybe even hug him, for proving he possessed one redeeming quality by not giving up on me. When I did, I was awestruck.

"What's the matter?" Donovan asked as I stared at him. His dark eyes narrowed.

"You're...glowing." A layer of light haloed Donovan's body, bright white with hints of green. I blinked to try and clear my sight, but the light was stubborn.

"Glowing? Like...with emotion?" He sneered at the likelihood.

"You! All around you. You're glowing." My focus strained until my eyes burned, and I was forced to look away.

"Let your power dissipate."

I concentrated on letting go of the magic, satisfied when my skin no longer itched. Trying to look at him again, I regretted it. "Fuckball-soup! Shit, what the fuck is going on? What'd you do?" When I looked away from him, my eyes still saw spots like I'd looked at the sun too long.

"Nothing!" Donovan snapped and shuffled me inside to consult Aunt Lacey. The process was slow and frustrating as he insisted on leading me with only voice commands. I couldn't open my eyes to stop from banging into walls because he was in front of me, blinding me with his glow.

Walking around without seeing was frustrating as hell. I kept trying to peek only to snap my eyes shut as soon as Donovan's glow seared them all over again. I opened my eyes again, a habit I couldn't refrain from, to look for Aunt Lacey as we reached the basement. I saw Kim on the couch with an old book in her lap, Bosco next to her. Kim had a glimmer of light around her, but I could handle that a bit better. I fluttered through a dozen wet-lashed blinks as my eyesight continued to fail while Donovan stood in front of me.

Light footsteps descended the stairs behind me. I turned to find help from Aunt Lacey only to backpedal so fast I cracked the back of my skull against the wall. The impact zapped my vision as my knees buckled, and my dazed ass slid to the floor. Sputtering back to life, I felt a hand on my arm and heard muffled voices around me as my hearing wasn't quite right.

Waterworks sprung from my eyes as my vision came back to see Aunt Lacey hovering above me, an intense glow assaulting my retinas like a two-hundred watt bulb an inch from my face. I was helpless under the weight of light.

My hands covered my face. "Get back! I can't fucking see anything!"

"What did you do to her?" Kim snapped at Donovan, though I couldn't see either of them.

"Shut your face-holes and get me to the couch!" Goddamned idiots.

"What do you see, Salix?" Aunt Lacey's voice floated around me.

I wiped away streaks of water from my cheeks and covered my eyes again. "First of all, I made the stupid flower grow. It was huge and awesome, and I didn't even kill it." The triumph felt insignificant now. "Afterward, Donovan was freaking glowing, and so are you."

"Can you look at someone again?" my wonderful, brain-breaking Coven Leader asked.

"Kim, stand in front of me. Everyone else get back."

I heard some rustling as people moved, gave them a second more, then cupped my hands around my eyes to block out my peripheral vision, just in case. I opened my eyes and saw Kim standing there, concern colouring her expression as a light made her look damn near ethereal.

"You're a Soul Seer!" The excitement in Aunt Lacey's voice was enough to make me want to slap her. Whatever this was, it wasn't exciting.

"A what?"

"You see the essence of people's souls. How did Wend look to you? Think of him."

Donovan had been glowing green in the backyard.

"This is marvellous, Salix!" Aunt Lacey bubbled over with joy. "Soul seeing is a rare gift. I have never had a Soul Seer within my flock."

"Glad to be of service,"—my sarcasm was heavy—"but this is like being told I'm the first person you've met with herpes. Sorry, but what use is it if I can't open my eyes? I happen to like seeing. I've kinda gotten attached to it."

Frustration bubbled inside of me as I heard people moving around the room, but I couldn't identify who was moving or see their faces. It made me paranoid they were communicating silently with each other. I realized I could see the difference in their glows through my eyelids and watched as Aunt Lacey paced.

"All souls are different," the pacing light explained. "With practice you will distinguish a soul's strength, colour, and even intent. Invaluable when distinguishing friend from foe."

"So, I'm like Denise? How is that anything special?"

Kim snort-laughed.

"No, darling, Lior's aura reading is nothing in comparison." Until Aunt Lacey reminded me, I hadn't remembered that was Denise's Coven name. "It is true her ability gauges a person's aura, however, many can accomplish such. Soul seeing is a direct view of a person's soul. Their inner selves reach out to you, become detectable to your talented eyes, and speak to you in ways few others are privileged to possess."

Great. Killing things wasn't enough, I had to get weirder.

"Special," Aunt Lacey amended my mental rebuke. "As for enduring these souls, your defences will strengthen in time. For now, sunglasses will suffice."

I sighed and dropped my head back onto the couch as Kim went to grab my glasses from my purse. Tonight I would be surrounded by a horde of Magics, all with their glowing souls daggering my eyeballs unless I hid behind sunglasses indoors at night. Looking like a douche was not the way I hoped to spend the night.

———

"Please tell me you got this with your incredible employee discount," I said to Kim as I shifted the one-shouldered, fully-sequined cocktail dress that shone gold and turquoise when light hit it. She had every detail down to the gold bangles and the sunglasses, which were a pair of vintage glasses from Aunt Lacey, the rim and arms made of metal lace.

"Clearly. And it's perfect on you." Kim wore a saucy fifties cocktail dress in a bright green that complemented the red of her hair. I followed her into the kitchen where we found Donovan behind the kitchen island. His glow hit me after being around Kim's low glimmer, but I reminded myself to suck it up as he would be the least of my issues when the others show up.

"Excuse me, buddy, no patrons behind the bar."

He turned with a short glass in hand, and I felt my mouth drop open. On any given day, Donovan wore jeans and a plain, dark t-shirt or something with a band logo on it. Nothing fancy. Tonight he was as dressy as Kim and I, wearing a suit with a vest and tie. Even his hair was somewhat contained from its normal mess—brushed back and styled with product.

Donovan's eyes hit me. "I really needed a drink." His voice was a hoarse whisper. Then, he drank down two fingers of whiskey in a single shot.

"Hello!" A voice from the front room called in a high-pitched tone.

"Great. While you two ogle each other, I'll start showing in the guests." Kim smacked my ass with a hard *twap* as she passed. "Places, chicky."

Switching places with an awkward Donovan who disappeared with another drink, I reverted into my role. I tugged a bit at the fabric of my dress, unaccustomed to wearing one, or heels, usually favouring jeans and Chucks, and feeling like the hem was too short. Thankfully, I got to hide behind the kitchen island, which doubled as a bar top tonight.

Once a few people had arrived, the rest filtered in quickly. I was mixing drinks quicker than cheap night at The Lush. The problem was every Magic who approached me, including some of the Coveners I had already met, blinded me with oppressive light from their souls. I didn't know if I ever believed in the soul as an actual thing in the past, but now, how could I argue its existence when a part of them was visible to me?

With Aunt Lacey's vintage sunglasses in place, I received more compliments than questions about why I was wearing them indoors, at night. Of course, Denise placed her order and sneered when she asked about the glasses.

"Eye surgery," Kim told her before I had a chance to blow her off myself as I served her another Cosmo. A lesser person would have spit in her drink. Instead, I made her drink perfect and gave her nothing to complain about.

While babysitting Aunt Lacey's Sect, as per Kim's job that night, Kim and I played a game as I served, rating the brightness of each Magic and relaying the colour their soul emitted. Regardless of their race, gender, or genetic details, all I could focus on was each Magic's drink order and what their soul looked like. Donovan's was white with hints of green. White was a constant with the others to some degree, if they had any light at all. Not all did. Of those who did shine, many were different colours. Green like Donovan, blue, yellow...and I had no clue why. Kim made notes on her phone since her retro dress had pockets, and my hands were busy. I hoped I could decipher what the colours meant.

As the night moved on, my curiosity about the souls I saw waned as it became harder to withstand the onslaught. A headache had been knotted behind my eyes from the beginning of the night. Many times I had to swipe away tears from strain, smiling the whole time and trying to keep my eyes looking at the glass in my hand rather than at the souls around me.

"You look like you're about to fall over," Donovan said as I passed a gentleman a vodka tonic and thanked him for the tip. The drinks were free but the crowd was not above tipping for good service. Aunt Lacey had insisted on a tasteful tip jar, even when I argued about it.

"I'm managing." I peeked at him a moment and noticed his bloodshot eyes. Besides the two drinks before the party started, I hadn't served him.

"Are you high?" I asked him in a tone lower than the hum of the crowd and poured two glasses of wine for the woman in front of me. I didn't smell anything, so maybe he had another stash of booze somewhere else.

"Tired. Let me take over for a while." He placed his hand on the small of my back. I spilled wine when the gesture sent a shudder up my spine, then fumbled to clean it up when Donovan tried to help me. I apologized to the woman who was sweet and laughed off the whole thing.

"Nitsa!" Aunt Lacey's voice trilled somewhere in the room behind the line in front of me.

"Who's that?" I asked Donovan to distract from my overreaction. As it was, standing so close to him was making my hands shake.

"Another Coven Elder. Those two have been friends since forever. You'd think they never see each other, but they're always like that."

"Salix!" I heard my name called next as Aunt Lacey raised her hand, her other arm around a woman whose soul shined as brightly as my Coven leader's. Colourless, blinding white. Both souls radiated in the space around us like searching fingers. Magnificent and frightening.

"Go. I got this," Donovan told me.

"You sure?"

"Yup. You mingle and find a moment to rest your eyes."

His look of genuine caring tripped me up before I made my way around the island bar to the women waiting.

"Is this lovely our Soul Seer? And in my vintage lace sunglasses no less," the woman asked Aunt Lacey in a husky voice as she looked me over. Her dark, short, blunt haircut was straight out of the 1920s.

Aunt Lacey gave her a playful swat on the arm. "Yes, this is Salix, our Soul Seer, a magnificent beauty in *my* vintage lace sunglasses."

The woman crossed her arms. "I beg to differ."

"Salix, this is Nitsa, my stubborn, delusional ally."

"Hey!" Nitsa complained.

"As well as a fellow Coven Elder," Aunt Lacey added.

"It's nice to meet you." I held out a hand to shake, and Nitsa gave a whoop of a laugh, which showcased a hint of snaggletooth, and pulled me in for a quick embrace instead.

"I've heard so much about you, Salix. Such a gift, I can't even imagine."

"Open your eyes in a tanning bed and you'll get the gist."

She found this hilarious, though I was serious about the comparison.

"I did hear there is a pinch of a problem." She put a hand on her hip, the other fisted beneath her chin. "One too many soul mates?"

"What?"

"Nitsa," Aunt Lacey scolded.

"Right," she waved off her friend. "We'll stick to the one still sleeping."

"Caine?"

"Of course. The other is—"

"Nitsa," Aunt Lacey scolded again, and Nitsa huffed but I caught the way she looked over my shoulder at people waiting for drinks. Donovan was still serving a constant line of people, now in only his dress shirt and vest, his tie gone, collar open, sleeves rolled to his elbows.

"Fine then, Caine." Nitsa regained my attention.

"What about him?"

She straightened at my attitude. "Try not to take offence. Bold conversationalists make the greatest companions, yes?" I didn't respond, which she didn't like. "I was going to offer my services during the Awakening Ritual, though I may have heard wrong about the worth of those involved." She looked to Aunt Lacey and back to me.

"Be involved if you've already made promises, but realize, I don't know you. Bold friends *are* ones to keep close, but we're not friends. You can't talk about soul mates, brush if off as nothing, then expect me to play nice."

Nitsa's smile creased her eyes and flashed a hint of a snaggle-tooth. "You are everything my dear friend promised."

Now I was really confused.

"You study the mind and behaviours of others. Better to learn early and save yourself the exhaustion empty relationships inflict. Though personal experience is our best teacher, isn't it?"

She looked at me like she knew everything about me, and I got the feeling she did.

"Yes, it is," I answered heavy-hearted, liking her much more than a few seconds ago.

Needing a moment, I excused myself to go to the bathroom, thankfully unoccupied, and took that break Donovan suggested. In a swimmer's chlorine-like haze, I removed the glasses and put them on the counter. The bridge of my nose ached. My make-up was smudged from swiping at my eyes as they watered.

Shaking off what Nitsa said and concentrating on her invitation to assist with the Awakening Ritual helped and, since I couldn't hang out in the bathroom all night, I used the facilities and washed my hands. I donned my sunglasses, ready to get back behind the bar.

Passing down the small hallway, Kim caught my attention with a wave, her dim glow awash in the sea of illuminated souls. Partway to each other, the doorbell rang. Weird since the door was always unlocked. Detouring to usher in the next guest, Kim opened the door with a spritely hello, then stepped aside.

The sight of the man on the porch's soul glow punched me in the solar plexus. I couldn't speak, muted by the threat standing feet from Kim, my voice too crippled to warn her. When I could breathe, it sounded like a gasp as magic sprung awake in my chest, cramping my lungs, making me dizzy.

The man's dark eyes looked straight into mine, at first curious, until a grin full of crocodile teeth creased deep wrinkles around his eyes. "A Soul Seer." His voice was full of gravel and an unsettling satisfaction.

19

WORTH MORE THAN YOU KNOW

Other Magics took notice of the man at Aunt Lacey's door as well as my reaction to him. Voices of the Coven rose, magic snapping the atmosphere like a whip, buckling my knees as I grasped my stomach and hinged over.

"A Seedling Soul Seer. How delicious." The smiling man let out a booming laugh that thrummed the already-vibrating intensity in the air.

All attention now on the door, the man raised his hands in a mock surrender before smug laughter boomed again. He adjusted the lapels of his suit jacket and stuck his hands in his dress pant pockets as a sweat broke over my skin.

What the tits? Get your shit together, Sophie.

Hands on my shoulder hit me with a spike of power and my head went down while my back arched until I felt a hand there as well. Donovan bent over me looking strung out, eyes wide and questioning before they turned venomous and fixed on the man at the door.

"Loring," Aunt Lacey spoke above the crowd, taking a step forward to reach the middle of the room. Nitsa was behind her with two other men. "This breaks—"

"What?" Loring barked. "The treaty? Come now, Elsa. You would cease to find meaning without my burr in your hide."

Elsa? Why would he call Aunt Lacey Elsa?

Aunt Lacey remained quiet, her expression conveying all the confidence and badassery I failed at. I leaned into Donovan when my equilibrium decided to punch out for the day. My skin trembled as I fought to gain control, my body tingling with the constant oppression of power emanated from those around me.

Loring was asked something, but I was too busy forcing myself to stand to hear what, only catching his gravelly response.

"Tales of elusive Coven Elders gathering in this garish replica of yours found my ears, Elsa."

Nitsa gave a throaty laugh. "Why don't you join us, old friend?"

Loring's grin grew, heavy creases enveloped his face. "Ha!" He barked a laugh and stepped forward. Kim matched his movement as she walked backward. Instead of entering the house, Loring surveyed the frame, licked his fingertip, and inched toward the empty space of the threshold.

Loring splayed his fingers and a man flew toward him as if pulled by an invisible string.

Shrill voices cried out as the man landed on the porch at Loring's feet. A few Coveners surged forward as more of Loring's people appeared behind him like they'd always been there: two redheaded beasts of men who eclipsed the suburban street behind them, and another man with dark hair, overshadowed by the first two.

The surging Coveners stopped short when Loring slammed a hand on the forehead of the man at his feet. The Covener grunted in pain, before Loring had him up in the air again. Tossed back toward the door, the man hit the empty threshold like he'd hit solid wood.

Light blinded me, and the man's screams were deafening.

It looked like he was being fried alive.

Pain shot through my thighs as my knees hit the floor, another spike of power blindsiding me and taking Donovan down with me. Above the screams of the man were the cries of the crowd and

Loring's bellowing, cruel laugh. When the screaming man quieted, Loring's laughter continued. A bright light burst from the man's body, and he ragdolled onto the floor. The loss of power in the room gave me my body back.

"So many uses..." I heard the thick gravel in my head, Loring's mouth never moving. I felt that smile over every inch of me.

His hand was out again. My body shot across the floor toward the door. I spun onto my stomach with flailing hands to grab Kim, seeing Donovan's panicked expression as he reached out from the floor where we had fallen.

I stopped only when I slid into the dead body spewing a pool of blood in Aunt Lacey's foyer. My spine cracked as I was lifted off the ground, the dead man's blood dripping down my thighs and toes.

The sensation of being pulled in different directions had the muscles in my chest seizing, my right arm cranked backward, stretching my shoulder muscle. I craned behind me and saw Donovan on the floor, straining backward, pulling on an invisible rope, his face red with effort. My left hand was pulled forward. Loring had used more of his power to bring my hand forward, examining Nya's ring before his dark eyes looked up at mine.

"Fascinating. You're worth more than you know, Soul Seer."

The man in shadow behind the red-headed beasts moved forward a step. I caught his eyes. Grey. An image of Caine came to mind.

"You're the infiltrator," Loring said. "Lost cause, Seer. Climbing trees won't save you."

Anger enveloped me. He knew about Caine.

Dangling in the air, I was still trapped in his grip. Loring's face screwed up and his free hand slapped down on the frame of the door. The wood splintered in a flash of light that caused a spike of power, overwhelming me.

I couldn't hold onto it anymore, and power flushed from my feet to my head, busting out of whatever cage trapped it inside me.

Blinking and struggling to lift my head, my body ached all over.

What happened?

My chest burned, and I remembered losing control. Now I was on the floor, looking into the charred, empty sockets of the dead man.

Loring.

I remembered him killing the man. I didn't understand how, but he did, and now the warmth of the dead man's blood soaked through my dress.

I scrambled to get away, bowling down Kim and Donovan in the process. I realized Aunt Lacey, Nitsa, and others from the party had gathered around me.

Still panicking, I searched the doorway, a piece of the framing hanging sharp and loose.

"He fled, Salix," Aunt Lacey told me. "You're safe now."

"Of course he fled," Nitsa said to a tall, blond man in a crisp navy suit.

"Loring will forever flee from those of greater strength," the blond man stated with pomp. His sharp features were as rigid as his ice blue eyes, his soul as bright as the woman next to him.

"I'm glad your ego's still intact." I earned myself a room full of attention as I stood and wobbled on my feet. Kim reached out to grab me, blood colouring her palms. "That fucker walked up to the goddamned door, fried this dude, threw me around, gloated about Caine and whatever else, and took off. What the fuck are you so proud about?"

Nitsa's lips pursed as she disguised a laugh. The man was clearly insulted, as I stared him down while trying not to pay attention to the feeling of blood running down my thigh.

"Profanity aside, I must agree." A dark-skinned man with a thick African accent and eye-piercing soul leaned on a cane. "What well does your endless pride sprout from, Hallden?"

"From the soil of centuries of success, Roon. Without the need to be questioned by a Seedling." His cold stare slid my way.

I couldn't believe them. "I don't care how old you are!"

"Sophie," Kim warned.

"No." I stood firm, blinking to offset the eye-watering effect of all the souls around me. "Someone needs to tell me what the fuck just happened and why no one's going after that piece of shit."

"While I love a feisty woman,"—Nitsa took a step toward me—"you need to watch how you address your Coven Elders in the company of the flock."

So Hallden and Roon were also Elders. I speared her with a look. "Well, my Coven Elders were as useful as the dead guy nobody seems to be making a fuss about. Or is death normal for you? For your Coven?"

"Loss is never without its appropriate time to grieve," Nitsa said.

"Appropriate? What are you waiting for? You let Loring get away."

"The moment we got close, Loring and his goons would have zipped back through the portal they used to arrive here." Nitsa fluttered a hand, dismissing my argument. "We gathered to discuss recent threats. Loring made sure we understood there was no question who the threat is. He thrust an image of evil intent into this man to ensure the spell would react."

"What spell?"

"The spell safeguarding this dwelling. You think a Coven Elder would allow herself and her Sect to gather without safety provisions?"

Now I understood why Aunt Lacey's door was always unlocked. A spell prevented Magics like Loring from entering. I thought back to my grandmother and her thoughts on where the power came from. After seeing Loring and his goons, I understood why Grandma Lizzie associated magic with the Devil.

"His desire for an audience is never-ending." Nitsa rolled her eyes. "Now watch that saucy tongue of yours and get cleaned up. We can chat afterwards."

I hesitated. "Wait...portal?"

Nitsa crossed her arms and lifted a dark, sculpted eyebrow that told me how uneducated I was about the world I now belonged to.

My rebellion drained into exhaustion as I followed Kim upstairs to take a shower that washed away the blood of a dead man whose name I didn't even know. An hour ago I'd served him a drink, and now he was a puddle of a human. My hands shook the entire time I showered with products that weren't mine. The scents were off, making me restless.

After pulling myself together, I went downstairs to find the Coveners in groups of serious conversation, their expressions drawn. The body of the dead man and his blood had been sanitized from the scene, and the doorframe was now intact. I took a peek at it and saw what I had missed before. I ran my fingers along grooved lettering I spotted in a few places, as on Aunt Lacey's dress during my Initiation. Once painted over in a matte finish, the words blended into the frame.

A few feet into the kitchen, Donovan handed me a drink, something golden in a short glass I downed in one gulp. I felt the heat of whiskey burning a path down to my stomach. "Thanks."

He nodded but didn't look happy. Restrained anger and something else glimmered in his eyes, and he seemed to have a hard time looking at me.

"Dead guy is gone."

"Yup," Donovan said.

"Gone where? Aunt Lacey doesn't have a wood chipper."

"Doesn't need one. He's already being returned to his family so they can do what they need to stage his death for the police."

"Stage it?"

"Bringing Blind police here is out of the question."

Whatever the setup it would have to involve a lot of juice to explain what was left of the man. This was, no doubt, not the first time they staged a crime scene and reminded me of seeing the Lush and how they sanitized that scene as well.

Before the memory of Jack took me to a dark place, I had more important things to worry about.

"We have to do the Awakening Ritual tonight," I told anyone

who would listen. "I can't wait. Loring knows something about Caine. He said—"

"We heard him, Salix," Aunt Lacey said. "His Tainted involvement complicates matters."

"Tainted?"

"Evil."

"Not always," Nitsa said.

"Debatable." Aunt Lacey gave her friend a look that ended the thread of conversation.

"Whatever. Tainted, dirty, butt-fuck ugly, either way, we have the Sect and Elders here tonight."

"Why should we risk any of our members for one outside our flock?" Hallden asked.

"Is this when I say I can't teach assholes empathy?"

"Empathy for a Blind man who became a target of one our great enemies?"

Hallden's eyes narrowed as I stepped toward him. "Maybe ask yourself what Loring would want with a Blind man. Or maybe why Aunt Lacey would waste her time with all the help she's given that Blind man so far. I won't pretend to know much about any of all this, but I've been dreaming about him while he's in a sleeping curse."

Aunt Lacey came into my peripheral vision. "On my word, fellow Elder, this man is more than the simple Blind. Explanation at this point is impossible without reeling Caine from his dream state, though I assure you and all our flock of the importance of such risk."

"Plus, you want to reduce the chances of your only Soul Seer being sucked into some dream realm, no? Without your help, who knows what the outcome might be."

Hallden wasn't a man of apologies, so I took his raised brows and glare at Aunt Lacey to mean he was following his co-Elders lead.

Aunt Lacey grabbed my hands, squeezing them. "You are more than your talent, Salix. I would be honoured to have you in my life even if you were Blind. Loring speaks of Magics like commodities.

Collects and trades for those talents he deems invaluable. That is not our Coven's way."

"Fine, but I need this to happen tonight."

We stared into each other's eyes, waiting for the other to relent. I wasn't giving up. I couldn't go on dreaming of Caine, watching him be tortured with the screaming of his brother, seeing the hope in his eyes that he could find Cole after all this time. They were right, it was a sleeping curse, and we needed to break it tonight.

The exhale and slight slump of my Coven leader's shoulders told me I'd won. Before she could say anything, I wrapped my arms around her in thanks.

"I know it doesn't mean I'll survive, but thank you for trying."

She held me tighter, and we stood entwined a moment.

Settled on having the Awakening Ritual that night, I went out back for some fresh air and to give my aching eyes and pounding brain a break. A few Coveners sat at the patio set smoking, so I went to the other side of the yard and found Bosco snoozing in the grass. As I came closer and called his name, his sleepy eyes opened, his curly tail going nuts before he stretched and howled at me.

"Hey, buddy."

I sat with him, wearing the clothes I'd arrived in. The beautiful dress was now in the garbage since I could never wear it again without thinking of the dead guy.

Someone died today and people were smoking and laughing and carrying on like nothing happened. Did the man have children? I hadn't known him, would never get the chance to, and he would never get the chance to live out his life because some dickhead with a grudge was sending a message.

My throat thickened, upset at the thought of leaving Bosco behind if I failed the Awakening Ritual tonight. I swallowed and smoothed Bosco's fur, trying not to get emotional. My family might be told, if Aunt Lacey would let them. Hell, Serena would be all over it and lead them right to Aunt Lacey's doorstep. Bosco would never understand why his girl didn't return. Somehow I found that most heartbreaking.

Bosco looked toward the door. I followed his gaze to Donovan. I squinted at his white and green gleam; it made him look like he was floating as he walked.

"If this is another attempt to talk me out of doing the ritual, be warned, you will annoy the fuck out of me, and I will walk away."

Donovan's cheeks dimpled. "Nah, you're set on that. But I do need to tell you something."

"Do you now?" My sarcasm unleashed.

The dimples faded as his expression became serious. He took a seat across from me. "You've asked before, now I'm telling you. Or getting annoyed and walking away, your choice?" The dimple flash said he wasn't going anywhere, yet his nervousness was palpable, and I didn't know if I wanted to hear what he thought he needed to say.

He readjusted his seat. "Give me your hand."

"Another palm reading?"

His head tilted. "We've established I can do more than read palms. Stop being a brat."

I smiled and gave him my hand. He flinched as I've seen him do before. I pulled my hand back, and he seemed to come out of it.

"I saw the day you got Bosco," he told me. "He was too small to be sold, but you took him anyway because you were afraid the people your ex got him from would mistreat him."

I felt my mouth open. "You saw—"

"Images, visions, whatever, every time I touch people. It's a version of psychometry. Reading palms is an easy cover since it requires contact, but if a turtle could memorize a book, it could palm read. Plus, palm reading doesn't freak people out as much. I see a sliver of their past, usually connected to a wayward thought. Happens with objects too. You're out here with Bosco, so it's not surprising what I saw was about him."

I crossed my arms. "So, you've seen other stuff. About me?"

He nodded. "Now that you've released your power, it's worse."

"Worse?"

"Stronger."

I nodded. "What else have you seen?"

"More than I wanted." His answer was too quick.

I lifted an eyebrow, urging him to continue while I remained on the fence about whether I wanted to know.

"Your ex. How he treated you. His addiction. His controlling—"

"I got it," I barked, needing him to stop. I couldn't hear a second more. I lived it long enough to know exactly what Donovan saw. I shuddered at the thought of him knowing. I thought Aunt Lacey got a glimpse of my thoughts while healing me, but I don't know what she saw. Seemed Donovan knew everything. His knowing this made me feel so raw and exposed that my skin itched. I contemplated leaving.

"We're supposed to be together." Donovan put his hand on my thigh with enough pressure to stop me from leaving, though I never tried, or at least I didn't think I did. "I don't mean that in a creepy, romantic way. I'm not that guy."

"Sure sounds like you're that guy."

"I'm not." He paused, pulled his hand back, and I waited, heart pounding. "When I touch you...I see a time when we used to be together. The way you used to look at me, like a husband. Sometimes they're mixed with images of how you look at Caine, though not as much, thankfully. Sometimes of your ex before things got bad, though I question how you saw anything in the jackass."

I was shocked, though I didn't take offence. After I was left with all of my electronics stolen and pawned, he fled the province, and I found out the extent of his drug problem. I wondered what I saw in him too.

"I wasn't lying when I said it before I kissed you. Before you kissed me back, I might add." The dimpled grin returned. "Between my ability and Aunt Lacey telling me so, it gets spelled out pretty clear. We used to be together and we should be now."

He looked at me with a yearning I couldn't escape.

"Dear heart."

He nodded.

"And you've known this for how long?" I asked him.

"Since the night we healed you. I tried to tie red yarn around your neck and got a flash. It freaked my shit. Later, I held your hand and was *flooded* by all this imagery." His gaze moved in the space around us. "Like watching an autobiography I never had a hand in making. Our names were different, we lived in a different country, I think, but we were together, and it all made sense. Whatever the healing triggered in you, it allowed me to see so much."

I waited for something in his expression to call him out as a liar. I saw nothing but grave honesty.

"And now," he sighed, "I have to suck it up and help you save Caine, knowing that as much as I care about you and as much as you care about him, none of it matters because you could die, and that outweighs all of this heartsick bullshit."

He was right, none of it mattered, but he still felt compelled to tell me regardless. I felt like a shmuck for it being an issue with so much at stake.

I put aside the thoughts of both guys, attempting to focus on the importance of the ritual and staving off hyperventilation.

Once it was time to get back inside, I squeezed Bosco before putting him back in the grass. Donovan looked at me with sympathy-soaked eyes. I tried to breathe away the encroaching tears and remain positive for the sake of the night's outcome, stopping him before we got within earshot of those on the patio set.

"If something goes wrong down there, I *need* you to take care of Bosco until you can get a hold of Serena." My voice hitched, and Donovan's lips twitched with a smile. "Kim can get into my apartment. She can help you too, but I need you to call Serena and tell her everything. She'll be pissed, but at least she'll know the truth. If I'm trapped in the dream, she can bring my parents to the hospital to see Caine's mom, and see Caine's and my condition, and at least not worry about me. They'll know I'm not scared or alone."

It took everything in me to fight back tears, but I managed. Could

I trust this in Donovan's hands? I hoped so. My family needed to know I wasn't some medical mystery, without an accident like Caine's to justify my unconsciousness.

Donovan pulled me into a hug, hesitant as he wrapped me in his arms. He was tense. This time I remained in his grasp, resting my head on his strong shoulder, finding my own strength while enveloped by him.

"Don't worry, I know you can do this." Donovan's voice was strained.

I pulled back. "Just promise."

"I promise, but I'm telling you, you *can* do this. Everything will be done to make sure you make it out." He grinned, but I saw fear in his smiling eyes.

CLIMBING TREES WON'T SAVE YOU

The basement was stuffed with members of the Sect, other Coveners, plus Nitsa and the two other Elders, Hallden and Roon. In the middle was my nest again, a small, deep-red pillow inside the oblong shape. As I sat surrounded by the light and colour of my fellow Covener's souls, Aunt Lacey wrapped some willow around a thicker branch, murmuring something in a different language, then instructed me to place it underneath the small pillow.

How did they expect me to fall asleep?

The Coveners moved into three circles, a tighter one around me consisting of Donovan on my left, Kim on my right with others between them. Another, a larger circle around the inner circle consisting of the majority of the Coveners. The four Coven Elders then stood spaced out surrounding all of us, Aunt Lacey holding the grimoire with the Coven symbol stitched into the leather.

A teacup was passed to Kim and then handed to me. "What'd you put in it?" I asked Aunt Lacey, hearing Donovan's low laugh.

She smiled. "Sleeping herbs."

I was never one to take sedatives, but the ritual called for me to connect with Caine, which meant I had to sleep. As exhausted as I was, that wouldn't happen with all these people watching me, so I drank it down like a shot, barely allowing it to graze my tongue. The liquid scalded my throat all the way down, making me cough and my eyes water.

I laid down, trying to instruct every muscle to stop gyrating so I could relax. I felt like an open-mouthed swine laid out for a feast in front of Donovan after what he'd told me. His stare was tangible as I closed my eyes.

The effects of the tea smacked me a good one, and I tried to wrestle my eyelids open. They were weighed down with leaded heaviness. The tea was potent. My vision was in and out of focus, like a broken camera.

Aunt Lacey spoke as I began drifting away, her voice distorted in my ears. "Those in the inner circle, place your hands on Salix's body. Wiccum, Wend, hold her hands. Those behind them, place your hands on the shoulders of those in the inner circle," Aunt Lacey instructed. "Do you remember what to do, Salix?"

I looked up at Donovan, my eyelids drooping, and squeezed his hand back, watching as his furrowed brows shadowed his unfocused, dark eyes.

Somehow I knew, maybe from what happened in the backyard or the sudden look in his eyes as they refocused on me, that he was there for me in the only way he was capable. His hand anchored mine as my surroundings took on a dream-like quality and moved like the height of a booze-filled night—it was worse than Kim's steam-mix.

"Do you remember what you need to do, Salix?" Aunt Lacey prompted again.

With my eyes closed, I recounted the steps. Falling to the tea's effects was taking what felt like a long time as I replayed my list of responsibilities over and over out loud, even though no one asked me to. I thought it was out loud though I was uncertain if my lips moved, feeling only the warmth of Donovan's hand holding me securely grounded as I lost myself to the tea.

Every part of me had given up the fight as my body languished.

Now I barely registered the spectators and their hands touching my body.

Suddenly, Donovan was gone. His touch disappeared, along with the sound of my voice. As I pried my leaded eyelids open, I knew I was no longer in the safety of Donovan's and Kim's grasp.

Obscured by overcast weather, the park was bathed in a light rain. I shivered in the slight breeze. The droplets were sparing, though large, as they dappled my body and splashed in depressions of muddy gravel.

I searched for Caine, but he found me first and ran to me, wrapping his long arms around me in a big hug, picking me up off my feet again. I held on tight, unable to comprehend being drawn to Donovan, considering my feelings for Caine.

I was not a fickle person by nature and hated this duality.

He placed me gently on my bare feet. "Are you okay? I saw you fall but you disappeared before I could—"

"Stop, I'm fine, but we have to get set up. The Awakening Ritual is happening right now." He stared at me in disbelief as I sped on. "The friends I told you about are good to go, but we need to do some things here first. You need to listen to *everything* I say. Can you do that?"

He nodded.

I ran to the nearest willow and attempted to break off some of its weeping branches. Instead of a clean break, my hands slipped down the water-soaked branch, stripping off its tiny leaves and causing a friction burn to sting my hands. I hissed a curse and turned to Caine. "We need to create a circle with these branches big enough that we can both sit inside it."

At first, Caine just stared at me. A moment passed before he ripped off a bunch all at once. I took them from him and began to knot and weave the branches when creek water started to rise over my toes.

"Come on." Caine grabbed my hand to pull me toward a tree, I assumed to climb it like before.

Loring's dark words came back to me, *"Lost cause, Seer. Climbing trees won't save you,"* and I tore my hand out of his.

"No! We have to stay down here." I blinked against the falling water, the rain now picking up speed.

"The water is rising."

"Just help me with this."

We didn't have time to argue. We grabbed the willow branches and troubleshot ways to get them to stay together, mirroring the nest back in the basement. It was less full and lacked finesse, but it would have to do.

Water grazed the back of my knees as we held the willow circle tight around our hips, forcing us close together.

"Now what?" Caine asked, looking at the rising water.

I tried to think of my objectives. With clumsy, wet fingers I spun my necklace around, fumbling with the clasp to remove it and wrap it around my wrist so the triquetra charm hung in my palm. I grabbed Caine's hands and watched as a smile crossed his lips, making it diffi-cult to focus on the worse to come.

As water lapped my thighs, I remembered something important. "Listen. Aunt Lacey said we'll be faced with whatever is holding you in this place, and she doesn't know what that is. But, and this is the most important part, Caine, whatever it is, you *have* to stay in this circle."

"That doesn't make sense, but okay."

"To be honest, it doesn't make sense to me either, but she said if you leave it, you could be trapped here forever and you may suck me in here with you." This may have been a negative or a positive for him, but I couldn't stay in this park until our bodies withered away in hospital beds.

"Would that be so bad?"

I held his hands steadfast and chose my words carefully. "I have family. I'd rather see them, and possibly have you a part of that, than stay here and let go of everything else."

He nodded in response.

Moments ticked by, the water rising to my hips, high enough that the willow circle was floating on top of the water instead of snug around us. My lower extremities were numb, the rest shook in the cold as time kept passing without anything happening, just rising water. I did my part, now it felt like the Coven was slacking in fulfilling theirs.

Pins and needles enveloped my waist as the cold water dipped into my belly-button, covering my tender sides and snaking up my ribs. Before long, it was grazing my breasts and panic began to set in.

"It doesn't usually get this deep," I yelled over the rain.

"No, it doesn't. Is it supposed to take this long?"

"No fucking clue." My chin shook and garbled my words.

"That's not very comforting."

"No kidding, but I left the manual back in my nest."

"Your nest?"

"A nest and sleepy tea got me here. This is what I was told to do, so we wait until something happens, and you keep your ass in this circle. Clear?"

"If the water gets any higher, it's not going to be my choice."

He was right. The rising water was our biggest threat. But we needed to stay together and within the circle. To ensure we did, he held my hand with the charm in our palms, our bodies pressed together as our other hands held onto the willow circle as it rose with the waterline.

Before long, that was no longer an option as the water grazed my chin.

Thankfully, Caine was tall. I wrapped my left arm around his strong shoulders, my legs around his waist to keep above the creek water, while he held onto the willow circle. With my muscles clenched and my limbs numb, I might have been crushing his ribs, but he wasn't complaining and I refused to drown in this place.

Lightning struck above us, thunder following in a crash that hammered my eardrums. The rain fell in sheets of water that blinded me, my hair whipped around. I had to bury my face into the crook of his neck to avoid inhaling frigid water.

Caine may have been tall, but he was running out of height. The water was now up to his throat and climbing. With our hands still clasped between our bodies, he let go of the willow circle floating around us to hold me tighter, his arm around me as I interlocked my feet around him to keep me in place. The trees and greenery around us were only visible when lightning struck.

Tilting our heads to keep our mouths above water, I was panting when Caine shoved the willow circle under the water and beneath our armpits to keep us within it. Above the roar of the rain, he yelled into my ear, "I'm so sorry, Sophie. I've killed us both!"

Leaded with sadness for this man who blamed himself for too much, I tried to make him see the truth. "You never killed anyone." Water rushed into my mouth, choking me. It was time to face the fact that the water was about to swallow us. "Hold on!"

Somehow Caine found strength to embrace me tighter, his heart beating against our clasped hands. We each took a deep breath, our last before the creek water rose above our heads. The water was icy as it filled my sinuses and a spray of bubbles escaped me.

My lungs screamed as I disengaged my legs from around Caine to swim to the surface while still holding his hand, careful not to lose the willow circle around us. The harder I tried, the weaker and heavier I felt, and the higher the water line grew. Too far above us, safety and oxygen were a luxury, as was the park floor that we no longer felt. The sense of floating in some black abyss at the bottom of an ocean was more terrifying than the thought of some dark figuring stalking me in my dreams.

Moments from losing the battle and succumbing to Caine's sleeping curse, my palm around the necklace warmed. Not burning, only a small perceptible difference against my icy skin, like it was raised to a campfire. Through the nothingness that encapsulated us, I lifted our clasped hands in front of us and saw light escape the spaces between our fingers, illuminating Caine's wide, terrified expression. Those grey eyes connected with mine in a question I could only guess at. Was this normal? I had no clue, but it was something different than drowning and as the warmth grew, I resisted the urge to let the necklace go by clutching Caine's hand tighter.

My vision spotted from the lack of oxygen, my knees pulled up from the pain in my chest as warmth now emanated from deep inside me. More of my oxygen reserves bubbled from my lips as I fought against a cough by clasping my hand over my mouth. I wasn't the only one struggling as bubbles of air escape from Caine's lips and nose. He refused to give up and fought to bring us to the surface, which seemed to only get farther away.

With my vision failing me, the heat grew between our palms as well as in my chest. I now recognized it as my power. Our tight grip loosened as Caine struggled to find the surface.

The pain in my chest stole every last reserve my lungs held, and the inky abyss swallowed us.

21

———

GIVING EVERYTHING

Donovan

An image of Sophie immersed in water and clinging to Caine clouded my vision as it did for everyone in the basement. Roon had fixed a spell to let us see what we were fighting for. It overrode my psychometric connection to me and Sophie's past. Roon probably figured if the Coveners could see who they were potentially killing, they would put some effort into saving them.

Seeing Sophie frantic to get the willow circle together, watching through her eyes as she peered around in the darkness, hearing the desperation in her voice as she waited for something to happen, was the most helpless I had felt in a long time. Why was this happening to her? Because she's a vessel? Because this dick attached himself to her and refused to let go? She didn't deserve this. Regardless of the reason, I needed to get her out of there. No way was I sitting here with a thumb up my ass while she drowned. I couldn't watch that without walking away half the person I was, and that was already less than she deserved.

"Wend, focus," I heard Aunt Lacey's voice in my head.

"It's not enough," I responded out loud.

"What?" Kim asked. She was blinded by what Roon was showing us, but still able to hear me.

"Something should be happening by now. I don't feel her. Shouldn't we be able to feel her? Her energy? Something?"

No one answered, which meant I was right. Even with so many Magics amassed in the basement, we weren't enough.

"Hold on," Kim said.

I took my hands off of Sophie so the sight of her in the park would drop from my vision. Kim was digging in the closet for something, taking out ingredients and muddling them together into a paste. She added more liquid to fill out the mixture and make it a more workable substance.

"I'm adding this to better connect us with Sophie." Kim moved around the circles, using the dark concoction to draw a line down everyone's forehead, with four straight lines jutting out from the side. I knew it as the Celtic symbol for the willow tree.

The difference was so immediate, I was impressed. Even Seedlings with little to no talent were tapped for more power, and the energy in the room amped up to the point it made me heady.

When Kim came around to me to add the symbol, the moment her finger touched my flesh I was hit with a vision.

I expected one, but not the one I got.

What I saw was a hospital room, not as depressing as I thought, though the body in the bed I saw was Caine. Or a version of the guy I saw in Sophie's dream world. Sunken features, sallow skin, little to no muscle mass, machines breathing for him, and this was a vision of whenever Kim saw him last. If he was any worse, the guy's body wouldn't survive the shock of waking up when the spell snapped him out of his sleeping curse, let alone be any more useful than a sack of potatoes after years of muscular atrophy.

I had seen too many die because Magics thought their power was a cure-all and ignored the body's natural reactions. Shock is a killer. If we didn't heal him before he woke up, shock would hit Caine before any of us was in his hospital room to attempt to save him from it.

My telepathy was flabby since I'd gone so long with my powers bound and Aunt Lacey was too focused on the vision of Sophie's dream and blocking the rest out to better focus on Sophie. I needed to change this.

I popped up out of my seat and stepped over the clasped arms of the sitting Coveners and took a more hands-on approach. When I touched her sleeve, it only took a moment for her to open her eyes and address me.

I told her what I thought of Caine's condition and what I could do about it. She paused a moment.

"Look ahead, can you see it? See what happens when he wakes up?"

Her eyes shifted from mine as they sought out what I needed. Before she answered, her lips parted on a gasp, and I knew I was right. Caine needed to be healed.

Without waiting, I raced back to my spot and changed tactics. If Caine died, and Sophie survived, she would never forgive herself. I would do anything to save her from that scar. She had enough already.

I touched her and reconnected with Roon's spell, seeing her now fighting to stay above the water as she and Caine clung to each other. The water was a slow-rising enemy, threatening to snuff them out. Able to see Caine through Sophie's eyes, and feeling the amp in power that Kim's spell provided, I felt a hint of Caine under Sophie's grasp and this was enough. Channelling what I could from the others in the room, I focused the energy into Caine and healing him, hoping to connect to his body in real life as we were with Sophie and as Sophie was attempting to do to wake him up.

Kim said something about the necklace glowing, that her spell was working, and I saw it too, using everything I could to get this done to make sure both came out alive.

When Gwen on my left slumped forward, I felt the energy wane a bit. I was channeling too much from the group. Being in the circle meant giving everything. Another dropped. They weren't dead. They'd wake up, but for now I needed more energy and took it from any source I could, moving around the room starting with those closest to me until they gave everything they could. The Elders weren't stopping me, and no complaints meant I was free to keep going, so I did.

I heard a few more bodies drop and didn't stop.

"Whatever you're doing, it's taking too much from people," Kim said. "We need them to help Sophie."

I ignored her, easy to do when I had more important shit to worry about than her opinion. The rest of them were working on Sophie, my doing this for Caine wouldn't take away from that. I didn't think.

Sophie was underwater now. I didn't know if I had done enough for Caine, I had no way to tell, and Kim was getting more frantic with every dropped body. What I was doing was helping Sophie in other ways too, I was sure of it. She was connected to Caine, anything that helped him helped her. Sophie's panic caused bubbles of air to blind her view of the glowing necklace in her and Caine's clasped hands. When I lost sight of Caine's face as Sophie's vision spotted and waned, I began to second-guess my tactics.

"Donovan!" Kim yelled at me.

I snapped out of my task and shifted my energy directly into Sophie. I heard Kim gasp. The energy I was packing joined with the others as Sophie's vision went dark.

22

———

HAVE FAITH

A floating sensation surrounded me, a weightless peace I let swaddle me until lead and ice were injected into my veins. My body seized, muscles clenched, as I sputtered into consciousness.

Opening my eyes, I saw trees around me, clouds above me, and felt rain dapple my face as I panted and coughed water from my lungs.

"You're alive," a relief-filled voice said as my body was hugged tightly.

When he pulled back, I saw Caine's pinched expression, his eyes filled with worry as I realized what had happened. I'd drowned, but somehow, was now alive and still in the park.

"Is it over?" I asked.

"You tell me."

I sat up and realized I was in his lap, the willow circle still around us. The fact it remained intact was a miracle.

"Do you feel different?" I asked him.

He shook his head, looking exhausted as he leaned into a hand that dug into the mud of the park floor.

If the Awakening Ritual was over, I thought that meant he should be awake.

Unless...

A moment of thinking the ritual failed railed through me and created a rock in my gut.

No. I couldn't be stuck in this place. This could not be it. It couldn't be.

I rose up on my knees and looked around. The clouds were a bit lighter than before, no more thunder or lightning, but the rain still fell. It was as it was before the water started rising.

Please, no.

I thought about my family and the devastation that losing me to a medically-unexplained coma could cause. I thought about Bosco in Aunt Lacey's backyard, still playing or snoozing, unaware of my failure, never understanding why I abandoned him. Even thoughts of Kim and Donovan flitted into my thoughts, my friend who brought me into the Coven life and the man with hidden talents who I shared a past life with, both back in the basement holding onto my limp hands and waiting for me to open my eyes.

A hiccup-like sob left my lips. A hand on my elbow brought me into Caine's arms. He held me tightly and smoothed my soaked hair, rocking us without words for the consoling we both needed. He'd spent years in the park, this would be new for me, and his embrace came with an apology that did little more than warm my chilled bones.

"CAINE!"

Our heads snapped up at the sound of Cole's voice. The continued torture of Caine's brother was agonizing, the voice closer than I had ever heard before.

Heat against my leg made me look down to find my necklace hanging limp around my arm, the now-illuminated charm resting on my leg.

The ritual wasn't over.

We hadn't failed.

"Cole!" Caine screamed for his brother. His desperation was a spear of guilt.

He scrambled to get me off of him so he could stand. I grabbed his arm and tried to wrap myself around him.

"Don't leave the circle! It's not over!"

"He can come with us! Cole!"

The atmosphere above us shifted. The sky grew darker, the clouds thickening and turning black. The rain quickened and grew violent. I shut my eyes as the pellets beat against my face. A fierce wind battered our sodden bodies, and my hair whirled around my face as I fought to keep a hold of Caine.

My ability to keep him in the circle was baffling. Somehow, I had exaggerated strength that I'd never possessed outside of the dream world. Push-ups were an issue for me, grappling a two-hundred plus pound man bent on doing everything to prevent being tied down was impossible.

"No, he can't, Caine. He can't!"

I manoeuvred myself between him and the voice.

"Caine! Caine! Where are you?!"

"We can't leave him here! He'll be trapped!"

Only that voice could get Caine away from the circle, and I needed him to stay put. This was what was keeping Caine in this place: the fear of leaving his brother behind. I needed him to understand Cole was dead, the voice an illusion, a manifestation of his denial. Whatever Caine saw was off in the distance behind me, but Caine's screaming painted a picture of what tortured him. His tow-headed brother, injured and in pain, somewhere far off in the distance, pleading for rescue.

I struggled to keep him circle-bound as wind and water battered us. With my eyes closed, I swore Caine pushing against me caused the muddy earth to fold around my feet. The earth held onto my ankles like shackles, keeping our bodies rooted.

"It's not him! You would have seen him by now if it was!"

Caine wasn't hearing me. His fingers dug into my skin with

bruising pressure as he tried to throw me off of him. Scream after scream, Caine hollered for Cole, his voice straining to best the wind and assure his brother he wouldn't leave him, that Cole should come find us, follow Caine's voice. I was the only thing stopping Caine from racing off to save his brother.

My bare feet slipped on the mud beneath us as he pushed against me like a football player. I dug in deeper to keep him in place, frantic not to lose my hold as he continued to scream for his brother and pleaded with me to let him go.

Hurting Caine would be the only way. Not physically, he could end me cleanly, but my body was shaking with exhaustion, and what I realized was also a dose of my magic, and I couldn't bank on this otherworldly strength lasting.

Terrified, my muscles burned as I yelled, "He's dead, Caine. Cole's dead!" My voice was hoarse. "The accident...you lost control. You killed him! Cole's dead because of you. He's not here. He drowned and he's never coming back!"

I craned my neck up to see his gaze fixed on the distance, his expression a mask of torment. With his weight easing off my shoulder, I let my hold loosen and grabbed his face, forcing him to focus on me. My hands vibrated with power I had little control over. He conceded for only a second. It was all I needed.

"Your mother buried Cole years ago." I strained to speak above the storm still battering us. "You'll be trapped here *forever* if you don't let Cole go. He's not here. Let him go."

Rainwater streamed down his face disguising the tears I knew were falling from his bloodshot, grey eyes.

Lightning and thunder crashed. Caine looked up at the storm and back to me as a cold hit of reality reached him through the fog. I didn't know if my power or what I said snapped him out of it, but his gaze flickered over my head to where the voice still screamed for him and then back at me for an immeasurable moment.

Whatever was going on in his brain, he wasn't speaking. I kept my hands at his sides, ready to grapple him again if he tried to take off. Instead, his fingers moved matted hair from my face, his eyes connecting with mine. I was desperate to know what he was thinking.

With the voice of Cole and the wind in my ears, Caine entangled his fingers in my hair and pressed his lips to mine, kissing me deeply, crushing me against his body. Passion chased away all rationale. Even with the abhorrent weather, my tattered heart, and the leafy prison around us, I went deaf to the screaming voice and focused on Caine.

My head swam when he pulled away, my thoughts chaotic and unorganized. I looked up into his smoky gaze and shared a look no words could express.

No matter if the ritual worked, something in Caine had changed, something in me had changed, and gratitude filled a hole in me I'd been too scarred to realize existed.

Still within the willow circle, the pelting rain softened. I had a moment of "holy shit" and looked away from him up at the sky. Quicker than was natural, the rain had already stopped.

Caine's eyes were on the sky, and his shoulders slumped with relief. All that had bound him to this world or realm or whatever Aunt Lacey would call it, was gone. His smile told me he'd shed the darkest part of himself in that moment.

Caine moved his thumb along my cheek, a light touch of pleasure. Wanting to resist him and the fairy tale notion that if we escaped unscathed, we would live happily ever after, I was still drawn, leaning into his touch instead of away. Happy endings were bullshit wrapped in glitter, too much Disney overload in my formative years. Happy moments only peppered my life, and I wanted to enjoy it while it lasted.

"Assuming we did it, what happens after we get out of this?" Caine asked.

"Caine, you're—"

"Pushing my luck, I know. I just...I don't want to wake up and never see you again."

Excitement to thank his "saviour" in person? An implication of wanting a relationship? I wasn't sure which option made me feel what. A thank you would be more than I needed. I didn't go through all this for thanks. I didn't do this for anything. And starting a relationship? I wasn't sure I had the emotional fortitude right now, and getting together based on our interaction in the dreams alone would head us into disaster. Neither of us needed the fallout when he realized his attraction to me was some hero worship.

"You've been in a coma a very long time. If you wake up, you may not remember me. Why don't we get through this first? It might not be over."

"It is. I feel different now. You saved me." He kissed me again, this time a brush against my lips so tender my cheeks flushed.

"Will you be there when I wake up?"

The fact he hadn't woken up yet made me hesitant to believe the ritual worked. Though he was right, something was different.

"I'm not in the same city as you. When you wake up,"—I refrained from saying if—"you can call me. My number's in a card I left you. If I don't hear from you, I'll know you don't remember me. Either way, I promised your mom I'd visit."

He nodded and gave an appeasing smile. I wasn't fooled. He wanted more from me, and I was reverting to old stall tactics.

He held me tightly again. We'd stayed like that for a moment when I heard him whisper, "Please let me remember you," before he vanished.

One moment strong arms enfolded me, our bodies touching, and then he was gone. No dramatic fade away, just gone.

Did vanishing mean the ritual worked? If it did, had he woken up? Did he die? This couldn't be how things ended.

Why was I still here? Was I stuck here now?

Panic lanced me. For the first time, I was alone in the park.

The clouds lightened further and morphed into odd formations I had never seen before, like dollops of whipped cream, completely smooth shapes and thick as they whitened. As soon as the odd formations developed, they flattened and dissipated with the soft breeze.

The sky had altered from its mass of torrential rain and nightmarish torment into pure beauty. Without Caine to share it with, to see the park was no longer a scary place, I felt nothing but emptiness. With the clouds mere wisps, they thinned and created fractures of warmth on my skin. The sun burst through and blinded me, throwing bands of colour across the park. The saturated greenery was now lush in earthy tones, highlighted with reds, oranges, and yellows, along with white that straightened my brow beneath its weight. The transformation was as abrupt as the lightning had been.

The sun became larger than possible, as if the earth had moved closer to be next to it. The sunlight blurred my vision and drowned out the beauty of the once terrifying park with fierce, blinding white light.

I blinked my dry, stinging eyes and realized the sun and lush greenery had been replaced with a white stuccoed ceiling. Another moment passed before my ears recalibrated to the whispering all around me.

To my left, Donovan still held my hand, his other on my stomach, though no one else was touching me. They all held each other's hands instead. I remembered everything that happened with Caine in the park, though the medicated effects of the tea still made me dopey as I looked around the room.

Donovan chanted in a soft murmur, his white and green soul glow framing his body, and I felt myself enamoured by his efforts to help me help Caine, knowing what he did of our past together and how I felt about Caine. I refused to feel guilt for what happened between myself and Donovan, and regardless of the situation, I was drawn to him, even now.

"I think it worked." This sounded more like a question than a statement. I cleared my throat, still trying to fight off the tea.

I rose up onto my elbow, tugged my hand from Donovan's grip, and watched his eyes shoot open. I touched Kim's knee. She gasped and ripped her hands from her neighbour's, who was bent over awkwardly and looked like they had fallen asleep sitting up.

"I think it worked," I repeated, looking from Kim to Donovan and squinting from the closeness of so many Magics' souls burning my eyes. I didn't know if the result was Caine waking up or dying, but he was no longer in the park. That meant success.

Heads perked up at the sound of my raspy voice. They waited for something, but I couldn't tell what. Donovan smiled in slight satisfaction, with eyes that spoke of something sadder.

He wished they failed.

When this occurred to me, I looked away, unsure I could keep from expressing my confusion over his regret.

When the Elders came to the end of their chant, Aunt Lacey raised her head, smiled, and said, "I knew it was in you."

Her confidence released the Coveners' ceremonial circle. Those laid out on the carpet or slumped over sat up with droopy eyes, shook themselves off, and stretched their muscles. Pride beamed from the Coveners, who celebrated with words of praise despite their exhaustion. A few collapsed back onto the carpet in fits of laughter. Kim, her eyes full of tears, reached her shaky hands out for me as I did for her, kneeling on the floor as we embraced over the nest in utter relief. Kim had gone from congenial neighbour to a close friend in a matter of weeks.

My head reeled and vertigo took hold for a moment as Kim helped me steady myself while I still sat within the nest. She handed over the sunglasses to partially block out my Coven, but I was more worried about the pressure of their attention and not their souls.

All eyes were on me. Moving to stand, Donovan extended a helping hand. I knew what accepting it would mean for his visions, but I took it anyway and watched his eyes flutter and shut. I released him, his expression guarded as I sat on a couch.

My back was as stiff as the floor. I stretched and let my head clear while I contemplated what to say to the others. Since they went beyond the call of duty, I owed them an explanation.

"Why do you think it worked?" Kim sat beside me, so excited she was pressed against me so close I thought she may perch onto my lap like Bosco.

My body quivered with unspent adrenaline as I started retelling the story, inches from breaking down, and working to separate myself emotionally. Then Denise interrupted telling me they'd all seen the whole thing, and I flushed in embarrassment as her smug expression said she enjoyed my discomfort. The others wanted to know what it meant when Caine disappeared. Was he alive? Was he dead? All the same questions I asked myself.

After hearing what Roon set up, I understood the necessity. But Donovan being amongst the audience, watching the intimate moment me and Caine had shared, flooded me with guilt.

Blake explained the odd cloud formations I was confused about, calling them mammatus clouds. He, being the storm chaser of the group, had seen them in the southern states, though Ontario rarely housed weather patterns capable of producing such clouds. An interesting factoid, especially since Blake looked more like the "duct tape fixes everything" kind of guy, now he seemed a hint smarter in my eyes.

Silver lining? The impromptu lesson proved a nice distraction, alleviating some pressure as I gathered my thoughts. Eventually the spotlight returned to me, but I had nothing else to add that they hadn't seen for themselves.

For all I knew, Caine was still comatose or maybe awake but uninterested in seeing me. He had family who cared about him and had been waiting for him to open his eyes.

I moved on as smoothly as possible. "It took a long time for it to begin. I thought something went wrong."

They had no problems recounting every measure with exuberance.

Gwen explained what Kim and Donovan did to help the process. I was floored by what Donovan did for Caine, though not too many of the Coveners were happy with him because they'd passed out after Donovan sucked the energy out of them. Maybe I should have felt bad, but I didn't.

I never considered Caine's physical state once he woke, assuming it would bounce back like any other coma victim. It was a ludicrous and unrealistic notion for anyone suffering a long-term bout of unconsciousness. Sleeping that long ruined his body, but he was in a hospital. I had to remind myself that when magic was involved, normal may not apply.

"Now I have to make sure he's awake." I dreaded meeting Caine, in person, with his real eyes open. He owed me nothing, but I hoped he remembered me.

"Have faith in your Coven, Salix," Nitsa said as she sat on the arm of the couch next to Aunt Lacey.

"Yes," Aunt Lacey said, "I could not be prouder." Her eyes glassed over as Nitsa placed a hand on her friend's shoulder. There was something else fueling the tears Aunt Lacey held at bay, but she didn't explain.

A cordless phone was passed through the crowd to Donovan, who passed it to me with exposed misery. I walked away from him and the crowd's intrigued faces to find privacy at the far end of the room.

Accessing my answering service, I found messages.

I skipped through a few, eager to hear Caine, fearing I wouldn't find a message from him until I finally heard his frantic voice on the line. "I remember everything! Sophie, come to the hospital as soon as possible. Visiting hours begin at eleven in the morning. And don't worry, my mom's a little confused, but I didn't tell her anything. Please...I need to see you. Your card promised." The call ended with a slam as he hung up.

I did promise, didn't I?

Standing with the phone still to my ear, taking a moment to get my head together, I pushed aside whatever it was I felt since I was beyond understanding it at this phase. Putting so many emotions off until later, I ignored the thought of the inevitable crash when "later" came to collect. For now, Caine was awake, and that mattered most.

The Coveners' attention was heavy on my back, waiting to hear if

Caine had called. I confirmed their eyes were on me as I turned, each face gearing up for the appropriate emotion given my response.

I moved a piece of hair from my face and readjusted the sunglasses. "He's awake."

They celebrated with actual high-fives and hugs, reinvigorated by their success. I was surprised at how intensely this angered me. Were they excited because this meant they were proficient at what they do, and not about the more substantial consideration that a man, comatose for years, was now awake and able to resume his life? I swallowed it back, reminding myself Caine was no one to them, just a name and a story. I tried to focus on the fact that their part in the ritual made Caine's awakening possible, remembering they didn't have to help me and had still done so without complaint.

Kim must have read the look of conflict brewing as she came over wearing that look that told me she saw right through me. I hated it, handing over the phone, giving a hollow smile I couldn't fill with anything remotely close to happiness. Kim gave me another tight hug, sympathy I didn't want flooding from her. I melted into her surprised by how much I needed it and needed Kim to be the one to give it.

Kim released me. "What do you want to do?"

"I want to go home. I doubt I can sleep, but I can't see him until visiting hours." Damn hospital policy.

"It's the middle of the night anyway. We can hang out until it's time, then head over."

"Hell yeah. No freakin' way am I walking in there alone."

"I'll distract his mom." She smirked and nudged me with her elbow.

"I seriously doubt privacy is an option with his friends and family popping in. He has a lot to catch up on." The prospect of enduring them alone was terrifying.

Kim relented. "True."

"What time is it?"

"Three-thirty." I gaped at her. "Yeah, you were under a long time."

It felt long, but not that long. Again, amazing how time moved in that place.

"Everyone's in the cheering mood. Do you want to stay and talk or head out?"

I sighed. "We'll stay and chat. I owe them that much."

"Yeah, you do," Kim smirked and I smiled, exhausted.

After another hour of forcing myself to socialize without listening to a single person, I decided to duck out.

I was stopped while retrieving a sleepy Bosco.

As before, Donovan embraced me, and I squeezed him back. I didn't know what to say so I didn't say anything, and neither did he. When he pulled back, he stared at me a moment before disappearing somewhere into the house. I had to stop myself from going after him. The only thing keeping me in place was that I had no idea what I would say if I caught up with him. That wasn't fair, so I remained in the backyard.

Aunt Lacey found me next.

"Caine may struggle with the life he has left behind," she told me. "Nonetheless, his soul is imbued with the very strength of the willow inside you, awakened like a bear from its winter's rest. Show him the way back to this world. He needs the guidance."

I nodded, having no idea how she thought I could do that, but figuring he might need someone to talk to who knew what he went through all these years. I doubted he would tell his mom. And if I was right, he would feel the need to talk it out.

I hoped I could keep it together and be what he needed.

Caine was safe and wanted to see me. Good news entitled me a fraction of happiness now that the dream would be over and a man's life restored, especially after the altercation with Loring. Thinking back to my first venture into the basement and Aunt Lacey's tea leaf reading, Loring was certainly my dragon bent on forcing his own agenda on me, whatever it was. I knew I'd see him again.

Aunt Lacey walked me and Kim onto the front porch. The warm

night was infused with fresh air I took into the deepest part of my lungs.

"I look forward to meeting him at the next Coven gathering."

A moment passed before I realized she meant Caine. "I'll ask," I responded. What a disaster it could be to have Caine and Donovan under the same roof. From the way Aunt Lacey said it, I assumed she "saw" it happened and figured I was sunk.

Fuckballs, that would be fun.

————

Back at my apartment, I showered, and then found Kim sleeping on the couch with Bosco tucked into the crook of her knees. I decided to lie down, needing a nap before going to the hospital.

Sleep took hold and I dreamt of nonsensical people and circumstances, all forgotten the moment the alarm sounded. I woke without disappointment.

The nap left me in a fog instead of refreshed. When I woke Kim, she popped up off the couch, red eyes begging for more hours of rest.

"Coffee, tea, toast, anything?" I never drank coffee or tea, but kept it on hand for company—mostly my mother—and even I could manage toast.

"Coffee would be sex right now," Kim said, yawning as I laughed. She took the cup I offered and sipped it, making a sound of immense gratification as her eyes rolled.

I took it as a thank you.

"So..." Kim started. When I didn't respond, her sculpted eyebrows raised. "When are we blowing this pop stand so you can meet Mr. Dreamy and have cute little grey-eyed babies?"

"Babies?" I revolted against the idea. "I'll leave the placenta to you, thanks. I'm hoping I don't pass out before the handshake."

"Handshake? This isn't a business meeting."

"You expect me to get down in his hospital bed and polish his balls with his friends and family in the audience?"

Kim shrugged. "It'd make an impression." I gave her look. "Better than a handshake. I swear if you shake his hand, I'm telling Caine's mom you're looking forward to giving her four point five grandchildren."

"What's with the point five?"

She took another sip of her coffee. "Bosco's half a person."

"Nah." I dropped and picked up my pug companion. "You're all man aren't you, buddy?" In answer, Bosco licked my cheeks. "Exactly," I said and returned him to the floor.

"Back in reality, when we going?"

"Visiting hours start at eleven. I'm not showing up too early and waiting in the halls like it's a Boxing Day sale. He needs time with his family."

"If you think he's not going to assume you're not coming at all if you wait too long, you're delusional. You didn't call him back. He might think you didn't get his message."

She may be right.

"Let's start with your wardrobe."

"Says Miss Fashionista."

"Yup. Though you could show up in a muumuu and granny panties, and he wouldn't care."

"Gross. Not that he'd see the granny panties. Why would I wear a muumuu?"

"Hey, don't knock GPs. They come in handy on occasion. And I know you wouldn't wear one, I'm just saying, regardless he'll think you're the hottest shit he ever laid his eyes on." Kim laughed into another sip of coffee.

"Considering his eyes haven't landed on another woman in years, you're probably right."

"Plus, he's only seen you in pyjamas, except for last night. Low bar to set. Be comfortable."

This took the pressure off a bit.

I vetoed Kim's first, cleavage-packed suggestion in case I bent down to Caine in his hospital bed and gave his mother an eyeful of my tits. I had the foresight to see the potential indecent event. And since hospital air conditioning was cranked in all seasons, long sleeves and pants were optimal.

"Maybe I'll get Bosco a girlfriend, and they could have adorable pug puppies," Kim said playing tug-of-war with him on the carpet as I finished getting ready.

"No offence, but getting dogs together to have sex just to sell their children for profit weirds me out. Can you imagine if humans did that?"

"I've never thought of it like that, but I guess you're right...in a twisted animal rights fanatic kind of way." She turned to Bosco. "Sorry, buddy, looks like your mama's keeping you a monk."

I laughed.

"Ready? You look good," Kim appraised after the odd direction our conversation had taken.

"Guess so," I said, but I was freaked. Piddle-as-you-tremble freaked. Eleven o'clock was closing in, and so was the room around me. I slumped onto the couch before I hit the floor. Petting Bosco helped.

"You gonna paper-bag it?"

"What?"

"Hyperventilate?"

"No. Just nervous." An understatement Kim saw through.

"Remember, he called you. He wants to see you. At least that's not part of the mystery."

"Yeah, I know, it's just so...so..."

"Fairy-tale perfect? YouTube-worthy weird? Killer-clown insane?"

"Exactly." It was all those things and more.

I was never the type to jump in the freezing swimming pool to get over its frigidness. Always slow and steady, and this was bone-chilling fast.

Before I could change my mind about going, we headed out.

When we arrived at the hospital, I wished I had eaten before we left. If I fainted in that room, in front of him, the embarrassment would send me headed for the door in a record-breaking sprint.

We made our way to his room in nervous silence, without stopping at the admittance desk to ask questions. Once we reached his floor and exited the elevator, I stopped and grabbed Kim's elbow, then fussed with the neck of the grey and yellow striped hoodie I had on. The light fabric was suddenly too tight.

"Do you think we should have brought something?"

"Like what? Change your mind about the GPs?"

"Kim! I meant like a gift. I feel empty-handed."

"We already brought flowers and a card he obviously read if he called you. Stop freaking out. I'm not going anywhere unless you want me to. Promise."

Bless her heart, Kim was in it for the long haul. I held onto her elbow tighter as we inched toward the open door. Laughter spilled out into the hallway. He had visitors, though it was impossible to tell how many.

I stopped breathing, my lungs kicking up a fit as I refused to draw in air. Kim knocked on the door and said, "Ready for more visitors?"

Everyone's attention shifted to us at the door, and my fingers started to tingle, my nerve-endings alive with anticipation.

Caine was sitting up in bed, arms crossed, free of machines, and no longer a shell of the coma victim I visited. His expression was free of the torture of the park, with an extra something I never expected. A soul glow framed his vital form, brighter than Kim's, with a hint of blue.

He was a Magic.

His mother stood to his right and a stocky, dark-skinned man Caine's age stood to his left. As everyone else did, Caine turned our way, his smoky stare meeting my eyes for the first time, its intensity far greater than within the park, more wolf than winter sky. I followed in behind Kim, still attached to her like a baby koala as the tingle crawled up my spine and tickled the nape of my neck.

All conversation lulled.

Caine shot out of bed. His mother shrieked as he sprinted across the room in his bare feet, white t-shirt, and hospital bottoms. He closed the gap between us with three quick strides and wrapped his arms around me, compressing my ribcage, pulling me up into a tiptoed embrace.

I wrapped my arms around him and buried my face into his neck. Containing the tears that poured from my eyes was impossible. That tingle was now a roar of exhilaration on the brink of overwhelming me.

We swayed just outside the doorway, engulfed in the euphoria of our first true introduction.

"I owe you my life," he whispered in my ear. The heat of his breath on my neck blanketed my skin in goosebumps. "Now that I've found you, I'm never letting go."

Donovan's face flashed before my eyes. My heart lurched. The urge to retreat and take off came alive in my bones. My arms squeezed tighter around Caine, an involuntary reaction to root me in this moment with him, one he interpreted as a positive response to his comment. He held me tighter.

Flushed with sudden panic, I was surprised at how quickly I wanted to give in to this stirring passion for him and then, equally, flee or reject him and his promises. A part of me was already Caine's. How could that be?

I wanted to fill my starving soul with purpose, to check off an item on my list and get my shit together. Finding a man, Caine or Donovan or anyone, was not on that list.

The tingle of magic grew. I fought to push it down before I burst.

What the fuck was happening to me?

Caine pulled back and looked down at me, concern clouding those beautiful grey eyes as the white and blue of his soul haloed his magically healed body and filled my vision.

Softened by his expression, I couldn't trust my voice, so instead I smiled as another tear escaped down my cheek. Oblivious to my internal struggle, Caine grinned so brightly I felt weak and my arms went around him again. This time without any hesitation.

———

Sign-up and stay current on book cover reveals, sales, giveaways, and more with S.J.'s newsletter! http://www.sjcairns.com/newsletter-sign-up/

———

Read on for DECEPTION, SOUL SEER CHRONICLES, BOOK 2 teaser now available for Kindle, Kindle Unlimited, and Paperback.

https://www.amazon.com/Deception-Soul-Seer-Chronicles-Book-ebook/dp/B0BH94H7MJ

DECEPTION TEASER

Deception, Soul Seer Chronicles, Book 2

When a long-standing truce with the enemy ends, Mother Coven members go missing.

Learning I was a Soul Seer changed everything and proved to be a dangerous discovery. Despite threatening warnings to back off, I dig deeper to expose baffling family secrets.

To complicate things further, my attention is split between two men. I don't know who I can trust, and I can't afford the deadly distraction.

My fledgling powers triggered Loring's evil obsession, requiring round-the-clock bodyguards, but the Coven's most vigilant can't protect everyone. No one is safe, not even within our most sacred space.

I am used to loss, but I am not ready to lose everything.